East Dunbart

3 8060 0

CW00376516

DISC
AND SOLD

DEATH AT THE KYLES OF BUTE

MYRA DUFFY

Published in 2014 by FeedARead.com Publishing

Copyright © Myra Duffy.

The author or authors assert their moral right under the Copyright, Designs and Patents Act, 1988, to be identified as the author or authors of this work.

All Rights reserved. No part of this publication may be reproduced, copied, stored in a retrieval system, or transmitted, in any form or by any means, without the prior written consent of the copyright holder, nor be otherwise circulated in any form of binding or cover other than that in which it is published and without a similar condition being imposed on the subsequent purchaser.

A CIP catalogue record for this title is available from the British Library.

DEATH AT THE KYLES OF BUTE

An Alison Cameron Mystery

MYRA DUFFY

www.myraduffy.co.uk
http://myraduffy-awriterslot.blogspot.com

Cover design by Mandy Sinclair
www.mandysinclair.com

Characters in this novel bear no relation whatsoever to any persons living or dead. Any such resemblance is coincidental.

A number of real locations have been used in the novel, but details may have been changed or added for purposes of the plot.

Also by Myra Duffy

THE ISLE OF BUTE MYSTERY SERIES

The House at Ettrick Bay

Last Ferry to Bute

Last Dance at the Rothesay Pavilion

Endgame at Port Bannatyne

Grave Matters at St Blane's

****

The prequel to the Isle of Bute Mystery series

When Old Ghosts Meet

THE ISLE OF BUTE

The Isle of Bute lies in Scotland's Firth of Clyde, off the west coast of Scotland, a short journey from the city of Glasgow. It rose to prominence in Victorian days when its proximity to a major city made it a favoured spot for holidays.

Bute is the ancestral home of the Stuart kings of Scotland and the 800 year old Rothesay castle (now ruined) was built by a hereditary High Steward of Scotland, from which the name is derived.

Today the island is a haven from the hustle and bustle of city life with quiet beaches, woodland walks and an abundance of wildlife, including seals.

For Peter

EAST DUNBARTONSHIRE CULTURAL SERVICES
Class
Barcode
Location __EDHQ__ Received __8/15__
Supplier __ Price __7.99__
DYNIX BIB NO

Prologue

'I tell you, I heard a noise.' Anna sat bolt upright in bed, scarcely breathing in the darkness, straining to hear.

'Oh, for goodness sake, go back to sleep. You're imagining things.'

Her husband Freddie stirred, then turned over, muttering and huddling under the duvet.

Anna swung her legs out of bed and felt for her slippers before pulling on her fleecy dressing gown. The heating in the hotel was turned down overnight and at her age she felt the change in temperature keenly.

'Where are you going?' Freddie asked, half raising himself on one elbow, but it was clear he had little interest.

Anna stood still in the middle of the room, listening. 'Shh - there it is again, a faint crying. Can't you hear it?'

Freddie grunted in reply. 'It's the ancient heating system in this part of the hotel, that's all. It sounds loud in the silence of the night.'

Ignoring this explanation, Anna moved forward and cautiously opened the door to peer out into the corridor.

'There's no one there,' she said.

'Of course not.' Freddie manoeuvred himself into a sitting position, pulling up the pillow to support his head. 'This is our second night here, supposedly for a pre-Christmas break and you've come up with the same nonsense each night. Come back to bed and let's get some sleep.'

Anna closed the door quietly and padded across the room, shrugging off her dressing gown before slipping back into bed. Thank goodness Freddie hadn't brought up the subject of why they were here on a *Tinsel and Turkey* week at the Kyles of Bute Hydro hotel, instead of the holiday in the south of Italy that had been his first choice. All because she was terrified of flying.

She tossed and turned and in spite of the many sheep she tried to count, sleep wouldn't come. It wasn't her imagination, no matter how much Freddie pooh-poohed her idea.

Both nights, in the middle of the night, she'd heard the same sound. A low weeping, as though someone was distressed, was in deep trouble. There was something strange going on in this hotel.

Eventually she drifted off to sleep, her last vague thought being that she must speak to the other guests, find out if anyone else had heard this disturbing noise.

If someone was unhappy, Anna knew she would have to find a way to help.

'Take the shore road out towards Port Bannatyne.' I'd been given exact instructions on how to find the Kyles of Bute Hydro hotel. 'Be careful - there's a sharp bend up to the entrance. You'll see the little lodge house beside the double gates. That was one of the buildings we were able to save.'

I didn't say there was no need for this information, having had many trips to the island for both business and for pleasure.

Even so, as I came off the ferry from Wemyss Bay I felt a surge of excitement. The Kyles of Bute Hydro had long been an important landmark on the island. If you said 'The Hydro' everyone knew exactly what you meant.

Although much of it had been demolished, the new company who had bought the semi-derelict buildings had managed to save the whole of the West wing as well as the lodge house. On Google Earth it looked very impressive and almost seamless in its structure, the way in which the old blended with the new and I was eager to see the reality.

I can't say my husband, Simon, had been as keen on my latest venture and said when I told him of my plans, 'But it's not the beginning of December yet. Christmas is ages away.' He put down his newspaper and stared at me, a perplexed look on his face. 'Why would people want to celebrate Christmas so early?'

'It's a way of bringing in customers to the hotel at a dead time of the season,' I replied, trying to keep the defensive note out of my voice. 'It's called *Turkey and Tinsel* and there are two separate weeks. This event has been running for a couple of years and it would appear it's very popular – or so it seems according to the brochure they've sent me.'

A shake of his head. 'Even so, even if they need all the custom they can muster, it seems an odd thing to do. Who wants to be thinking about the festive season already?'

As Simon belongs to that group of men who think shopping for presents before Christmas Eve amounts to deviant behaviour, I didn't pay much attention to his comment.

Trying to stifle my disappointment at his lack of enthusiasm, I said, 'Well, I've agreed to go. It won't involve much work over the two weeks I'll be there. My task is to spend the time chatting to guests, answering their questions about the island's history, and the talks I've been asked to give are already prepared - a maximum of three each week.'

Even my suggestion, 'You can come down for the middle weekend, fit in a game of golf,' didn't change his opinion.

So ignoring his concerns I'd headed for the study to phone the Manager, Clive Timmons and accept the contract.

'Delighted to hear from you, Alison. We've tried to recreate the original as best we can, but with all modern conveniences of course,' he said. 'We'll accommodate you in the old West wing if you would like - much more atmosphere, though not all the bedrooms in that

4

part of the hotel are ready for occupation. We're still working on the renovations.'

It sounded an excellent plan. I'd heard so much about the history of the old Hydro the offer to stay for the two weeks of my contract in what had been the original part of the building was too good to refuse.

The only reason I'd been offered this contract was because the hotel had been let down at the last minute by one of the speakers booked for these *Turkey and Tinsel* weeks, a way of encouraging visitors to Bute in the quiet days of late November.

'It won't be difficult,' the Manager had assured me. 'All you have to do is give a few short talks about the island: the history, or any stories you think might be of interest. It's only something to fill in the time for the guests for an hour before dinner. Then there's entertainment like a cabaret or dancing or a film organised, though some of the group may prefer to chat to you about times gone by. A few of the guests may elect to stay for two weeks, but with many of them short term memory can be a problem, so don't be concerned about repeating yourself. I'm sorry you won't be here for the Saturday night Welcome dinner to start our week, but you'll be here for the next one.'

There was a pause, then he added, hurrying on before I could answer, 'I'm very grateful to you for agreeing to do this at such short notice. The speaker we'd engaged has been taken ill and the other two we tried were already committed. We were getting desperate, I have to say, when someone thought of you and that book you wrote about St Blane's. You were our last resort.'

I ignored this put-down of my skills. Since publishing a short book on St Blane's, the ancient ruined monastery at the south side of the island, I'd been at a loss, wondering if this career as a writer, the one I'd left my previous job as a teacher for, had been the right decision. So when the opportunity presented itself, I was happy to take the commission.

Not that it had been an entirely easy decision. Simon and I were now the proud grandparents of a baby boy, Connor, thanks to our elder daughter Maura and her husband, Alan. They were currently living in Edinburgh, near enough for regular visits, but far enough away from our home in Glasgow to allow them some privacy. I'd a feeling baby Connor would create changes in our lives we didn't as yet suspect.

But with a contract to write health promotion materials for schoolchildren recently completed, I was at a bit of a loose end, with no other work on the horizon and this seemed a good option. In spite of several pleading phone calls from the Head teacher at my old school, Strathelder High, the last thing I wanted to do was return to teaching.

And now, disembarking from the mid-afternoon ferry, I immediately headed out along the road beside the bay, resisting the temptation to call in at the Electric Bakery in the main town of Rothesay to buy one of their home-made fruitcakes. That would be a treat for another time.

Then, as I drove through Ardbeg and headed towards Port Bannatyne, little doubts began to creep in. I'd never done anything like this before. I'd given talks, but I hadn't tried to be particularly entertaining in any of them. Most of my previous audiences had been interested in the facts rather than anything else. Now I was expected to come up with amusing anecdotes and I wondered if I could be as entertaining as the Manager anticipated. Too late now, I thought, as I reached Pier Street in Port Bannatyne.

Once upon a time, many years ago, the steamers had called in at the pier at the bottom of the road leading down to the Bay. All that remained of the original pier was a series of blackened stumps, like so many fingers pointing skywards and I stopped the car for a moment to gaze at this reminder of how busy the original hotel had been.

Immediately before the War Memorial at the junction of the Shore Road and the High Road, I looked for the sharp bend of the road up to the Hydro and sooner than expected found myself outside the large stone pillars marking the beginning of the driveway leading to the main building.

I passed the Lodge house, shuttered and dark, before driving slowly up the long, winding drive towards the imposing building that was the hotel.

As I came nearer I couldn't help but marvel at the skill with which the original West wing had been blended with the new addition. The embellished stonework of the front, with its mock towers and castellated turrets, made it look exactly like the Hydro that had been such a popular choice in Victorian times.

Of course, in those days the island had been a destination for the rich (many of whom had large summer villas on the island) and the not-so-rich who took lodgings wherever they could find them cheaply. This often meant a whole family being crammed into one room, which might be the only bedroom in the

7

house, while the owner and his family made do with the kitchen or farmed the children out to a neighbour in return for a small fee.

But the Hydro had no such problems. Elegant and spacious, it filled the skyline as the original once did and I drove through landscaped gardens towards the imposing oak front door.

There was little to see at this time in November, but there were several young lime trees at the entrance, now lifeless and bare and I spied the outline of flower beds stretching into the distance. Near the dilapidated greenhouses there was a large pond, but it was difficult to tell if it was real or artificial. Plenty of time to have a walk and explore the grounds later. With a sense of eager anticipation I parked my car on the gravel drive and hurried to the front door where a large fir had been adopted as a Christmas tree and the multi-coloured lights winked and twinkled invitingly.

At the side of the door there was a large metal bell and I gave the chain hanging from it a good hard yank, startled by how easily it moved. No detail had been ignored in the desire to recreate the grandeur of previous years.

Almost before the booming had died away, the door opened and the Manager stood before me. At least I guessed that was who he was because his name, Clive Timmons, was prominently displayed in large gold letters on the badge he was wearing.

I stepped forward into the inner lobby. 'I'm Alison Cameron,' I said, putting on my brightest smile.

'Oh, yes, glad you could make it, Alison.' He steered me into the main entrance hall and for a moment I was speechless.

Tinsel and shiny Christmas baubles glittered everywhere in the light from several chandeliers and the overwhelming impression was of warmth, a contrast to the grey day outside. A large staircase, carpeted in red, swept upwards in grand style and a marble and oak reception desk ran the length of the other wall. On closer inspection it was clear the make-over had been rather sketchy, but first impressions were encouraging.

Behind the desk a plumpish young woman wearing a dark blue uniform sat at a computer. Her fair hair was cut in a short bob, her make-up faultlessly done, unlike my own lipstick hastily applied in the *Ladies* on the ferry as it rolled towards shore.

He gestured towards her. 'This is Kelly, our senior Receptionist. She'll be able to help you with any queries if I'm not around. Or even if I am around. She knows a lot more about the place than I do.'

Kelly lifted her head and smiled as though this acknowledgement of her abilities was no more than she deserved. Her voice was low and husky. 'Always glad to be of help,' she said and went back to typing non-stop at her keyboard.

A large musical Santa on the corner of the desk suddenly sprang into life with a loud, 'Ho, ho, ho' and she grimaced as Clive led me away saying, 'Anyway, first things first. Let's get you settled in your room and then we can discuss the arrangements for your talks over a cup of coffee.'

'Great idea,' I said, remembering I hadn't eaten since breakfast several hours before.

'This way.' He walked briskly in front of me towards the stairs on the far side of the desk. 'We'll walk up. The lift takes ages. As I said on the phone,

9

I've put you in the original West wing. I hope that'll suit. Don't worry; some of the rooms, including the one you're in, have been refurbished. We've a full house, but we had a last minute cancellation - one of the guests who was supposed to be coming died. ' He said this as though it was a personal insult. 'So I thought you'd like to have that room, see what the place was like in its heyday.'

'Sounds fine,' I said, though that wasn't how I felt about his choice of room for me.

'We've had to open up the very top floor for a couple of the guests. We gave them a discount, of course.'

All the time chatting non-stop, he trotted up the stairs and then stopped suddenly so that I almost bumped into him. 'Luggage? What about your luggage?'

'I don't have much,' I said. 'I can bring it in later.'

'If you leave me your car keys, I'll get one of the porters to fetch it.' He headed off again at the same brisk pace.

We reached the second floor and as we went through the corridors, twisting and turning, I wondered if I'd be able to find my way back to the main desk.

Almost as though he read my thoughts, the Manager said, 'Don't worry, you'll get used to it,' stopping in front of a large door to Room 213.

'Here we are,' he said, producing a key with a flourish from his pocket. 'The new rooms have electronic keys but it seemed wrong to mess about with these doors, so they still have old-fashioned keys. Leave yours at Reception when you go out.'

He pushed open the door and I found myself in a large airy room with a view over Port Bannatyne bay, stunning even in the gathering gloom of the winter's afternoon.

He reached over and switched on a couple of lamps, sending pools of light into the darkness.

'I'll leave you to settle in,' he said. 'Any problems give me a call on the house phone.' He indicated the old-fashioned telephone on the table beside the four poster bed. 'It may look ancient but that's all for appearances. It works fine. Dial 100 and that will get you through to reception.' He looked at his watch. 'If I meet you downstairs at the main reception in about half an hour would that suit?'

'Fine,' I said, but I was already eyeing up the hospitality tray in the corner where a kettle, cups, coffee sachets and a plate of biscuits sat temptingly. I doubted I'd be able to wait half an hour.

He turned round as he reached the door. 'I am most grateful you've agreed to do this at such short notice.'

'Not a problem - I'm delighted,' I said. And I meant it - seeing the hotel more or less as it had once been was a great thrill and I was glad of this opportunity to spend time in it.

Now I could relax. Apart from the problem of inserting a few funny anecdotes my talks were well prepared and nothing could go wrong. My previous experiences should have set warning bells ringing, but sadly, that was not the case.

2

If this speaker went on for a moment longer, I'd soon be fast asleep. After an hour in this over-heated room, I could scarcely keep my eyes open. The topic was a problem, as was the monotonous tone of voice he'd adopted. Perhaps this was in deference to the average age of his audience, which was far from young, judging by the number of grey heads in the room.

A brief glance round the ornate carvings, the dusty crystal chandeliers and the scuffed wooden floor (in spite of a brave attempt to polish it) in this original ballroom, now made me wonder if rebuilding the Kyles of Bute Hydro Hotel and Spa had been such a good idea after all.

'Look closely at this next slide,' the speaker was saying, 'and you can see the consequences of not using the right knot when securing your boat to the jetty. It causes a fluctuation in the stability which can be a serious problem when it's high tide. It could even be fatal.' He chuckled at what he considered a joke, but there were many people in this room who would fail to find his comments funny.

He fiddled with the old-fashioned projector, eventually succeeding in putting the picture up on screen. A grainy shot of an upturned day boat, scarcely visible in the surging waves, flashed up. 'The important thing is to make sure you keep hold of the boat, use its buoyancy to keep you alive until help arrives.'

A rapid survey of the audience confirmed my belief none of these hotel guests would be in need of this information any time soon. Several were asleep and others were chatting in soft tones to their neighbours.

I must be more positive. I reminded myself the offer of a contract to give a series of talks on the history of the Isle of Bute combined the skills from my early job as a teacher and my more recent work as a writer. And with no other employment in view, it was an offer too good to refuse.

With a jolt I came back to the present. The speaker had finally ended his talk and Clive Timmons, the hotel Manager who was doubling as the compere, stood up, a little too quickly it seemed to me. 'Thank you, Mr Gibbon for a most interesting and helpful lecture. Are there any questions?'

But those in the audience who were still awake seemed stunned into silence after being bombarded by information about double hitches and bowlines and reef knots. I made a mental note to be sure to inject some light-hearted moments into the first of my talks scheduled for the following night. One good thing - I didn't have much of a reputation to live up to.

Clive gazed around in desperation and rather than have this embarrassing silence continue a moment longer, I raised my hand, as yet not quite certain what my question might be. Finally I managed, 'What's the most dangerous experience you've had with your own boat?'

This was a mistake, a big mistake. Vincent Gibbon leapt to his feet before the compere could repeat the question and started on a long, rambling story about one time he'd been foolish enough to go out in bad weather,

13

the difficulties he'd faced trying to keep the boat upright, the problems with the rigging in the wind.

From a little further along the row came the sound of gentle snoring and I glimpsed an elderly lady digging the man beside her in the ribs. He came to with a start, shouting, 'What, what's happened? Is there a fire?'

Fortunately the speaker was too absorbed in his story to notice this interruption, but the rest of the audience did and a subdued titter went round the room.

Clive finally interrupted him saying, 'Well, thank you so much for a most interesting and enlightening talk. I'm sure we're all much wiser about what to do should we find ourselves in the kind of emergency you've described.'

Scarcely pausing for breath, he went on, 'And now the bar is open for the pre-dinner drink included in your holiday package.'

If I hadn't seen it with my own eyes, I'd have found it hard to believe so many elderly people could move so quickly, bumping into one another, jostling for position as they hurried and scurried out of the door, heading for the bar.

It was a wonder there wasn't an accident as this group of guests pursued the free drink on offer. Perhaps that was their reward for sitting through a boring lecture, because I'd heard this talk about boats by Vincent Gibbon hadn't been the first event of doubtful interest. Trouble was, there was no choice. The management had organised a talk for every evening before dinner and it appeared it was compulsory to attend.

Well, compulsory for most people. As we reached the bar I could see one of the guests, already firmly ensconced in the best position, downing a large whisky. And by the look of him, it wasn't his first.

'Oh, there you are, Norman. I wondered where you'd got to.'

A tall, thin woman, dressed from head to toe in pale lilac, with her hair coloured to match, strode over to him. I guessed her calm demeanour was for the benefit of the other guests, because she grabbed him by the lapels and whispered something in his ear. We couldn't catch what she said, but it was obvious he was being scolded, as he jumped up with a start, splashing little drops of whisky onto his trousers.

She tutted and fussed over him as he turned red with embarrassment, hissing, 'Leave it alone, Calla, it's not a problem.' As he was short and stout, they made an odd pair.

Calla Pratt shook her head and turned away. 'Well, I'm going in to dinner, even if you prefer to stay here in the bar all night.'

As she moved off his look at her retreating back was murderous, making me think this wasn't the first time they'd had this disagreement.

A voice beside me said, 'Are you going to have the dinner on offer here, Alison, or shall we play truant and try one of the restaurants in town?'

I turned round to greet Hamish McClure, the member of staff responsible for organising the week's entertainment.

'I don't think that's allowed,' I laughed, thinking he was making a joke. 'It wouldn't look good if the organiser opted out of the meals on offer.'

He frowned rather than returning my smile. 'I've already had enough of what they serve up here,' he

15

said. 'The quality of food isn't what I'd anticipated when I signed up for the job.'

Now it was my turn to frown. 'What do you mean?' I said, remembering the various phone conversations we'd had after I'd accepted the contract.

He shrugged. 'For one thing, it's not exactly the kind of group I'm used to dealing with. Nor,' he waved his hand expansively to take in the sweep of the antiquated bar, 'is this my usual venue. I'm used to somewhere more modern, much sharper.'

A nippy reply sprang to my lips, but on reflection I decided to keep quiet. If he hadn't taken the time to investigate properly, that was down to him. Instead I said, trying not to sound as annoyed as I felt, 'I've promised to sit beside the Herrington sisters at dinner. They seem VERY interested in the talk I'm giving tomorrow night about the legends associated with the St Blane's site at Kingarth.'

If he thought most of the events he'd organised were rubbish, I wasn't letting him put my talks in that same category.

He shrugged, not in the least put out by my response. 'Suit yourself. But I warn you, don't have the shepherd's pie. It's suspiciously like the mince and potatoes served up yesterday at lunchtime.'

Without another word he turned on his heel, leaving me staring after him, before the Herrington sisters, elderly twins dressed identically in flowing garments of many hues and adorned with a wealth of sparkling jewellery, came bustling over to claim me as their table companion.

It wasn't an evening I was particularly looking forward to if I was honest, but their company was much preferable to that of Hamish and I smiled encouragingly as we headed for the dining room, each of them twittering like a little bird as we went.

As we left the bar I glanced back to see Hamish failing to persuade any of the guests to agree to his plan and with a shrug he joined the rest of the group slowly making their way to the dining room.

It was only later, much later, it became clear Hamish should have taken his own advice about the shepherd's pie.

3

There was no sign of Hamish at breakfast the next morning. Having had my company at dinner the previous evening, the Herringtons had clearly decided I was the kind of person they wanted to adopt as a friend. They made straight for the table in the corner where I'd tried to conceal myself in the vain hope of having a few moments of peace to eat what was a fairly scratch meal.

I kept reminding myself that being sociable, chatting to the guests, was part of the contract, but as they rambled on I let my mind drift to the first talk on my schedule. It was becoming increasingly clear the lecture I'd prepared would be totally unsuitable for this particular group. I'd have to come up with an alternative pretty fast.

'Don't you agree, Alison?'

The question from Iris brought me back to the present with a start. At least I guessed it was Iris. The sisters with their short white hair, their pale blue eyes and almost unlined round faces looked identical. What had I missed and could I manage to find a way of asking her to repeat it without revealing I hadn't been paying attention?

Fortunately I was saved by Lily chiding her. 'You shouldn't ask Alison a question like that, Iris. She's one of the staff. She couldn't possibly comment on the other members of staff in the hotel.'

Iris ignored this attempt to silence her. 'We were talking about that so-called events Manager, Hamish. He seems to be a bit of...'

'...a nuisance,' ended Lily.

This was a tricky one. 'I don't really know him,' was the best reply I could think of.

'And the food isn't...' said Iris as Lily butted in '...too good either.'

I smiled non-committally, but resolved to pay more heed to the conversation.

By way of diverting their attention I said, 'So your parents were keen gardeners?'

Lily looked at me strangely. 'Oh, I see what you mean. Because we were named after flowers?'

Iris frowned and leaned closer. 'What did you say?'

Lily smiled. 'It was a family tradition. There were five of us – Poppy, Rose, Iris, Jasmine and me.' She gave a little sniff. 'Iris and I are the only two left.'

Iris nodded in agreement, though I wasn't convinced she was following this exchange.

It was difficult to tell them apart. Although Iris had a decided limp and used an ornate walking stick, this was no help when they were seated.

'Yes,' murmured Iris, 'how little did I think all those years ago that one of the plants father disliked so much would provide medication for me.'

'Oh?' This was a surprising turn of conversation.

'Yes,' said Lily hastily, 'Iris means foxgloves - digitalis. She has a heart problem.'

Iris smiled as Lily added, 'Did you remember to take your pill today?'

'Of course,' said Iris, 'you're in charge of them. You always remind me.'

The information package for the *Tinsel and Turkey* weeks proudly boasted "All Meals prepared by our renowned chef and a glass of wine included." This claim was more than a little exaggerated: if the chef was indeed renowned it wasn't anywhere I knew of. The food was of the most basic kind and the buffet breakfast was worst of all: watery orange juice, a choice of supermarket own brand cereals or the full Scottish which consisted of one fried egg, one thin rasher of bacon, a fried potato scone and a quarter of a tomato.

There was a rumour the chef had been spotted in the local supermarket, rummaging through the end-of-line food items. On the off-chance there was some truth in this, I'd opted both mornings for the continental breakfast - a croissant with butter and jam and a cup of milky coffee. The croissants were bought in, so there wasn't much the chef could do to spoil those.

'We're so looking forward to your talk tonight, Alison,' gushed Calla as she and Norman approached our table. 'Can we join you?' And without waiting for a reply, they sat down on the remaining chairs.

Calla was as imposing as I remembered from the previous evening: her husband scarcely uttered a word, though he did a lot of nodding in response to his wife's comments. Today, in deference to the early hour, she was dressed in pale cream trousers and a highly embroidered top in a lurid shade of pink, but her hair was light brown rather than the lilac of the night before.

I squinted at her, trying to decide if she was wearing a wig, but it was hard to tell.

'I'm almost finished,' I said, standing up, 'but you're welcome to use this table.' To make the point I began to lift my cup and my empty plate and push them over to the other side.

'Oh, you must stay and have some more coffee. There's no need to rush off, is there? The tour bus won't be here till ten o'clock. Plenty of time.' She wagged her finger at me. 'You young people rush about so much, you'll end up with an ulcer, mark my words.'

I couldn't object to this comment, considering her description of me as "young".

But as I was about to make an excuse about having to go over my notes for the evening, there was a great commotion at the far end of the room and the Manager came rushing in as though pursued by demons.

'Good gracious, what's happening?' said Calla, clutching her chest.

Clive's first words were as unexpected as they were breathless. 'How many of you...I mean who...had the...shepherd's pie last night?'

There was a murmur in the room, an exchange of glances and Iris said, 'What is he asking? Someone's telling a lie, did he say?'

'No, dear, he's asking who ate the shepherd's pie last night,' Lily shouted.

A burly man at the table nearest the door stood up, his waistcoat straining over his considerable paunch.

'That's Major Revere,' whispered Lily.

'He was in the army, you know, and he's well used to taking command of any situation,' added Iris.

'Now what's all this about, sirrah,' boomed the Major, looming over the Manager who shrank visibly at this loud interruption.

'I'm trying to find out how many people had the shepherd's pie at dinner last night.' Clive Timmons stood wringing his hands.

'Why? Is it rationed? Or are we to have it tonight if we didn't opt for it last night, eh? Nothing would surprise me about this place.' He waited, appreciative of the titter that went round the room.

'No, no.' The Manager shook his head. 'Is everyone here?'

'I think so,' replied the Major, who'd clearly appointed himself as spokesperson for the group.

'Anna hasn't come down yet, nor Freddie.' Lily Herrington ventured, her voice trembling with the effort of taking centre stage.

'Anna? Freddie? The Burrows? No, come to think of it, I haven't seen them since last night.' The Major frowned.

'And did they have the shepherd's pie?' Clive Timmons was wide-eyed.

'Good Lord, man, I didn't go about inspecting what everyone was eating.' The Major was getting into his stride now. 'Though I must say the quality of the food isn't of a very high standard.'

The Manager ignored this slur on his hotel and the chef and turned to the slim young woman who had appeared beside him, her severe hairstyle and black framed glasses giving her a decidedly retro look. 'Yvonne, perhaps you could go and check on them?' He took out a large handkerchief and wiped his face.

'Hope nothing's wrong,' growled the Major as I added, 'Hamish hasn't appeared either.'

The Manager dismissed this comment with a wave of his hand. 'I've seen Hamish, but he's not very…'

I was sure he was going to say 'very well' which might be his reason for questioning the assembled company, but he side stepped this and ended with '…very keen on breakfast this morning.'

Ah, that was the problem. Hamish was ill and while I hoped it wasn't serious, I couldn't but help think it served him right if he'd eaten the shepherd's pie.

There was a hush in the room. The Manager stood in the doorway and although many of the guests sat and stared at him, others went on with their meal.

'No sense in letting this get cold, eh?' muttered the Major as he sat down heavily and drew in his chair to finish a plate heaped with food. He must have been able to sweet-talk the girl serving breakfast to have such a large portion.

I sipped at my now cold coffee. There was no point in asking for a re-fill - it would all be cold.

Then, as I was about to stand up and bid the Herringtons and the Pratts farewell with a, 'I won't be going on the tour, I've too much to do,' Yvonne came rushing back into the dining room.

The Manager turned to her, lifting his hand as if to calm her. 'All well, Yvonne?'

'No, it isn't,' she gulped. 'I went up to the Burrows' room as you asked, but there was no reply to my knocking.'

The Manager grabbed her by the elbow to usher her away, hissing, 'Don't make such a fuss. You'll upset the other guests. If they're ill we can call a doctor.'

Yvonne stared at him, then burst into tears. 'It's not a doctor they need, it's an undertaker. I think you'd better call the police.'

4

Any sudden death is a tragedy, but I'm sorry to say my first thought on hearing this was, 'not again'. I'd been so sure this visit to Bute would pass off without incident, unlike many of the previous ones. Then, almost as quickly, my second thought was, 'What on earth will Simon say?'

For some strange reason he seems to believe I deliberately become involved in murder and mysterious happenings every time I take up a commission on the island, though nothing could be further from the truth.

'What do you mean? They were absolutely fine last night.' I turned my attention to the Manager as he visibly bristled at Yvonne's interruption. 'You're being silly. Did you actually go into the room? Check they weren't merely asleep?'

Yvonne fidgeted with a strand of her hair and blushed, wiping away her tears with the back of her hand. 'No, but I did knock very loudly and there was no response. I peeped through the keyhole and they were in the room, lying on the bed. What's more, there was no sign of movement from either of them.'

The Manager stood wringing his hands again, before finally saying, 'You're mistaken. I'll go and see them. They are both elderly, you know, and probably slightly deaf. You may be alarming us for nothing.'

His rapid dismissal of her worries seemed to me to be more than a little premature. Surely, even if they were deaf, they would have heard Yvonne's frantic knocking? In my experience, most elderly people didn't sleep well and would be more likely to rise early than sleep late.

I sat down again as the Manager hurried out, closely followed by Yvonne. 'I'm sure there's nothing to worry about,' I said soothingly to the Herringtons as they gazed at me open-mouthed.

Iris frowned. 'Do you think it was the shepherd's pie? The Manager seemed very concerned to know how many of us had eaten it.' She shuddered. 'I'm so glad I opted for the meatballs.'

'Me too,' added Lily. 'Shepherd's pie is so often no more than re-heated meat of inferior quality. It wouldn't surprise me if they had food poisoning.'

I refrained from saying that the meatballs might also have been made from the same meat, but there was no point in alarming them further, though Calla said, 'Well, I had the shepherd's pie and I'm fine.'

'Constitution of an ox, my dear,' muttered Norman, but if Calla heard this remark she gave no sign.

A strange quiet had descended on the room; those still eating murmuring as they finished breakfast. One of their fellow guests might have died suddenly, perhaps from the suspect shepherd's pie, but everyone was aware that it was a long wait till lunchtime and although there would be a stop on the tour at the tearoom at Ettrick Bay, they had to eat as much as possible to keep hunger at bay.

Even Calla seemed to have lost the will to speak, which was one blessing. I didn't feel like engaging in conversation and certainly not in giving an opinion about what had happened.

Norman looked at his watch several times and then said, 'The Manager's been gone a long time. Do you think Yvonne was right?'

I also found this hard to believe. If the shepherd's pie had been responsible, then surely other guests would also have suffered. And so far there had been no sign of anyone else being affected.

Then, as I was about to make my excuses and leave to find the Manager or Yvonne, unable to contain myself any longer, the door to the dining room was flung open with a flourish. A beaming Manager ushered Anna and Freddie in to the room, one on either side of Yvonne and decidedly unsteady on their feet. Anna was wearing her slippers and an oddly mismatched top and skirt while Freddie's jumper was on back to front. Both looked dishevelled and peculiarly attired, as if someone else had dressed them.

'Here we are,' said the Manager in an exaggerated jovial tone, pushing them forward into the centre of the room. 'All a great mistake. Nothing to worry about. And no, they didn't have the shepherd's pie last night.' He laughed loudly at this last remark, but no one else in the room joined in. They were all too busy staring at the strange appearance of Anna and Freddie. The dining room was so silent you could have heard the proverbial pin drop.

Between them, the Manager and Yvonne hustled, then almost carried, the couple over to the empty table beside us and rather unceremoniously pushed them down into the seats.

'Now what will you have for breakfast?' he said with a false gaiety. 'No, don't get up. Yvonne and I will bring over whatever you want.'

'Very strong coffee would seem to be in order,' muttered Yvonne.

I was no longer able to contain my curiosity as the Manager bustled off to the buffet table, leaving Freddie and Anna staring zombie-like into space.

I stood up and joined Yvonne at the corner of their table. 'What on earth happened?' I whispered to her.

She stared at me blankly, then made a face. 'It appears they couldn't sleep and accidentally took a double dose of their sleeping tablets.'

But Anna had overheard - there was nothing wrong with her hearing. She turned round. 'It was that noise, that sobbing,' she said. 'It's wakened me for the past two nights and I disturbed Freddie. The only way to get some sleep was to have our tablets, but I forgot we'd already taken them.'

Before I could question her further about the 'sobbing' she claimed to have heard, there was a commotion at the far end of the room where some of the guests were beginning to leave.

'Come quickly,' said Kelly running from the front desk and rushing over to the Manager. 'You've got to come at once.' She tugged at his sleeve.

'Not now, Kelly,' he said, trying to shake her off. 'Can't you deal with it? I'm busy here. Or ask Hamish to help. He must be feeling better by now.'

'That's the problem,' said Kelly, wild-eyed as she grasped his arm yet again. 'It's about Hamish. He's collapsed in the foyer. The Major tried to help, but it was no use…and I think he's dead.'

Oh, for goodness sake, I thought, not another false alarm. This was proving to be far from the easy week I'd anticipated …and it was only Monday.

27

5

I wasn't the only one whose first reaction had been selfish. Especially as Kelly was right and this time there had been a death.

'I told you, I told you,' she repeated, snivelling into a damp tissue as several of us rushed out of the dining room to cluster around the prone body of Hamish.

As though suddenly realising the seriousness of the situation, the Manager began to move the eager spectators back, waving his hands and narrowly missing smacking Calla in the face.

'I suggest you all go into the lounge and wait there. The tourist bus will be along in,' he quickly consulted his watch, 'ten minutes.'

The small group of guests began to disperse reluctantly, given this was the most interesting event of the week so far and he had to repeat himself several times, eventually enlisting the help of one of the porters and ushering everyone away with the promise of free coffee.

I suspected he'd no intention of providing coffee as there wasn't time and sure enough, no sooner had the area been cleared than there was a sound of the scrunching of tyres on the gravel on the forecourt and a few minutes later the bus driver came breezing in.

'Came a bit early,' he said. 'I know how long it takes to get these old dears on to the bus and settled and...' His voice trailed off as he took in the scene before him:

Yvonne and the Manager standing protectively over the dead body of Hamish.

I'd retreated to the bottom of the stairs but as one of the employees, albeit a temporary one, I felt I should linger in case there was anything I could do to help.

'Heart attack, was it?' The bus driver shook his head. 'I knew him well. He never would listen, Hamish. Too many fags and too much booze, not to mention a liking for fatty foods. Bound to happen sometime.' He raised himself up on tiptoe the better to view the body, patting his own slim stomach.

Before the Manager could reply the police car arrived, siren blaring, and I made a quiet retreat. I hadn't witnessed what had happened and given my previous form, it would be better if I kept a low profile. I sidled into the lounge to tell the guests the bus had arrived and they would be off as soon as the police had finished questioning them, a comment that appeared to alarm more than a few of them. Perhaps the Manager would have to pay for that coffee after all.

What I hadn't anticipated was the barrage of questions that met me as I came in.

'What happened?'

'Did he have an accident?'

'Was he ill?'

By now the word had spread (though goodness knows how) that Hamish was dead and Norman said, 'Was it his heart? Or did someone attack him?'

'Where did you get that idea from?' I said, astonished at this ghoulish comment. Then I realised most of these guests were only too glad this hadn't happened to one of them.

'He was a nasty man,' muttered Iris.

'Yes, I didn't like his manner at all,' added Calla.

'I think it would be better if we all took up the offer of coffee,' I said and went off in search of the kitchen staff to make sure the order was delivered. No point in delaying this any longer: the guests wouldn't be able to join the bus until poor Hamish's body had been taken off and the police had finished taking preliminary statements.

In the kitchen the staff had clearly downed tools on learning about the death and they were huddled together with no sign of coffee... or anything else.

'The Manager suggested coffee could be provided for the guests while they were waiting,' I said in what I hoped was a firm tone of voice. I didn't have any authority here, but luckily the kitchen staff were too stunned by what had happened to dissent.

'And perhaps a biscuit or two?' I ventured. This was a step too far.

'Biscuits? You want biscuits?' The chef glowered at me. If I'd asked for caviar, his response couldn't have been less helpful.

'Yes, surely the hotel can stretch to a biscuit?'

He turned away, muttering to himself something about, 'I'd get on better if people didn't keep interfering in my kitchen, coming in and questioning this and that. Keep those awful old sisters out while I see what I can do.'

With coffee now ordered, I returned to the lounge to advise the guests it was on its way, carefully keeping to the side wall. I needn't have bothered. In the few minutes I'd been in the kitchen the police had cordoned off the area where Hamish had been found.

The Manager was standing by the front desk with Yvonne, Kelly and the bus driver and as I approached they suddenly stopped talking.

'I've organised coffee with biscuits. I hope that was okay,' I said. 'Will the guests be ready for the bus tour when the police have finished here?'

The Manager shifted uneasily. 'Thanks, Alison. It's been quite a shock to everyone.'

'And so it seems to have been a heart attack?' I said.

No one replied then, 'Not exactly,' said Yvonne, looking at her feet, avoiding my gaze.

Noticing my expression the Manager chimed in. 'No one's sure at the moment exactly what happened to Hamish. That's for the post mortem to decide.'

There is always a post mortem in the case of a sudden death and this would be the way with Hamish, no matter how much of an upset it caused for the hotel. But in the silence that followed my only thought was – surely it wasn't possible he'd been poisoned by the shepherd's pie?

6

The police had arrived quickly, but my intention was to keep a low profile for as long as possible, though I couldn't avoid being questioned along with everyone else. Quite a task, given the number of guests in the hotel at the moment. Nagging away at me was the memory of Hamish cautioning me against the shepherd's pie, so surely he would have chosen any meal except that?

At some stage I'd have to tell the police about his warning, but this wasn't the right moment. Everyone else who'd eaten it seemed fine and why create problems when he might have died from something as easily identifiable as a heart attack?

I retreated to my room, saying quietly to Kelly who was back on Reception, 'You know where to find me if I'm needed.'

As I passed the Manager I heard him mutter, 'So like Hamish to cause a problem. It's the last thing we need right now.'

A rather unfeeling comment in the circumstances.

The Herringtons were sitting beside the Major on the little sofa at the bottom of the main stairway and as I passed, he rose and grabbed me by the elbow. 'What's going on, eh? Have you any information about what happened to the poor man?'

Unwilling to become involved in speculation, I shook my head, put on my sweetest smile and headed upstairs saying, 'Absolutely not. Your guess is as good as mine, but no doubt the Manager will make an announcement shortly.'

He growled, dissatisfied with this answer, but I was out of range before he could think of a response.

I hadn't a clue if the Manager did intend to make a statement about Hamish, but there was no point in encouraging gossip and I reached my room unhindered.

But as I closed the door behind me I was at a loss. Would this mean my talks would be cancelled? And if so, what would I do? I supposed a certain amount of my fee would be reimbursed, then chided myself for such a mercenary thought at this time. Poor Hamish was lying dead and here was I worrying about my contract. Besides it was unlikely this week would be cancelled halfway through. That would cause more problems than it solved.

I rummaged in my bag and eventually found my mobile to call Simon. The job he'd started the previous year with Scottish Alignment Ltd had grown into a full-time post. He'd started with them on a part-time basis, following his early retirement from his position as head of department in a further education college and his training skills were exactly what the company wanted.

He was the first to admit working on his own as a freelance didn't suit him one little bit, whereas I loved it, in spite of all the uncertainties. He couldn't conceal his delight at being back in full-time employment, although for the moment it meant he had to stay in Inverness during the week and come home to Glasgow at the weekends.

I don't know if it was because of the new job, or a more settled time in our lives, but we seemed to be getting along very well at the moment, with none of the ups and downs in our relationship we'd experienced over the past few years. Perhaps the arrival of Connor had something to do with it, but whatever the reason, I was grateful we'd managed to make it through the difficult times.

And his sound advice was exactly what I needed at this time. Of course, as luck would have it, the call went straight to voicemail and feeling very frustrated, I sat down on the bed to consider my next move.

As I mulled over the options for the rest of the day, there was a soft rapping at the door. I held my breath. I couldn't think who it might be and I wasn't in the mood for more speculation about Hamish. At the moment I wanted time on my own, time to think.

The knocking came again, fiercer and more insistent.

I sat motionless, scarcely daring to breathe.

A voice said, 'Are you in there? I really need to talk to you.'

My heart sank. I recognised that voice - it was Anna Burrows. Then I felt downright mean. She and her husband Freddie were among the oldest of the many old guests at this event and how could I ignore her request? Besides this was part of my duties, something I'd signed up for.

Reluctantly I stood up and went across to open the door, putting on my brightest smile. Thankfully the concerns of most of these guests usually turned out to be trivial, nothing of any great concern. Perhaps she merely wanted reassurance after the earlier episode of the sleeping pills.

There was nothing in Anna's first words to make me suspect this might be anything different. 'Is everything okay? You aren't involved in that stramash downstairs?'

'No, no, everything's fine,' I lied, keeping the door only slightly ajar.

But she wasn't to be so easily deterred. 'I'm glad of the opportunity to have a word with you,' she said, pushing her way in, demonstrating a strength that belied her years and her recent state of health.

Closing the door firmly behind her, she edged me further back into the room. 'There's something strange going on in this hotel,' she said, dropping her voice to a whisper.

I stifled a desire to say, 'Of course there's something strange, given the sudden death of Hamish.' But it wasn't my duty to start gossiping about what might and might not have happened. The post mortem would provide an answer soon enough.

'I'm sure Hamish's death was unfortunate,' I replied. 'He was very overweight and these sudden heart attacks can happen.' I didn't mention the belief the shepherd's pie might have hastened his end.

She looked at me, perplexed. 'I'm not talking about Hamish. Of course it's likely his death was no more than an unfortunate occurrence. I'm talking about the noises in the night, the sound of someone weeping, but when I check there's no one there. Do you believe in ghosts, Alison?'

This conversation was becoming more and more peculiar. Assuming a hearty voice, I attempted to end it. 'Of course there will be noises during the night. This is a very old hotel, there are bound to be creaks and groans as it settles down.'

I'd no desire to be involved in her wild imaginings. Anna and her husband probably lived in a brand new retirement flat somewhere, well insulated from the usual noises of an old building. 'And,' I added, 'in spite of all the renovation, it's still very draughty. I've been wakened in the night by the wind whistling through the cracks.'

'It's not any of your usual old building noises,' she replied, a trifle tartly. 'Freddie and I live in a large Victorian villa in the south side of Glasgow. We're well used to the sounds that an old house makes. This is something different.'

So much for my theory about a modern, sound-proofed flat and resigned to some odd tale, the result of a vivid imagination or the medication she had to take, I flopped down on the bed. 'What kind of noises have you been hearing?'

Perhaps once she'd told me about her worries she'd be able to forget whatever it was she'd heard. I could always say I'd pass on her concerns to the Manager, as though he didn't have enough problems at the moment.

But as she sat down in the wicker chair by the little table at the window too late I realised my sitting on the bed had been a mistake. She seemed to be settling in for a long story. Pointedly I looked at my watch as she began to speak again.

'It's not what you think,' she said leaning forward in a conspiratorial way and glancing around, though there was clearly no one else in the room. 'It's not an old building settling for the night, nor is it sounds made by other guests.'

Without pausing for breath she went on, 'It's a soft, crying noise, as though someone was in great pain, or great trouble. But there's no one there.'

This was nonsense. 'I don't think so,' I replied, more abruptly than intended, but I didn't want her to be spreading rumour, or panic, among the other guests. 'Are you sure you weren't dreaming?'

She bristled visibly, pushing back a lock of grey hair that had fallen over her face. 'I'm sure. And we've heard it each night since we've been here. I get up and look out into the corridor, but there's nothing to be seen.'

'Freddie has heard it too?' This put a different slant on her story, if her husband had also been hearing these strange noises.

She sniffed before continuing a little more hesitantly. 'Well, not exactly. But then he isn't as tuned in as I am. He's a much heavier sleeper.'

I relaxed a little. This was more like it. She was probably dreaming and, in that halfway state between sleeping and waking, she was imagining she heard a noise. A speculation borne out by what had happened earlier when they'd taken a double dose of sleeping pills.

'I'm not making it up,' she said as though she'd read my mind. 'I'm telling you I heard it clear as anything. Someone in trouble, someone looking for help.'

She stood up, grabbing on to the chair as she tottered a little unsteadily. 'If you don't believe me, why don't you come along and listen for yourself.'

She sounded so cross, so upset, I felt I had to soothe her somehow. I certainly didn't want her complaining to the Manager about the curt treatment she'd received. 'Which room are you in?'

'We're in one of the rooms at the top of the building, on the floor above you. The Manager said it was the only one available. There's no one else on that floor as far as I know. I believe the building was a house originally, before they added several wings and converted the place into a hotel.'

'Yes, yes, this is the oldest part of the building. I believe he only opened up your room because there was such a good response to the *Turkey and Tinsel* weeks.'

'So you will come along tonight? Nothing happens before two in the morning but you're welcome to have a cup of tea while you wait.'

Reluctant to become involved in this nonsense about ghosts I tried to think of a way of putting her off and said, 'Have you spoken to the Manager about this? Told him what you've heard.'

Anna looked scornful, as though this was a ridiculous suggestion. 'He's absolutely useless. Of course I tried him first. Dismissed me out of hand, saying it must be my imagination, almost threatened me if I told anyone. Too worried about the reputation of his hotel, no doubt. About how the other guests would react.' She sniffed. 'He warned me in no uncertain terms against saying anything in front of the others.'

She paused. 'That's why,' wagging her finger, 'that's why I've asked you. If you come along about half past one that will do.'

Without waiting for an answer she stood up and made somewhat unsteadily for the door as I sprang to my feet ready to catch her.

She waved me away as she regained her balance, saying, 'I know I can rely on you. You strike me as being a very sensible woman.'

And with that she left, closing the door quietly behind her. I sat on the bed, pondering what she'd said. No doubt the compliment of being a "sensible woman" was meant to flatter me into doing what she wanted, but it didn't make me in the least inclined to agree to her request.

This story was all nonsense of course, the imaginings of an elderly woman who probably didn't sleep well, who confused dreams with reality. And as for the idea of a ghost, that was even more ridiculous.

And yet, and yet. Much of the top floor had yet to be renovated. In spite of my reservations, my inclination to dismiss her account of someone crying in the night, I couldn't help but be intrigued by her story.

It would be no trouble to go along to her room as she suggested. It could do no harm and would scotch this silly tale for good. Or so I hoped.

7

After Anna left I sat in silence for a while, trying to think of a way to deal with this request. If the story was nonsense, it would be easy, but if there was something to this tale that would be a different proposition.

There was no reason to become involved: there were plenty of problems already. There had been several jokes about the quality of the food on offer, particularly the shepherd's pie, and the way in which Hamish had died, but no one seriously believed it. Given his girth and his (rumoured) very unhealthy lifestyle it wasn't much of a surprise to anyone who knew him that he'd died so suddenly.

In the meantime there was the evening's talk to prepare for and as I came downstairs later I met the Manager.

My intention was to request Clive to rearrange the seating in the large chilly ballroom. I didn't expect there would be much of an audience, in spite of the lack of alternative entertainment for the early evening.

The week was clearly defined: the Saturday evening was taken up by the Welcome dinner. On the following three nights guests were offered talks on subjects deemed to be of interest, followed after dinner by entertainment much more to their liking. These included a revue show, a tribute night or a film.

If Hamish had arranged the early evening programme he'd little idea of the interests of a group such as this, but it was a job, I was being reasonably well paid and it was only two weeks out of my life.

What's more this week, thanks to Vincent Gibbon, I'd only two talks scheduled.

The Manager was standing with his back to me, in earnest conversation with a very large lady carrying a large bright blue handbag.

On coming closer, my first thought was that it must be a struggle to carry around a handbag of that size all day and I started back in fright at the sound of a high pitched yapping noise coming from somewhere nearby.

'Hush, darling,' she said, apparently to the handbag, her heavily made up face creasing into a smile of sorts, though her forehead remained suspiciously taut beneath a mass of frizzy blonde curls. I looked round, but there was no sign of a dog.

Then I realised the yapping was coming from the handbag itself and suddenly a tiny dog, much smaller than its bark suggested, poked its sharply pointed head out of the top.

The lady smiled again as the dog continued its high pitched yapping. 'He gets quite excited when he sees new people. He's such a friendly dog.' She gazed fondly at the little head looking out of the bag, now accompanied by a quivering upper body and a set of paws. This was the smallest dog I'd ever seen. Its size was no indication of the strength of its yapping, nor of its growling as I approached it.

Don't misunderstand me - I like dogs, even though it's a cat, Motley, we have at home. But as with all cats, Motley is nothing if not independent and only meows if there's a good reason. This was more like one of those toy dogs you would give a child at Christmas. Its sharp face peeped out under a cloud of silky gold hair and its tiny paws latched on firmly to the edge of the bag.

She turned round and close up I could see she wasn't as young as I'd first thought in spite of her dyed hair and the carefully applied make-up.

'This is Sylvia Openshaw,' said the Manager, almost bowing as he introduced us. 'Alison is one of our guest speakers. She's very knowledgeable about Bute and I'm sure her talks will be most entertaining.'

Sylvia raised an eyebrow, though she did this with some difficulty as she fiddled with the gauzy scarf carefully draped round her neck. 'So you're a Brandane then? You were born on Bute?'

I shook my head. 'Sadly, no. But we've been coming here for many years so I suppose I could consider myself an honorary Brandane.'

'There's no such thing. You're either born on the island or you're not.' As though to emphasize her point, the little dog began to yap again, wriggling within the confines of the bag. 'He's so excitable,' she said fondly.

Even at this early stage I could tell we were unlikely to become friends.

Lily came out of the lounge and walked over to join us, closely followed by Iris who was leaning heavily on her walking stick.

'A dog? How delightful,' she said, reaching out her hand to pat it, only to be greeted by a snarl and a snapping of jaws.

'Dear me, not very friendly, is he,' she said, drawing back in alarm, backing into Iris and causing her stick to clatter to the floor.

'Oh, I'm sure he's lovely once he gets to know you,' cooed the Manager, tentatively putting out his hand to stroke the dog only to have it snapped at by a set of very fine sharp teeth.

'There, there, Jasper,' said Sylvia, 'he didn't mean to upset you.' She patted the wriggling, trembling animal and then said, 'I'll go up to my room. You can send up some tea on a tray. And make sure it's a decent brew, not that rubbish you serve to the other guests.'

With that she turned on her heel and started up the stairs, lugging the large bag with some difficulty, leaving us staring after her.

He grinned at me, a little shame-faced. 'She is really very pleasant when you get to know her,' he said. 'She's so fond of her dog.'

'And I suppose the dog is also delightful when it realises you mean it no harm?' Lily was being sarcastic, but he failed to notice the tone of voice and smiled uneasily as he said, 'Yes, usually Jasper is fine. He has a sensitive nature, is easily upset.'

'He's a dog, for goodness' sake, or I assume he's a dog, though it's pretty difficult to tell what kind of dog he might be.' The words were out before I could help myself.

'I can't stand dogs like that,' muttered Lily. 'We had a dog at home in the old days, a Labrador, not that excuse for an animal. Nasty creature.'

With that she turned and headed back to the lounge, followed by Iris who was clattering her stick loudly as if to show her agreement with her sister's words of disapproval.

Yvonne had pretended to be busy at the computer on the Reception desk all through this conversation, but she stifled a laugh and seemed engrossed in her screen as the Manager whirled round to her. 'I don't know

43

what's so funny, Yvonne. Sylvia is a very important client for us, very important indeed. We have to make absolutely certain her every whim is catered for ... and that includes Jasper.'

'Yes, Mr Timmons,' said Yvonne meekly, bowing her head, but I could see she was having the greatest difficulty in controlling her mirth by the way her shoulders were shaking. She dived underneath the counter and came up a moment later with a handkerchief clutched to her mouth, coughing loudly to disguise her amusement.

As though in agreement, the Santa on the desk burst out with a loud, 'Ho, ho, ho.'

The Manager ignored this and turning to me said, 'She's coming along to your talk tonight, Alison. She has a great interest in the history of the island. I hope you've prepared well, because she's a stickler for accuracy. She considers herself an expert.'

This distrust of my ability was so unexpected it was a moment or two before I could think of a reply, by which time the Manager had scurried off, muttering, 'I must make sure the kitchen staff prepare her tea at once.'

A soon as I was left alone with Yvonne, there was a decided lightening of the atmosphere and she sat back, evidently no longer feeling the need to pretend to be absorbed in her computer. 'Bit of bad luck her turning up like that,' she said. 'Mr Timmons didn't expect her, though she always comes to stay over Christmas and New Year.'

'That's unusual, surely?'

Yvonne grinned. 'Not for her. There's nowhere else for her to go, I guess. She does have a son, but I hear

44

his wife can't stand her. Or perhaps it's that dreadful dog they can't stand. She treats it like a child, spoils it rotten. She comes here three times a year, regular as clockwork – Easter for a month, the first two weeks in July and Christmas and New Year for two weeks. Apart from that we don't see her at all. It's strange she's decided to turn up so early.'

Not that I wanted to defend Sylvia, but Yvonne seemed rather harsh. 'That's the thing with animals, you intend to be strict with them, but you can't help spoiling them. At least that's what happens with our cat, Motley.' I thought guiltily of all the times I'd given him 'treats' much to Simon's disgust.

'I don't think any dog could be as spoiled as Jasper,' Yvonne said with a loud sniff. 'Did you see it? It's like a large furry rat rather than a dog.' She shuddered. 'I wouldn't have that animal in my house.'

It was clear Yvonne couldn't stand the dog or its owner and I had to be very careful. In a small place like this word and rumour spread like wildfire and there was no way I wanted to offend Sylvia.

'Each to his own,' I shrugged my shoulders. 'I have to go. I've a few bits and pieces to sort out before tonight. No matter how often you do this kind of thing, you still get nervous.'

But Yvonne wasn't prepared to end the conversation like this. 'You know who Sylvia is, don't you?'

'No…I thought she was one of the guests, one who comes frequently.'

Yvonne laughed and tossed back her head. 'There's more to it than that.'

Now I was curious. 'So tell me, who is she?'

Yvonne pursed her lips and took a deep breath. Whatever she was about to say, she was aiming for maximum impact.

'Her family once owned this hotel. It was in the family for years - her husband's family that is. They bought it some time after the war, tried to make a go of it, but its heyday was over. When her husband died her son persuaded her to put it on the market, though she was very reluctant to sell a place that meant so much to both of them. The new owners had the place rebuilt using what was left of the original. I suspect that was what caused the difficulties between them. Trouble is, she still thinks she owns the place and Clive does nothing to make her face reality. She's a guest like any other.'

This explained a lot, but at that moment the phone rang and Yvonne changed her tone of voice as she answered it.

I went up the stairs slowly, thinking about what I'd heard. This might be why the Manager had been grovelling so much, but not why Sylvia had decided to break her usual routine and turn up early. I didn't flatter myself it was because she wanted to hear my talks. There must be some other reason.

8

Thank goodness Simon phoned me back later that evening before I was due in Anna's room to test out this absurd idea she had about hearing noises during the night. The more I thought about it, the less inclined I was to continue and bitterly regretted agreeing.

He sounded so upbeat I hesitated to tell him of my problems and when I did so it came out in a rush '... but it wasn't anything to do with me,' I said, 'none of these events were my doing.'

There was a long pause and I could hear him breathing deeply, trying to calm down before answering. Eventually he said, 'Alison, do you not think it best you come home, forget all about this commission. I'm earning well now, there's no need for you to worry about money.'

'I don't think so.' Unwilling to have an argument during a phone call and knowing he had my best interests at heart, I had to qualify this terse statement. 'It was difficult enough for Mr Timmons to find someone at short notice. A couple of his first choices pulled out.'

'Shows how sensible they were,' he grunted. 'I don't see why you can't do the same. Surely they could fill the time somehow.'

But I wasn't to be persuaded. 'All I wanted was a little support,' I said huffily. 'It's only two weeks after all and then we can discuss what I do next.'

'I guess that would be a good idea,' he replied and I detected a note of caution in his voice.

'Is there something wrong?' A sinking feeling as I had an awful premonition this new job of his might have run into difficulties.

'Nothing at all,' he said. 'In fact everything is going well, very well. They've asked me to go to London to talk to the parent company about training some of the staff there.'

A wave of relief hit me. 'Well done,' I said, adding hastily, 'You'll enjoy a trip back there.' London was where we'd met, where our romance had blossomed, more years ago than I cared to remember.

We chatted for a few more minutes and then he rang off saying, 'Remember, Alison, coming home is always a possibility.'

In spite of what he said, I didn't feel any more confident as I ended the call, but determined to be positive about the time remaining at the Hydro.

As I sat there, contemplating the options or lack of options open to me, my mobile rang again and I checked the display before answering. I was in no mood for idle chit chat, but this time it was Maura.

'Hi, Mum, sorry to phone so late but Connor only fell asleep a few minutes ago.' She sounded tired, but that's normal for most parents of young children and I wasn't unduly worried. Even so, it wasn't like her to call at this hour. Once Connor was sound asleep I suspect she and Alan collapsed on the sofa. I remembered that stage of life well.

After a few general comments it became clear she had something on her mind.

'I thought you'd want to know,' she said with a studied casualness, 'Alan's been asked to go back to the London office.'

There was a pause as she waited for my response, but it was a moment or two before the implications of this struck home. They didn't live very near us, but it was near enough and now with our first grandchild, the wrench if they left would be very difficult. Yet what to say without sounding selfish?

'It could have been worse,' she said defensively, hearing my sharp intake of breath, 'it's because the colleague who was sent out to Boston was poached by some big company there. Fortunately Alan's immediate boss jumped at the chance to replace him. It's a big opportunity, a big promotion for Alan. Thank goodness we only rented out our house in Kent.'

'That's good news,' I said forcing myself to sound happy for them. 'It's a bit unexpected. When do you leave?'

'Sometime early in the New Year,' she said airily. 'The tenants' lease is up at the end of February, but Alan will have to start a bit earlier. I'll be on my own during that time in Edinburgh, organising everything here.'

Well, that probably took care of the next few months after this work at the Hydro finished. I'd be spending a lot of time in Edinburgh helping Maura.

'Oops, think I can hear Connor. I'll have a longer chat when you're back home.' And with that she rang off, leaving me staring at the screen and contemplating how you think life is on an even keel, things are settled for a while, then some surprise or other pops up. All that was needed now was for my younger daughter

Deborah to make some outlandish decision or my son Alastair to surprise us with his news.

It was all overwhelming, more so because I was stuck in this hotel for another ten days before I could have a proper chat with Maura.

I was startled out of my reverie by the sound of loud knocking on the door and reluctantly I got to my feet to open it. Anna was standing there, her woolly dressing gown round her shoulders.

'Ready, Alison?' she whispered, casting a furtive glance behind her into the empty corridor. 'You hadn't forgotten, had you?'

'No, I hadn't,' I replied and grabbing my bag and a large sweater, I followed her up to her room.

This would be a complete waste of time, an undertaking that would leave me tired and out of sorts the next day and I'd no idea why I'd agreed.

9

What on earth am I doing here, I thought as I sat in the
armchair in the bedroom belonging to Freddie and
Anna. I hadn't been in the top floor of the old wing and
it was clear this was where the servants or staff had
slept. I recalled some story about the place having
started out as a house, Swantonhill House, before
becoming a hotel back in the days when a large number
of staff were required to keep the Hydro running
smoothly.

Anna was right. Theirs was the only serviceable
bedroom on this floor and it appeared many of the
others had been used as store cupboards, since most had
no numbers. Even so, there was bound to be a simple
explanation for the noises Anna had heard, or thought
she heard.

I shivered, snuggling deeper into the spare quilt
she'd found in the cupboard. The sweater I'd brought
wasn't nearly warm enough to combat the chilliness of
the night in this top corridor of the hotel.

I peered at my watch, squinting to see the time in the
soft glow of the nightlight beside Anna's bed.
Regardless of her promises to keep awake, Anna had
drifted off to sleep and now I could hear the sound of
gentle snoring coming from the direction of her bed.
This together with the louder snoring from Freddie,
'You can't expect me to stay awake for this nonsense,'
he had snorted, made sure there was no way I would
drop off.

Two o'clock and nothing had happened. In spite of straining my ears to catch any sound, the only noise had been from a couple of late night revellers returning to a room on the floor below somewhere around midnight with a lot of 'Hush, hush,' and giggling.

I shifted this way and that to ease my aching limbs, struggling to find a more comfortable position in this small chair. This was a waste of time and effort. I'd wait another half hour, I promised myself, until two thirty and if there was nothing happening by then, I'd sneak back to my own room.

It was all I could do to keep my eyes open after spending the evening giving a talk on St Blane and his connection with Bute.

I must admit I'd been more than a little apprehensive about the topic, but in the event the audience had been most welcoming and not only listened attentively, but asked a good number of questions at the end. Perhaps after the talk of life saving in a boat from the night before, mine was welcome. At least it didn't raise the prospect of sudden death.

There was only one silly question and that was from Sylvia. 'But how do you know all this is true?' she said, when I finished speaking about the medieval custom of burying men and women in different cemeteries and the legend it was because St Blane had been refused help by a woman he'd met on the shore. 'I mean we do like some proof.'

She'd turned to the rest of the audience for approval, but there was a stony silence, most people deliberately avoiding her gaze.

Sylvia was beginning to get on everyone's nerves. Thank goodness the dog in her bag hadn't made a sound all during my talk. I'd been prepared to ask her to leave if Jasper started barking, but fortunately that wasn't needed. And my answer seemed to satisfy her, because there wasn't a peep out of her for the rest of the evening.

Or perhaps it was the way I delivered it in a determined tone of voice. I hadn't spent all those years facing down boisterous teenage boys to let someone like Sylvia frighten me.

Even so, I'd forgotten how tiring it was giving a talk, trying to keep an audience engaged, and now, as I counted the minutes ticking by, it was all I could do to keep awake.

I must have dropped off into a micro sleep because the next thing I remember was jerking awake at a sudden sound. For a moment I couldn't think where I was and had to shake my head a couple of times to rouse myself.

Yes, this most certainly hadn't been my imagination. There was a noise and it was coming from outside this room. Awakened so suddenly, my heart started to pound and before I could lose my nerve, I stood up and headed for the door. It was definitely from somewhere further along the corridor, a soft moaning and crying sound, as though someone was in deep distress.

I padded over to Anna and shook her gently awake. She sat straight up in bed. 'What's wrong? What's happening?'

I put my finger to my lips and nodded in the direction of Freddie who was still sound asleep, oblivious to the disturbance.

'I can hear a noise like someone sobbing,' I whispered.

53

Anna swung her legs round and stood up, steadying herself. 'I told you. Now you've heard it you'll believe I was telling the truth.'

Together we crept over to the door, though why we were being so cautious I don't know. If there was anyone out in the corridor they would hardly be troubled by our presence, not if, as Anna claimed, this was a nightly occurrence.

'What do you think it is?' Anna grasped my arm as I made to open the door.

Sounding bolder than I felt, I said, 'The best thing we can do is go out together and try to track down the cause.'

Anna looked doubtful.

'Come on,' I said abruptly. If I was to be kept awake half the night I wanted some answers.

Carefully we opened the door and crept out into the corridor, the carpet muffling any sound from our footsteps.

The only illumination was from the soft nightlights on the wall half way down, but all they did was cast long shadows. 'Have you been out here before when you heard it?' I asked.

Anna shook her head. 'No, only peered out. Truth to tell I was too scared and as Freddie would sleep through anything, he refused to help me. Said I must have been dreaming.'

'Well, now's our chance.' With Anna close behind me, I tiptoed down towards the entrance to the lift.

Suddenly there was a great rattling sound and I almost jumped out of my skin before I realised it was only the lift heading for the ground floor to pick up the last of the late night revellers. In this old part of the building the original lift had been restored - or at least restored in that it did work, even if it made a terrible din as it creaked its way up and down.

'Stop.' Anna grabbed my arm. 'There it is again. Can you hear it?'

We stood rooted to the spot. For a moment there was silence and then it came again, a low sobbing sound.

'It's further down the corridor,' said Anna and we inched our way towards the source of the noise.

I hoped no one would suddenly appear and we'd then have to think of a reason why we were creeping about the hotel corridor in the middle of the night like a pair of thieves, listening intently at one door after another.

We reached the end of the corridor and stood looking at each other.

'It's not from any of the rooms on this floor,' said Anna.

I looked round again. The crying had stopped, but she was right. None of the rooms on this floor seemed to be the source of the sobbing.

'Could it be from the floor above?' Anna gestured towards the ceiling.

I shook my head. 'I don't think so. There's nothing up there except the turret and it's purely decorative from what I know. These walls are really thick, there's no way a sound as low as that could travel any distance.'

What were we to do now? There had definitely been a noise, Anna hadn't imagined that and neither had I, but there seemed to be no way to track it down, find out where it was coming from.

We stood absolutely still for a few minutes longer, but there was no repetition of the sobbing we'd heard and 'There's no point in standing here, getting cold,' I said, noticing how Anna had only had time to throw a thin cardigan over her nightie. 'There's nothing more we can do here.'

We crept back into the room where Freddie still lay sound asleep, oblivious to the excitement. I lifted my bag and prepared to leave, whispering, 'This noise you heard - was it at the same time every night?'

She paused for a moment and frowned as though trying to recall the details. 'Yes, I think it was. No, I'm sure it was.' She smiled at me. 'Will you come back tomorrow night and we can try again?'

'Sorry, I don't think I can do that. You can let me know if you hear it again.'

She looked so wretched at this abrupt dismissal of her concerns that I'd no option but to say hastily, 'Well, I might manage one more night. Let's see how things stand in the morning,' ignoring the fact it was already morning.

This seemed to satisfy her at least temporarily and with a hasty 'goodnight' I left and went down the stairs to my room on the floor below. There was no way I intended to trust myself to the creaky lift.

As so often happens, shattered though I was, once back in my own room sleep evaded me. I lay in bed, tossing this way and that, willing myself to fall asleep, but to no avail and eventually I got up, put on the light and made a cup of tea, aware I'd be fit for nothing later. Fortunately I didn't have to give a talk on Tuesday evening, merely chat to the guests and I might manage to snatch a nap sometime during the afternoon.

There was no doubt in my mind Anna had heard something in the corridor outside her room. I'd also heard it. But what could it be? I shut my eyes and in my imagination I went back along the corridor, counting the doors.

Anna and Freddie were in Room 302 in the far corner and there was no one in the room opposite. There were two rooms on either side until you reached the entrance to the lift and then by counting the doors there were a further three on one side and four on the other until you reached the end of the corridor.

And I was certain I was right; with the thickness of these walls there was no way a sound as low as that weeping we'd heard would travel far.

It was a great puzzle. Though I'd said to Anna I might be willing to spend another night in her room waiting to hear if the noise came again, I might go up on my own round about the time the noise was said to start. I'd manage a lot better by myself and there was sure to be some simple explanation for this strange event. In my experience there usually was. I certainly didn't believe in ghosts.

My mind now made up, I fell sound asleep and didn't waken till the alarm startled me all too soon a few hours later.

10

'Sylvia's been looking for you,' Yvonne called to the Manager as I made my way down to breakfast next morning.

As soon as I'd wakened I'd begun reflecting on the events of the previous night and wondering if the whole episode might be no more than auto suggestion, some kind of sympathetic concord with Anna. The more I thought about it, the more sensible this idea seemed and made me decide to take up Anna's suggestion to check it out one more time.

'She's very distressed,' I heard Yvonne say. 'Very distressed.'

The Manager sighed as I crossed beside the desk to go into the breakfast room. 'You see what it's like, Alison, you're completely at the mercy of your guests.' He looked worried.

He went over to Yvonne. 'So what is it about this time? What has displeased her majesty now? Her darling Jasper being kept awake by noisy guests?' He laughed but it was a mirthless laugh with more than a hint of fear in it. 'Whatever it is, it won't be anything serious. She's always complaining about something or other.'

Yvonne began to signal to him, raising her eyebrows and making faces.

The Manager frowned. 'What on earth's wrong with you?' as a voice behind him said, 'No, my darling Jasper wasn't kept awake by noisy guests, thank you very much,' and he whirled round to see a very irate Sylvia had come up behind him so quietly he hadn't registered her presence.

'Only joking, only joking.' But his laugh was hollow and the way he was twisting his hands together showed he knew he was in trouble.

Sylvia ignored his attempt to explain his comments. 'It's something much more serious. As you can see I'm quite on my own this morning.'

For a moment the Manager looked baffled but Sylvia went on, 'It's Jasper, you silly man. Did you not notice he's not with me?'

And sure enough where there was usually a giant bag housing her pet, there was now a dainty handbag dangling by her side.

'I hope nothing's happened to him?' said the Manager, trying to sound sincere, though both Yvonne and I knew what was going through his mind and it wasn't concern about Jasper.

'Only that someone's tried to poison him, that's all - a mere trifle to you, I'm sure.'

She pulled a handkerchief from her bag and dabbed at her eyes. 'My poor, poor Jasper, who would want to do such a thing?'

'Is he dead?' Aware his tone of voice was too eager, the Manager retreated and hastened to say solemnly, 'I mean, I do hope he's okay.'

'Thankfully, yes,' snapped Sylvia. 'The vet said he would be fine, but they're keeping him in for observation. I had to call him out in the middle of the night – not that you'd have noticed.'

'I don't see how any of this could be my fault,' the Manager protested.

'Of course it was your fault. I asked the chef to prepare something for Jasper and it was almost immediately after eating it that he fell ill. Poor mite, shivering and vomiting.' She shuddered. 'It was quite awful to see.'

'He didn't by any chance have leftover shepherd's pie, did he?' I said.

She turned as though only just noticing I was there. 'Shepherd's pie? Why on earth would I give my pedigree dog shepherd's pie? If I wouldn't feed him that terrible dog food people buy in tins, I wouldn't dream of feeding him that.'

She tutted loudly, as though considering me particularly dim.

But I was persistent. 'So what did he have to eat?'

She sniffed. 'I asked the chef to prepare him a portion of finely minced beef, if you must know.'

I refrained from comment, but silently thought this was likely to be the same meat as went into the shepherd's pie. I'd have to have a word with the Manager, tell him of my suspicions. But now wasn't the moment to do so as he said, 'I'll have a word with chef, but I can assure you that all our meat is of the best quality, sourced from local farms.'

Having made her point and given the Manager a dressing down, Sylvia was satisfied. 'I can't stand round here all day: I have to collect Jasper from the vet. I'll speak to you about this later...once you've had a word with chef.'

The Manager stared after her as she swept out, shaking his head. 'I don't understand it, I really don't. It couldn't be anything to do with the food we have here.'

He turned to me, a pleading look on his face. 'I'm sure all our meat is quality.'

'Unless,' muttered Yvonne waspishly, 'chef did it deliberately, fed up with her and her demands for her pet.'

The Manager looked horrified. 'There's no way he'd do that. It's more likely she's been over-feeding it with titbits. He's completely spoiled.' Having found a reason for Jasper's illness, he began to look more cheerful.

'I suppose people do become very attached to their pets, especially when they are lonely.' I stopped. Why on earth was I defending Sylvia? She was a nuisance to everyone.

The Manager straightened his tie nervously. 'I'll speak to chef, but really the very notion that the meat could have caused Jasper's upset is nothing short of ridiculous.' He was becoming more certain of his case by the moment. 'Anyway,' more briskly, 'there are other guests to attend to.'

'Yes, but don't forget to have a word with the chef,' Yvonne said, perhaps fearful she'd have to deal with Sylvia if he didn't. And if she had additional information about the chef, surely she would voice her suspicions to Clive?

'Yes, yes.' But his manner was offhand as he hurried away to other duties.

Yvonne stood looking after him and shrugged. 'I don't envy him one little bit. It's bad enough to have had Hamish die like that, but to have this happen…' Her voice tailed off, but it was clear she thought Clive Timmons had little future as the Manager of the Hydro.

61

It was a pity she hadn't stressed the need to talk to the chef, especially when word came through later in the week about the initial post mortem on Hamish.

11

At first it seemed the rest of the week would pass without incident. I did go back to Anna's room on Tuesday night, but in spite of being there for a couple of hours there was no sound of anyone sobbing or crying. After waiting till almost three o'clock I left saying, 'Whatever it was, it looks as if it's been sorted.' I could almost swear she was disappointed.

Jasper made a full recovery and if anything seemed yappier than ever, though the Manager went out of his way to be nice to Sylvia at every occasion.

Sylvia wasn't to be so easily pacified. 'Poor Jasper,' she kept saying, 'Mummy was quite worried about you.'

And then she would glare at Clive Timmons as though daring him to make any comment. At least he'd stopped trying to pet the dog: he'd almost had his finger bitten off the last time he'd tried it. 'It's not everyone whom Jasper likes,' Sylvia had said, 'he's very discerning.'

It was too good to last. Wednesday started off with a beautiful clear crisp morning and several of the guests had ventured outdoors for a walk in the grounds. Lunch had been surprisingly good, with not a single complaint. It was later that the trouble started.

And as is the usual way, everything that could possibly go wrong went wrong as I prepared to give my second talk of the week. This time I wanted to focus on the Rothesay Pavilion before the war.

I'd plenty of material and, being sure many of the guests would remember stories about the place, my aim was to have the audience participate. But when I came into the ballroom to check my heart sank. All my carefully arranged chairs had been equally carefully re-arranged back to their original places and the note of informality I'd hoped for by placing them in a semicircle was completely ruined.

Row after row of serried ranks of chairs faced the front where a temporary stage had been erected with a table designed to hold a slide projector. This wasn't right either: I'd specifically requested a clear table so that I could use a laptop for the presentation. This was a lot more serious than the rearrangement of chairs.

I hurried out in to the Reception area where Kelly had been replaced by Phyllis, a student who filled in from time to time. She was engrossed in her mobile and had every appearance of not wanting to be disturbed, but too bad. I needed someone to sort out this predicament.

'I've a big problem here,' I said, 'and I need some help pretty quickly.'

She raised her eyebrows. 'What kind of help?' A look of irritation crossed her face.

Briefly I explained my difficulty, but the expression on her face didn't change. 'Bertie usually deals with that,' she said.

'Well, could you call him and tell him it's urgent?'

'Oh, he's only here during the day. He goes off duty at four.'

'So who deals with any emergencies?'

'We don't usually have any emergencies. Bertie is a kind of general handyman, that's all.'

This was ridiculous. 'There must be someone who can deal with a crisis like this. I have to have the room the way I want it, if the talk is to be a success.' I wasn't about to try to rearrange the room on my own.

She frowned. The notion of an emergency was one she appeared to be unfamiliar with. I know on Bute there is a different attitude to time, which seems to move a great deal slower than it does on the mainland, but even so.

'Can you call the Manager?' Surely there was someone available to help.

'That's the problem if you depend on the technology,' said Phyllis cheerfully. 'It always goes wrong.'

'I won't have the opportunity to find out, 'I replied frostily. 'I have no technology.' Why had I relied on the Manager's assurances that they would be able to provide all the necessary equipment and I didn't need to trouble myself about bringing my laptop over to the island? The slide projector was of no use whatsoever as I didn't have any slides: my talk and all my photos were on the memory stick in my bag.

I could feel waves of panic beginning to rise and I took a deep breath before speaking. 'No matter what, I do need some help,' I said. 'If you don't find it the evening will be ruined...and,' I added darkly in an attempt to move her, 'there are bound to be lots of complaints.'

Reluctantly Phyllis lifted the internal phone and spoke in to it, turning away so that I couldn't hear what she was saying.

'Bertie will be with you in a few moments. You're lucky to have caught him – only because he was delayed fixing some new light bulbs in the top corridor in the West wing. They seem to go out with alarming frequency.' She went back to her mobile, scrolling through rapidly, appearing annoyed at this interruption.

The top corridor? That's where Anna and Freddie were, but there was no time to think about that now. I looked at my watch. Did we have time to put the chairs out the way I wanted? Bertie, when he arrived, would give me help. I was cross with myself for lingering over that last cup of tea, but I'd been so sure everything was in hand. That would teach me not to be so trusting.

After what seemed like an eternity, but was in fact no more than a few minutes, Bertie came sauntering along the corridor. First appearances did not inspire confidence. For one thing, he was a tiny man who looked as if a puff of wind would blow him over and his grey hair and lined face put him well above the age at which most people retire.

I should have guessed that this would be yet another item the hotel would economise on. He didn't look as if he had the strength to wrestle with the ornate ballroom chairs at the speed my approaching talk demanded.

'So, what seems to be the trouble?' He grinned, displaying a mouth with several teeth missing. 'I hear you're having problems?' He wagged his finger at me. 'You see, I always say that the speakers should make sure things are done well in advance. But do they listen? Oh, no, not at all. They leave it all to the last minute and then other people have to bail them out, others have to...'

I was in no mood to stand listening to a lecture from Bertie who I suspected of having been responsible for upsetting my careful plans. I interrupted him. 'I'm giving a talk tonight and I'd arranged the chairs to my liking and now someone (with a heavy emphasis on 'someone') has rearranged them…and I'd asked for a laptop computer and I've been given a slide projector and the talk is about to start …'

He held up his hand to stop me in full flow. 'Whoa…wait a minute. That's more than one problem.' He frowned. 'I wasn't told there were so many things wrong.'

'Can you help?' I was conscious of time running out and perhaps it would be better to try to coax Bertie into helping me. The first of the audience would soon be heading for the ballroom in the expectation of getting the best seat. I didn't want to be trying to move the furniture about once they had arrived. Apart from looking unprofessional, most of these guests wouldn't be fit enough for this task.

'Can you lend a hand? It's really urgent.' By now I was desperate, but my anxiety didn't appear to communicate itself to Bertie.

'Let's see,' was as much as he was prepared to say as he followed me as I hurried back towards the ballroom. At least, I hurried and he sauntered behind me.

'Oh, ho,' he said as we pushed open the large double doors. 'I'm not sure about this, not sure at all.' He stood looking around and then shook his head, a glum look on his face.

As I hadn't spoken, hadn't identified the problem, this wasn't encouraging.

'So you don't think we can move at least some of the chairs? I'm trying to make the place look more informal.'

I paused. 'If it's too formal, people won't ask questions and it would be really boring for them were I to speak all evening.'

This plea to his good nature didn't move him. He shook his head as though in sorrow. 'Naw, not a chance. Health and Safety, you see. This has been specially arranged for maximum safety.' He waved his hand in the general direction of the chairs and then pointed towards the front. 'All the spacing will have been specially calculated to allow safe passage through and the optimum space for comfortable sitting over a long period of time. We can't tangle with that.' The way he said this made it clear he'd culled it from some handbook or other – not a good sign.

This was not what I wanted to hear, but with the first of the audience due any minute, there was no time to get into an argument with him.

'Fine, fine. If it can't be done, then I'll have to deal with it as best I can.' Perhaps I could rescue the situation. For part of my talk I could come down to the front of the first set of chairs and could take questions from there. It would be slightly less formal than the current set-up allowed. 'What about the laptop?'

'No one mentioned any computer to me,' he said. 'All I was told was that there would be photos to illustrate the talk - that means slides doesn't it?'

'No, no, it's meant to be a Power Point presentation.'

He stared at me. 'Never heard of that. What on earth is it? Some new fangled computer thing, is it?'

I sat down on the nearest chair and put my head in my hands. This was worse than useless. The evening would be a shambles.

When I looked up, Bertie was standing looking at me with a baffled expression on his face. 'I'd like to help, but I'm not sure what I can do.'

Nothing at all, I thought bitterly, but aloud I said. 'Let's forget it. I'll manage somehow.'

'That's the spirit.' For the first time in our conversation Bertie smiled before saying, 'Well, if that's all I can help you with, I'd best be getting back.'

Before I could trouble him with any more requests for assistance, he turned on his heel and made a swift exit.

I went over to the platform, trying to come up with a scheme that would help me rescue the evening. Next time I did anything like this, I'd be sure to bring my own equipment with me rather than trust to others.

I ferreted in my bag and put the now useless memory stick to one side. As I pulled out my notes, I remembered I did have some photos. They weren't ideal, but they were better than nothing. I could pass them round during the talk.

No sooner was I semi-organised than the first people came in, laughing and talking loudly, no doubt in expectation of an entertaining evening. I could only hope they would find the few jokes I'd come up with hilariously funny, funny enough to ignore the old-fashioned nature of the event.

The seats filled up quickly and I don't know if I was pleased or worried to find they'd all been taken.

For the first part of my talk I decided it would be better to stand on the platform and then come down in to the audience to make it less formal, taking this opportunity to pass the photos around.

An expectant hush fell on the audience as I mounted the podium, the whispering and giggling ceased and many pairs of eyes fixed me with their gaze.
Bereft of my props of a computer and the memory stick, I felt totally exposed, but I took a deep breath, smiled and gripped the edge of the desk to stop my hands from trembling.

'Good evening, everyone,' I said, trying to keep my voice under control. 'I'm pleased to see so many of you have come along tonight for my talk. It's not going to be the one I intended, but I hope you'll enjoy it and be happy to ask lots of questions.'

There was a look of anticipation from the audience and a few people leaned forward the better to hear. Perhaps this wouldn't be the disaster I feared.

I lifted my notes, prepared to begin …and suddenly all the lights went out.

12

A few shouts of surprise, then a sudden silence before the clamour began in earnest.

'What's happened?'

'Who put off the lights?'

And a few, 'I can't see a thing.'

It wasn't complete darkness. There was some light from the hallway beyond, but I scrabbled in my bag for a torch and flicked it on, though it made little impression.

Instead of staying put, waiting for someone to take charge of the situation, people were beginning to move from their seats, bumping into one another, tipping over chairs. I had to act swiftly or there would be an accident and there were enough problems in this hotel already without adding more.

In a moment of inspiration, I turned the torch to shine on my face, shouting, 'Please keep calm and stay where you are. Someone will be along in a moment or two to sort this out. In the meantime it's too dangerous for you to be moving about.'

There were several muttered comments, 'That's all very well for her,' 'We can't see,' but I ignored these and said, even more loudly, 'Please stay in your seats. Help is at hand.' The priority was regaining control.

I used my torch to find my mobile in my bag and dialled the main number for the hotel. It was answered on the first ring and luckily Kelly was back on duty.

'Keep everyone as calm as possible,' she said, 'and I'll call Bertie.'

'Is he the only person available?' He hadn't exactly proved himself helpful so far.

'Yes, he is the only person on hand.' Kelly's reply was curt and I rang off with a hasty, 'Thanks,' before calling to everyone, 'Someone will be here soon. It'll all be fine.'

Bertie announced his arrival with a great clatter and banging of the chairs nearest the door.

'Ouch, mind where you're going,' said the voice of Major Revere from the audience, but instead of apologising Bertie replied, 'I can't make out a blooming thing here.'

I swung the torch from side to side to provide some light as he came down the passageway towards me.

'What have you been doing this time?' he grumbled.

'I haven't touched anything,' I said. 'You'll remember there was no possibility of finding the equipment I wanted, so I wasn't using anything that could have fused the lights.'

He ambled over to the wall and flicked the switches on and off several times but apart from a soft click nothing happened.

Meanwhile the audience was becoming restless.

'Have you not found the problem yet?'

'Are we going to have to sit here in the dark all night?'

'I'm sure it will be sorted very soon,' I called out in what I hoped was a reassuring tone of voice, but the grumbling only grew louder.

'I've no idea what you've done,' Bertie said again, 'but it looks as if the whole system is buggered.'

'Excuse me.' This was a criticism too far. 'I keep telling you I haven't done anything, didn't touch any of the switches. The lights were on when I came into the hall and I haven't so much as looked at them.'

'Hmm,' was the reply in that infuriating way when you know someone doesn't believe you.

'Well, no point in standing around here,' he said, shuffling off back down the passageway.

I grabbed his sleeve. 'You're not going to leave me here like this, are you? I have to get all these people out of the hall and I can't do that on my own.'

'Well, I can't help – health and safety and all that. It's not part of my job, evacuation of guests, except in an emergency.'

'This is an emergency,' I hissed.

He was not to be persuaded. 'I can't decide if it's an emergency or not, and neither can you. If something goes wrong, I could be sued.'

What more could I do? 'So what happens now?'

'I'm sure it's some problem at the main fuse,' he said. 'I'll go and check and...' a tad pompously, 'I'll inform management of the situation. They can send someone along.'

With that he scuttled up the passageway and out of the room, leaving me staring after him, trying hard to control my anger at being left alone in this impossible situation.

A moment or two later, as I was wondering how to manage evacuating this number of people on my own, Clive Timmons came bursting through the door, shouting, 'Stay calm everyone, stay calm. The situation is under control and Bertie will arrange for the problem to be fixed in no time.'

The presence of the Manager seemed to help and the mutterings subsided to a low murmur.

'Don't worry, Alison, this is no more than a bit of bad luck.'

We stood in silence for a bit. I wasn't in the mood for small talk, but at least someone else was now in charge.

Suddenly, all at once, the lights came back on, dazzling us. I shielded my eyes against the glare.

'Thank goodness,' said Clive Timmons. Then to the audience, 'Well, folks, sorry about that, but it'll make a good story, won't it? The night the lights went out at the Hydro.' He laughed, but it was a forced laugh and no one joined in. They were all too busy blinking and covering their eyes, trying to adjust to the sudden brilliance.

'You can carry on now, Alison,' he hissed from behind his hand.

'What? Do you think that's wise?' The last thing I felt like was continuing: a stiff gin and tonic would have been more in order.

'Of course. These guests have paid for a full programme. I don't want any complaints about lack of value for money.'

Clive Timmons wasn't to be dissuaded. He moved to the front, rubbing his hands together, saying, 'I'm sure we all want Alison to go on with her talk, don't we? It would be a pity to miss out because of a little unfortunate problem. I daresay it was a fuse or some such, but we're back to normal now and...'

As he spoke the door at the back of the hall flew open and Bertie almost fell into the room.

74

'Ah, Bertie,' said the Manager with forced gaiety, 'here's the person who has saved the day, or rather the evening. We should give him a round of applause. Come on, folks.'

Bertie looked startled at the sudden accolade as most of the audience started to clap and made his way down to the front to join us.

'Now that all is well, you can return to your duties,' said the Manager, plainly eager to usher Bertie out now that the problem was fixed. 'I'm sure it was a simple fuse that caused the problem?'

'Simple fuse, nothing,' shouted Bertie in a loud voice that carried to the back of the hall. 'Some bugger had tampered with the electric system.'

13

The atmosphere at the hotel was so suffocating, so febrile, I had to escape and early next morning before most guests had surfaced, I crept downstairs and with a hurried, 'Good morning,' to the few early birds loitering in Reception almost ran out of the door.

Once outside I was immediately hit by a blast of cold air. The wind had sprung up during the night and the grass was speckled with frost. The fir tree by the entrance had a glossy sheen and sparkled in the light shining from the hotel windows as I went to collect my car, shivering as I did so.

After a few attempts to get the key in the frozen lock I turned up the heater and sat for a few minutes waiting for the car to warm up.

Perhaps this had been a stupid idea. This wasn't the height of summer, where I could grab a coffee and a sandwich and head down to the beach.

Even so, there was no way I was going back in to the hotel, not yet. I could always take the next ferry across to the mainland and head for the Seaview Cafe at Wemyss Bay.

As I drove towards Rothesay this seemed a perfectly good idea, but on reflection that would be cowardly. No, best to find somewhere local for a coffee and drive off to stop at one of the bays to watch the sun rise.

Time on my own would give me an opportunity to think about events at the Hydro. I didn't believe in ghosts, I was far too practical for that, but what was the explanation for the strange sounds I'd heard outside Anna's room?

And she'd grabbed me at the end of my none-too-successful talk the previous night. 'You heard that noise,' she'd said. 'You have to help, Alison. Freddie keeps telling me to shut up about it all but that's because his sleeping pills knock him out. He wouldn't hear if a ten ton truck came down the corridor. Part of the problem is that mine don't seem to work as well.'

In spite of my reassurances, she and Freddie were about to pack up and go home early, though I'd the distinct impression her husband was doing this with some pleasure.

'I can't stand another night of this,' he said.

Anna looked tired, drained, the dark shadows under her eyes proof of how little she had slept since coming to this *Turkey and Tinsel* week.

'Have you tried approaching the Manager again?' I asked, wishing I hadn't become involved.

'Of course, but he doesn't want to know. He wants to brush it all under the carpet. "No point in alarming the other guests with this tale," is what he said.' She made a face. 'What does he know?'

That was all very well, but in spite of Clive's desire to sweep her concerns aside there was something odd happening. I scarcely knew Anna but even if I made allowances for her being highly imaginative, the noise had to be coming from somewhere. I'd heard it myself.

Decision made about a place to have coffee, I drove through Craigmore and headed towards Kilchattan Bay, feeling calmer with every mile between me and the Hydro.

Perhaps I was taking this all too seriously? Possibly it was no more than one of the other guests having a nightmare and the sound was carrying.

Could you have the same nightmare night after night? I'd no idea.

The Kingarth Hotel, the oldest coaching inn on the island, blazed forth lights. Tempting as it was to stop here, remembering the many good meals I'd eaten over the years, I made the decision to continue into the village.

As I reached the signpost marking the beginning of Kilchattan village the sun was rising in a fiery red sky. Christmas lights winked and twinkled, in a sequence of red, blue and green, strung out between the poles along the single street by the side of the water.

Across from the cottage I'd rented while writing a history of the Pavilion in Rothesay, down by the quay, a Christmas tree, resplendent with decorations, added to the festive look of the village. It was good to see that, apart from the many Christmas decorations, nothing much had changed since my last visit.

The tide was out, the waves gently lapping at the shore on the curve of the bay and the little mid-terrace building was in darkness, but that might be because the occupants were not yet awake.

When I reached the far end of the street I pulled in and sat gazing out over the water, watching as the morning sky became streaked with orange and then purple, changing to blue as the sun rose. Wraiths of mist spiralled up from the grassy verge as the chill of the night gave way to winter warmth.

The little shop must be open by now I thought, gazing back to see the van pull up outside. I knew they sold coffee and the thought of a warming cup made me shiver even more as I started up the engine and headed towards the café.

The young owner greeted me with a smile I found hard to muster at that time of the morning. I didn't recognise him, an indication that perhaps the business had changed hands since I'd last been there.

'What can I get you?' he said, as he easily swung the newly arrived bundles of newspapers on to the counter. In spite of the cold he was casually dressed in a pair of well-worn jeans and a short sleeved shirt.

The coffee pot bubbling on the hob behind him was invitation enough and a grin creased his weather-beaten face as he poured some of the fresh brew into a large polystyrene cup. 'I won't ask what size of coffee you want,' he said. 'I can tell only a large cup will be enough. You look frozen.'

'Coffee will be most welcome,' I said through chattering teeth as I cupped my hands round the container, though sadly there was no heat generated.

'You won't get warm by holding it like that,' the shopkeeper pointed out in a kindly tone of voice. 'That's the whole reason for having a polystyrene cup.' He indicated the corner of the shop where there were chairs and tables at the window overlooking the bay. 'Why don't you have a seat in the warmth? I'll turn the heating up for you. I'm used to the early morning chill, but I guess others aren't as lucky.'

'Something to eat?' He held up a plate of fresh rolls. 'I can do you bacon or sausage.'

'A bacon roll sounds exactly what I need.' I sat down and sipped my coffee in anticipation of this treat.

As the bacon sizzled in the pan and the enticing aroma wafted towards me, he came over and sat opposite me, ready for a chat, something I didn't feel in the mood for. With no desire to be unsociable, in reply to his, 'Here on holiday?' I shook my head. 'No, I'm at the Hydro - the Kyles of Bute hotel. I'm one of the staff giving a talk or two to the guests during the *Turkey and Tinsel* weeks.'

He laughed. 'And you're escaping? Can't say I blame you. It's a rum place that. I hope they haven't put you in the old West wing.' He shook his head. 'It's not somewhere I'd want to stay, let me tell you.'

'Why ever not?'

Before he could reply, he jumped up saying, 'I must catch the bacon before it's done to a crisp.'

He busied himself at the counter, making an elaborate show of buttering a roll and carefully putting the bacon in before bringing it over and setting it down with a flourish.

About to say, 'What's so strange about the Hydro,' I was stopped by the door being flung open and an old gentleman, clad in so many layers that only his nose and eyes peeped out, came stumbling in to the shop.

'You'll have to get that doorstep fixed, Donald,' he said. 'Someone is going to have a nasty accident.'

'I know, I know,' the shop owner dismissed this concern with a wave of his hand. 'It's on the list. Now you'll be wanting your morning paper? And how many rolls is it today, Angus?'

Any hopes I had of quizzing Donald as soon as Angus had departed were soon dashed as, one after another, the villagers began to arrive. After dawdling over my bacon roll and coffee I decided any stories

Donald had to tell about the Hydro would have to wait for another day.

In the meantime I'd have to head back. I paid for my coffee and bacon roll and nodded to Donald who was sitting beside another couple who were tucking in to a full Scottish breakfast.

He waved in reply. 'See you again – perhaps very soon if rumours about the food at the hotel are to be believed.'

Busy as he was with other customers, Donald scarcely noticed my departure, but what he'd said had intrigued me. Sure, the West wing was part of the original building, but it had been added to, sanitised. Sure, it could do with a little more work. Much of it had been hastily done, probably as cheaply as possible.

And yet, and yet…there was still that strange noise in the night. Perhaps I should suggest to Anna that I'd give it one more try, would come to their room again and make a determined effort to find out what was going on. It was no longer something I would do to help Anna: now I was intrigued about what it could really be.

Once outside the café I stood for a few minutes savouring the fresh air, the smell of brine. The early morning promise of a bright, cold day had receded and grey clouds were beginning to build, scudding overhead, bringing a threat of sleet or snow. It wasn't a morning to be lingering out of doors. No matter what my concerns about the Hydro might be, I'd no option but to return.

14

At the hotel guests were milling about in the Reception area and there was a lot of shouting and jostling. Whatever could have happened in the short time I'd been away?

The Manager came running down the stairs and leaned on the Reception desk, panting for breath. 'Is the ambulance on its way, Kelly?'

'Said they'd be here in a few minutes,' Kelly replied, her face pinched and pale.

'What's going on?' I said, almost afraid of the answer.

Neither Kelly nor the Manager made a reply but Calla, who was standing next to me, pursed her lips as she said. 'It's that lovely elderly lady, Anna. She and her husband often sit at our table. They are so pleasant to talk to, so considerate of my debilitating arthritis…'

'But what's happened to her?' I cut Calla off, whirling round to look for someone to give me more information.

The Major, who was standing close beside her, leaned over towards me and growled.

'It happened at breakfast, m'dear. She suddenly said she didn't feel very well and keeled over. It all happened in the space of a minute.'

'And is she okay? I assume the paramedics will take care of her?'

'Okay?' Calla gave a screech. 'I don't think so. If you ask me there's no point in bringing an ambulance.'

I moved away. This news disturbed me greatly, given what I knew and I tried to reassure myself.

The food in the hotel might be of suspect quality, but surely after the incidents with the shepherd's pie rigorous checks would have been put in place. A hotel like this couldn't afford another case of suspected food poisoning. That would be a way of making sure the place had to close.

I leaned over the desk. 'What is going on, Kelly? I'd really like to know.'

She sniffed and I could see she'd been crying. 'It was all too awful…so sudden.'

Just then, Clive Timmons, who'd disappeared a few moments before in the direction of the kitchen, came thundering along, hotly pursued by someone who looked like the chef, though it was hard to be sure judging by his grubby white overalls.

'Don't give me any more excuses,' the Manager yelled. 'It's very strange two of our guests have now had an 'episode' as you like to call it. A very serious episode. And both of them to do with something they ate.'

The chef, of a build more suited to a boxer, his bare forearms completely covered in tattoos, was equally loud in his denial. He scowled and hunched forward to Clive Timmons, who now cowered and retreated under his gaze.

'You are blaming my cooking? Is it because I am Polish? You think my meals are not the right ones? I have been cook in lots of places before coming to this terrible place with its need to buy everything as cheaply as possible. The cut-price sausages, the eggs from the poor locked up hens…'

83

The Manager turned to face him, the veins on his forehead standing out, his face bright red. It looked as if he was about to explode. 'Don't you dare put the blame on me. You're the one in charge of the food. It's down to you at the end of the day.'

'I would have no problems if the guests did not always be interfering, coming in to the kitchen, demanding to see what I am cooking, nosing about.'

'Nonsense,' replied Clive, making an effort to regain control of the situation. 'You should be able to control your kitchen, make sure you don't allow such behaviour.'

'You try it. Some of your guests are not nice. And you are mean, penny pinching man,' the chef yelled, banging his fist on the counter of the Reception desk 'and I do not stay here one minute more to be insulted. I am proud man, trained by the best chefs in Poland. I cook well.'

'Oh, yes? And who might that be? Name one.' The Manager seemed to have regained his nerve, but unfortunately this was the wrong thing to say.

The chef whipped off his apron and threw it at the Manager's feet. 'I quit your job. Find some other cook. I will not do it any more.'

'You can't do that,' shouted the Manager. 'You can't quit.'

'Oh, no? And who will make me stay? You? I think not. I am proud man; I do not need job in this terrible place.'

By now Clive had taken several deep breaths and glared at the chef before playing his trump card. 'It's nothing to do with me. The police will want to speak to you. What's happened to Anna now makes Hamish's death look very suspicious indeed.'

Now it was the chef's turn to look pale: it appeared as if he'd suddenly been deflated, like a balloon. He stopped, all bravado gone, as he said in a whisper, 'Why would police want to speak with me? What have they to do with me? I have done nothing wrong.'

Having gained the high ground, the Manager was determined to make the most of it. Those guests standing by were looking from the chef to the Manager and back again, engrossed in this exchange of insults, eager to see who would be the winner.

The Manager took a few seconds to let his gaze travel over this captive audience, confident he was once again in charge.

He pulled himself up to his full height and said, 'They will want to talk to you because you were the one who served up the food that both Hamish and Anna ate immediately before collapsing.'

'Not forgetting my poor Jasper.' Sylvia Openshaw said loudly as she pushed her way to the front of the crowd and pointed accusingly at the chef. 'He said he would prepare some food especially at my request and no sooner had my darling eaten than he became quite ill.'

The chef's face took on a hunted look: he crumpled visibly before us. 'Not true. Not me,' he whispered. 'Not to do with me. I only did food for that horrible dog because she pestered me. Someone is trying to cause trouble for me.'

'We'll see about that,' said the Manager, a note of triumph in his voice and we heard the sound of the ambulance screeching to a halt outside, closely followed by a police car.

The police came bustling in and as all eyes turned towards them I looked over to the chef. He was shrunken into his whites, his shoulders hunched and then, without warning, he burst into tears.

15

In a way I felt I owed it to Anna, after what had happened, to keep watch that night and try to find out what had been troubling her, find out if the noise was real or the product of our imagination.

Freddie, understandably distraught, said, 'I can't stay here a moment longer.' He was shaking all over and the paramedics had to spend some time tending to him.

Given the nature of Anna's death, the police were reluctant to agree to his request to leave the hotel. Though perfectly polite the sergeant said, 'I'm sorry at a time like this, but we'll have to question everyone, have a clear picture of what happened.'

In the end, they agreed they'd allow him to leave the Hydro, as long as he stayed on the island.

It was Kelly who came to the rescue. 'My mum's friend has some holiday flats at Port Bannatyne,' she said, 'and most of them are vacant at this time of year. I'm sure she'd be happy to let you have one of those.'

Freddie, numbed by grief, was all too ready to take up this suggestion. 'I don't care where I go as long as I don't have to stay here.' He sat on the chair in the corner, trembling and biting his nails.

The Manager bristled at this. 'It's been most unfortunate that your wife should die in these circumstances, but she was elderly and the fact she passed away immediately after eating could be no more than a coincidence.' Clive Timmons was well aware he had an inquisitive audience and there was no way he wanted the hotel blamed.

Freddie shook his head, refusing to engage in this insensitive conversation. He kept on saying, shaking his head, 'I can't believe it, I can't believe it'

'Nor can I,' Sylvia Openshaw interjected. 'If I hadn't called the vet so quickly Jasper might have suffered the same fate. Anna might still be alive if you'd done the same.'

Freddie turned to look at her and said in a perplexed tone of voice, 'Why would I have called the vet to Anna?'

It was obvious he was completely dazed, so I took him gently by the elbow.

'The police can talk to you again later and in the meantime I can take you round to the flat in Port Bannatyne,' I said.

He turned abruptly. 'Do you think it's anything to do with those voices she thought she heard? Could that have been the cause?'

'She mentioned that to me,' said Iris who had suddenly appeared beside us.

'And to me,' said Lily.

'Nonsense,' said Clive, glancing round nervously. 'That was all her imagination. There's nothing on that top floor except the one refurbished bedroom and various store cupboards and disused rooms. There's nothing else up there.'

About to say I'd also heard the strange noises, for some reason I decided to keep quiet. This wasn't the moment to become involved in this discussion. There were more urgent concerns.

But Sylvia had overheard. 'There might be something in that. As the Manager you should investigate, or at least inform the police.'

It was clear Clive Timmons had no intention of following her advice.

'Elderly people who take strong sleeping pills imagine all sorts of things. Look what happened when she and her husband took a double dose.' He turned on his heel without waiting for further comment.

By now most of the guests had been shepherded back into the lounge by several police officers and Anna's body had been taken off, leaving me with Freddie and Kelly.

'It would be kind if you could arrange accommodation elsewhere,' Freddie said, sinking further down into the chair beside the desk and burying his head in his hands. Tears trickled between his fingers and he sat up and wiped them away with a grubby handkerchief he pulled from his pocket.

'You'd better clear it with the police,' said Kelly, 'and I'll ask my mum to phone her friend about the flat.'

'Of course.' Reluctantly I headed for the lounge, hoping none of the police officers would recognise me from previous trips to the island and my involvement in other cases.

Fortunately the police officer nearest the door was a new recruit. At least I didn't recognise him and judging by his youthful appearance he hadn't been on the island long.

'You'll have to check with the sergeant,' he said doubtfully as I explained my request. 'I know he wants to interview everyone as soon as possible.'

'Oh, come on,' I coaxed him, 'what possible motive could Freddie have for murdering his wife?'

He frowned and pursed his lips. 'Most people aren't murdered by strangers. They're murdered by someone they know and often someone they know well.' He folded his arms to emphasize his point. 'It's not up to me. You have to speak to the sergeant.'

This was the last thing I wanted to do because I could spy the sergeant in the far side of the room, talking to a little group of people and was sure he was the police officer who'd been in charge of investigations last time I'd been on the island working on the visitor guide for the ill-fated theme park at St Blane's.

'Look,' I said in a wheedling tone of voice, 'all Freddie wants to do is get away from where it happened. He's not going to leave the island. You can put a guard on him if you like. Could you not ask the sergeant for us? It would sound better coming from you, more professional.'

I hoped this appeal to his vanity would stir him to do as I asked and fortunately I'd judged rightly because he drew himself up and said, 'I suppose I could help in such difficult circumstances.'

From behind one of the large marble pillars at the entrance to the lounge I watched as he strode over confidently to relay my request.

There was a moment of doubt as I saw the sergeant frown and then shake his head, but the young constable must have pleaded my case with some skill because a few moments later he came across and said, 'Sergeant isn't too keen, but he understands the circumstances might make Mr Burrows want to leave the hotel.'

He frowned. 'He's prepared to agree if details of the new place are left and Mr Burrows understands that under no circumstances should he leave the island.'

'Of course, of course,' I agreed eagerly. 'I'll go and tell him and take him over to Port Bannatyne right away. Kelly at Reception has the particulars of the flat he's going to - her mother's friend owns it. She'll give you the address.'

Before he could give me further instructions, I hurried back through to the entrance hall to tell Freddie it was arranged and we had permission to leave. He was sitting looking very forlorn on the little couch beside the front door, as though eager to leave as soon as possible.

'If you want to organise packing some things, we can go,' I said.

Kelly came over. 'Don't worry about that. I'll do it and drop your case off at the flat. I'll bring what I think will tide you over meantime. You can come back and collect anything else you need once you're settled.'

Freddie, still looking dazed, nodded in agreement, then rose slowly to his feet and shuffled out behind me without a backward glance. As I helped him into the car to drive to Port Bannatyne I explained the rules about this new place. 'You mustn't leave the island,' I said, 'no matter how you feel about it. The police will want to question you again about what happened to Anna.'

He seemed not to hear me, made no acknowledgement of my instructions, but gazed out of the window as we headed down the hill and along Marine Road past the War Memorial, past the Post Office cum general store, past the Coronet Hotel and towards the far end of the village.

The Coronet was a blaze of lights, the giant Christmas tree in the window brightly illuminated. The lights strung between the lampposts along the bay had been switched off, but the glitter of decorations in the windows of the houses along the front more than made up for this. The entire village, it would appear, was gearing up for the festive season while poor Freddie's world had been turned upside down.

I turned left to drive up Duncan Street as Yvonne had directed and there at the top was a little block of flats within a terrace of old sandstone buildings emblazoned with the name *Chateau Holiday Flats.*

I drew up outside and cut the engine. 'Are you ready? This is the place. Kelly said her mother's friend would be here with the key.' No sooner were the words out of my mouth than a small woman came bustling along from the direction of Upper Quay Street, pulling her bright red coat tightly around her against the chill wind from the bay.

'Sorry. I hope you haven't been waiting long,' she said a little breathlessly, leaning in as I wound down the window. 'I'm Mrs Underwood. I was about to step out of the door when the phone rang. I felt I had to answer it in case it was important, but of course it turned out to be no more than a cold call. The usual nonsense. We seem to get so many of these at the moment and I'm not sure how to stop them. I'm always tempted to let any calls go to the answering machine but of course you never know, do you...'

As she rambled on, I opened the door which caused her to draw back suddenly, but didn't interrupt her flow '...and it takes so much time to tell them not to call again, to stop bothering you.'

I went round to the passenger side to help Freddie out of the car.

'It's absolutely no problem to have Mr Burrows. In fact it's always a pleasure to have as many of the flats as possible occupied during the winter. So close to the sea we have a problem with damp and...'

I held up my hand to stop her. Freddie was looking pale and on the verge of collapse. If we stood out here in the cold much longer, goodness knows what would happen so I said, 'It would be good to get Mr Burrows inside out of this freezing wind.'

'Of course, of course.' She drew a bunch of keys from her pocket and we followed her up a set of well worn steps to the front door. She wrestled with the key for a moment. 'Sorry about this, it sticks a little at this time of year. It's the damp as I said. It never happens in the summer time which is when these flats are mostly used. The flat won't be too bad - once you have all the heaters going it will be quite cosy...' She kept up a stream of chat as we went in to what had evidently been the original hall of a large house with several doors leading off, each with its own lock and nameplate on the door.

'I've put you in the *Ardbeg*,' she said. It's on the ground floor and is large enough for a couple...or one person,' she added hastily, realising her mistake.

But if Freddie was upset by this, he gave no sign, merely nodded as she handed him the key. It was clear he was still in shock.

The flat was indeed small but did look perfectly suitable for Freddie at the moment. The main room was boxy but big enough to accommodate a pair of comfortable chairs, a television and a fold down table with two dining chairs by the window.

From the window there was a glimpse over the rooftops of Kames Bay in the distance, scarcely visible in the gloom of the winter's morning. An archway led to a tiny kitchen and through the half open door on the other side I could glimpse a bedroom.

She insisted on explaining in minute detail all the quirks of the flat ('the heating is set, but you can change it'), how everything worked ('the cooker can be a bit temperamental, but it's safe enough'), how the bedroom had an en-suite ('since the flat is only for one or two people that seemed all that was needed'), what to do in an emergency ('if I'm not available any of the neighbours will help. They're all very kind, you know, no need to worry about asking them') before finally producing a large book from the table by the window saying, 'It's all in here, anything you might need.'

It was as well she had provided this back up, because Freddie hadn't taken in a word she'd said and apart from the odd grunt had scarcely registered her presence.

'I'm sure it will be fine,' I said, trying to edge her towards the door. 'We'll be sure to contact you if we need anything. You've been most helpful.'

Freddie meanwhile had sat down on the chair at the window and was staring out over the bay.

At the door she turned to me and said in a low voice, 'Awful about his poor wife. Do you know what happened? Kelly's mum was only able to give me the briefest of details. Or so she said, even though I asked her lots of questions.'

Ah, perhaps she has the measure of you, I thought, but aloud I replied, 'I don't think anyone knows the details at this stage. It's all been a terrible shock.'

'Yes, and coming on the death of that other poor man, Hamish. We all knew him well, you know. He was quite a local character. Have you heard any more about him? Mrs Strang in the village said there was something suspicious about his death, but my understanding is that it was no more than a heart attack. Still, two people dead, even by natural causes, is something for the hotel to be concerned about, isn't it?'

She paused for breath. 'The Manager must be very worried. It's not the sort of reputation you want any place to have, but especially not a place like the Hydro. I've heard they're in financial difficulties, you know, it's not been the success they hoped, though that's probably no more than local gossip...'

All the time she was speaking I was trying to edge her further out of the door and eventually succeeded in getting her as far as the hallway. But something in her last remark made me pause. 'What do you mean? I thought the new hotel was doing well, building on the history of the old hotel, getting lots of people in?'

But now that she had at last said something interesting, Mrs Underwood decided to clam up. 'It's only rumour, of course,' she said. 'I'd better be getting along.'

And with that she hurried out, slamming the main door behind her and leaving me staring after her, wondering what on earth she meant by that last remark. Surely the Kyles Hydro hotel wasn't in financial trouble as she suggested? If it was, two deaths in a short space of time would only add to their troubles.

16

My contract with the Hydro was for two weeks, but I was becoming increasingly reluctant to stay. Okay, so part of the deal was I'd be around to chat to the guests, answer any questions they might have about the history of Bute, but these topics appeared to be the last thing on anyone's mind. When they could be diverted from concerns about the recent deaths, they were more interested in the Charades night or the Elvis tribute night than anything I had to offer.

The police had questioned everyone again, though they indicated these were only preliminary enquiries. No doubt they'd want to chase up all the possible reasons for Anna's death, but for the moment they had gone and left us to continue with the rest of the week's activities.

So I was very surprised, when I came down later for afternoon tea, to find two burly constables at the Reception desk.

'Ah, Alison, the very person. These policemen want to speak to Mr Burrows.'

'We gave the address to one of the other officers when he moved to the flat at Port Bannatyne.'

'That's the problem - he's not there.'

This stopped me in my tracks, then I said, 'Not there? Perhaps he's gone for a walk. He's not a prisoner.'

Poor Freddie. None of us had given him much thought since I'd dropped him off at the flat in Port Bannatyne that morning.

'That's as maybe,' said the one of them in a voice that indicated doubt, 'but do you think an elderly gentleman would go out walking in weather like this?'

One of the problems about being in a hotel is that you are cocooned from the rest of the world and a glance over the policeman's shoulder through the large side window showed why he was so surprised.

The rain was battering off the glass, driven by the wild winds you only get on an island, made worse by the darkness of the afternoon.

'Even so,' I said lamely, 'he might have stepped out to buy something. You could try again later.'

'I'm afraid there's no point in doing that. Given his age and his circumstances, we were concerned when there was no reply. Mrs Underwood let us in, in case the old fellow had had an accident. She'd left food for his lunch, but it hasn't been touched.' He paused for dramatic effect. 'Not only had he gone, but there was no sign of any of his belongings, nothing.'

He concluded on a note of triumph, as though challenging me to come up with an answer to this puzzle, but there was nothing I could say except, 'I've absolutely no idea where he could be. He seemed all right when I left him earlier.'

All the while my mind was whizzing through the possibilities, but I couldn't think of any sensible reason why Freddie might have left the flat. Or perhaps I'd underestimated how upset he was.

'I'm sure there's some simple explanation,' I said firmly. 'I repeat – he was fine when I left him, seemed

97

relieved to have somewhere to stay away from the hotel. And he took very little with him – only the bare necessities.'

A gleam came into the officer's eye. 'Ah, that's exactly the point. You were the last person to see him.'

This was nonsense. Did the officer think I'd helped Freddie leave? 'I can assure you he was perfectly fine and Mrs Underwood said she'd keep an eye on him, help him with anything he needed. He wouldn't have gone off the island. He knew you'd want to speak to him. The only reason he left the Hydro was because it was too painful for him to stay here after his wife died.'

'So you can't think of any reason why he might be missing.' It was a statement rather than a question.

'I'm sure you're making too much of this,' I said with a show of confidence I didn't feel.

'We'll put out a call. It's possible in his distressed state he's wandered off somewhere.'

But surely if he had decided to leave the island he wouldn't have left most of his luggage at the hotel, I thought, but didn't say so. I'd no inclination to detain these police officers any longer. I'd no answer for them, had no idea where Freddie might have gone and besides after all the problems of yesterday I was more than ready for a cup of tea.

With a hasty, 'I'll be pleased to help you if I can,' I made for the dining room. How on earth had I become involved? You'd have thought I'd have learned from previous experiences.

Unfortunately the only seats available were at a table in the far corner and it was easy to see why. Sylvia was sitting there in front of an enormous plate of food, feeding titbits to Jasper. I wondered if he ever left that handbag.

For a moment I considered turning tail, but the rumbling in my stomach got the better of my judgement. My plan was to have a cup of tea and a slice of cake and head off as soon as I'd finished it, without becoming drawn into conversation with her, but this was not to be.

'Sorry, I'm in a bit of a hurry,' I said, pouring a cup of tea from the enormous brown teapot in the middle of the table.

She wasn't put off by this abruptness. 'Poor Jasper,' she said, 'he's had such a fright. He needs a lot of loving care.'

She paused to feed him another piece of cake from her plate. 'Here you are, darling. Mummy knows you're not feeling quite well. Never mind, you'll soon be back to your usual self.'

As Jasper's "usual self" was a vicious, snappy beast, I thought it would be better if he stayed the way he was, but that would no doubt cause a quarrel if I hinted as much.

She began to regale me with stories about Jasper: his latest problems, his recovery from illness, why the chef should be sacked for what had happened. On and on she went, scarcely pausing for breath, which at least let me concentrate on my tea and cake.

Suddenly noticing I was making no reply, she leaned forward and demanded. 'What do you think about it all? Don't you agree with me? That chef should be out of here as soon as possible. I know it's hard to get someone to take over, but you can't employ someone who is poisoning the guests. The Manager should have

99

let him go when he said he would, instead of persuading him to stay on like that. It's a wonder the police haven't arrested him. I'm sure they suspect him.'

I noticed concerns about the quality of the cooking hadn't put Sylvia off her food.

'I don't think you should be accusing him,' I said, looking round to see who might be listening, but fortunately everyone was too busy eating to eavesdrop.

'I'm telling you,' she shouted, 'he shouldn't be here.'

'Who shouldn't be here?'

Kelly came over with a cup of coffee and sat in the only remaining seat. I acknowledged her presence gratefully, seeing a way to make my escape.

'Sylvia will explain,' I said, leaving my unfinished tea as I stood up and hurried out of the dining room. Perhaps Kelly would be more sympathetic to Sylvia and to Jasper's problems, though I doubted it.

Once in the foyer I considered what to do next. If Freddie was indeed missing, I could think of no reason for his disappearance.

Unless of course he believed there were suspicious circumstances about the death of his wife. But that was highly improbable.

Lily came bustling out of the dining room, with Iris trailing behind. 'Ah, there you are, Alison.' She came up so close I could smell her distinctive perfume, an old-fashioned lavender that was rather pleasant, unlike the very strong musky perfume favoured by Kelly - a modern one that left a strong after-scent.

Iris glanced round as though to make sure no one could overhear. 'Do you think Anna's death was anything to do with what she ate? She ...'

100

'Oh, for goodness sake, Iris,' Lily butted in sharply. 'You know fine well it wasn't, not on this occasion. How could it be?'

Iris frowned at her sister as Lily nudged her with her elbow. 'Of course,' she said brightly. 'No more than coincidence. Not like that awful man, Hamish.'

Arm-in-arm they ambled off, leaving me staring after them. A chill went through me as I remembered other occasions when I'd been on the island, when events I'd rather not remember had occurred.

And the sisters were so trusting, so amiable. I hoped they weren't in danger. Surely I wasn't caught up yet again in some crime or other. This couldn't be happening. But I had a terribly sneaking suspicion that it was.

17

As it happened, events were taken out of my hands. With no sign of Freddie in spite of extensive searches round the island, the police were fully occupied. They were now concerned (according to my trusty source Kelly) that Freddie had had some kind of breakdown, something that should have been foreseen and there was a worry the local press might get hold of the story before he was found.

Something Sylvia said, in an off-hand manner, made me stop and think.

We'd met again over dinner. In vain I'd scoured the dining room as I'd come in, hoping to find a spare seat at a table with a more congenial group.

It appeared the Herrington twins had abandoned me after our conversation. Perhaps they thought I was bad luck, and yet again the only remaining seat was beside Sylvia. Jasper seemed to be sound asleep: the only reason I could think of for his non-appearance.

As I sat down beside her, determined to make do with one course she said, 'It was strange how upset the Burrows were in that room they were allocated. Mind you they're not the first people to have been worried about staying there, but others asked for a switch earlier on.'

'Why? What's wrong with the room?' Now I was alert, wondering what she could possibly mean.

She leaned forward and whispered, 'I shouldn't say anything, it's nothing to do with me, but that West wing is part of the original hotel and there have been rumours that there's a ghost that stalks the place.'

'A ghost?' I raised my voice in disbelief and Sylvia said, glancing nervously around, 'Hush, quietly. The Manager doesn't want people to know - thinks it will be bad for the reputation of the hotel.'

'How long has this been going on?'

Sylvia shrugged. 'The hotel hasn't been open all that long. The West wing was the only part of the building that survived - the rest had to be demolished it was in such a bad state, but there's no doubt old buildings often retain the aura of people who once lived there. I should know.'

She sat back, appearing mightily pleased at my reaction to this piece of information.

'This is the twenty-first century,' I said, trying hard to keep the scepticism out of my voice. 'Surely no one believes in ghosts nowadays?'

'You'd be surprised, very surprised. The old Hydro saw plenty of action in its day. Who knows who or what might still be here? I wouldn't dare go into that part of the hotel. I have this way of feeling any aura, any spirit unable to find rest. That's why I spend so much time here. I can sense my dear husband, can feel his presence, even though he has passed over.'

Before I could ask any more questions, the Manager came bustling along. 'Kelly's been delayed. Her little one is sick and she has to wait for her mother to come to look after her. We have to think about engaging extra staff for next week if she's not back. We're fully booked.'

'Not our problem. That's your job,' replied Sylvia dismissively and I took this opportunity to make my escape. I'd have to find an opportunity later to ask for more details.

Surely Sylvia was wrong with her talk of ghosts.

This was no more than someone's febrile imagination. Most likely Anna had heard or read the story somewhere and with an overactive imagination, or a surfeit of sleeping pills, she had imagined hearing the sound of sobbing. Yes, that was all there was to it. Freddie certainly hadn't mentioned it, had in fact been scornful of Anna's suggestion. And why had none of the other guests mentioned hearing the noises? Did they sleep so soundly or think it was something they shouldn't concern themselves with?

Then again, I was sure I had heard something that night I'd stayed in the room with Anna. Perhaps I should try again, should go in to their room later and check. As far as I knew, the room hadn't been re-allocated. All I had to do was come up with a reasonable excuse to get back in. Surely I would think of something?

And if I did hear the sound of sobbing again, what would I do? That decision I'd worry about later.

18

I shouldn't have done it, shouldn't have been drawn in, but I couldn't help myself. Now that I suspected there was something odd going on at the hotel, I wouldn't be able to rest till I discovered what it was.

In spite of everything, in spite of arguing with myself that I was only storing up trouble, I decided to spend one more night in the room Anna and Freddie had occupied and hopefully make some sense of that sound of sobbing. That would be an end of it.

One explanation, the one I clung to, was that Anna had convinced me to hear something that wasn't actually there.

This plan needed careful timing. My idea was to tell Yvonne I'd left something in the Burrows' room (quite what I hadn't yet decided) and say I'd return the key within the hour, by which time it was shift changeover and someone else would be on duty.

I only had to cross my fingers that with everything else she had to do, including find a substitute for Kelly, Yvonne would forget she'd given me the key and I'd be able to slip it back in the morning before she returned.

At least, that was the plan, but of course with the upsets in the management of the hotel, I'd no idea if the usual arrangements would apply.

Luckily when I went down to Reception after dinner Yvonne was still there. 'I suppose you have to fill in for Kelly,' I said affecting a studied casualness of manner, attempting to disguise my nervousness.

She frowned as if she considered my interests in the staffing arrangements of the hotel rather odd.

'No, Kelly will be on in a few minutes. Her wee one is much better though I'll always help her out when the need arises. We work together - neither of us counts the minutes, you know. But thank goodness she's back. I've an emergency dental appointment for a terrible toothache and I've already had to cancel twice because of some problem or other with staffing. This is the night they open late. We really need more help, but Clive ignores any suggestions.'

My attempt at a laugh came out as a kind of guffaw and I quickly covered it up with a cough, lest she think I was making light of her toothache. 'I wonder if I could have the key for room 302,' I said.

'The one the Burrows were in? Why would you want that key?' As Assistant Manager she was trained to be polite, but curiosity had kicked in.

'Yes, how stupid of me, I left my camera there the other night and with everything that's been happening I completely forgot.'

'Your camera?'

This wasn't going to be as easy as anticipated. Why hadn't I said Freddie had forgotten something? Though as he was still missing that might arouse her suspicions even more.

'Yes, I was showing Anna and Freddie some photos I'd taken of Kames Bay and I must have left it lying there when I left. I only missed it this afternoon when I went to take some photos and realised the only place it could be was in their room, so...' Aware I was gabbling on, I stopped abruptly.

'I'm not sure,' said Yvonne, frowning at this muddled explanation. 'I'll have to ask Clive. I think the police wanted that room to be out of bounds for a while yet, especially with Freddie's sudden disappearance.'

'Oh, it won't take long and I can return it to you. By the time you find the Manager I could be in and out.' Now I was relying on the fact Kelly would be here within the next few minutes and Yvonne would want to keep her urgent dental appointment. Besides the Manager could at this moment be anywhere in the hotel.

'I suppose so,' she said, still doubtful, 'but make sure you return it to Kelly. I don't want anyone to get into trouble. There's been enough disruption already.'

'Yes, this will be between us and I'll make sure the key is returned as soon as possible.' I didn't add that that meant early the next morning.

To my relief, she turned to the board where they were kept, but seemed to take an inordinate amount of time looking for the one for Room 302.

All the time, I was keeping a lookout for the Manager. It would be my luck if he came marching along the corridor and scuppered my plans, but fortunately Yvonne turned back at that very moment and passed the key across. 'I'm still not sure about this,' she said, wincing a little in pain as I made to take it from her.

'Honestly, I don't think anyone will be bothered.' I almost grabbed the key from her outstretched hand. 'This is only a matter of collecting my camera. I really, really need it tonight to get some evening winter shots for my new project.' Hopefully she wouldn't ask me what the project was, because I didn't have one.

'Okay, then, but don't tell anyone that I gave it to you - try to slip it back on the board. Kelly goes for a break about eleven and you can do it then.'

I nodded, not trusting myself to speak. I'd told enough lies as it was.

'Thanks, Yvonne, you've saved the day, or rather the night,' I said as I pocketed the key and hurried away before she could change her mind. As it was, I could feel her staring after me as I made for the stairs.

Before going to the Burrows' room, I stopped at my own room. It was going to be a long night and I'd no idea if I'd have to be there through till early morning or whether I might find an answer to my questions within the first hour.

I grabbed my fleece, a packet of biscuits from the hospitality tray together with a cup, some coffee sachets and some little cartons of milk and stuffed everything into my tote bag along with that day's newspaper, the book I was currently reading, a notebook and pen and my micro recorder.

In my rush I almost forgot my camera, my excuse for being in the room, and had to go back for it. I crept upstairs and along the corridor to the Burrows' room, in case someone might see me. In my haste I had to fumble with the key in the lock and it took me a moment or two before I could make my way in.

The room appeared to be exactly as they had left it with clothes strewn on chairs, the bed unmade, the door to the ensuite ajar showing Anna had possessed a fine collection of creams and potions. A book lay on the bedside table, face down as though someone had finished reading a chapter a few moments before.

At this intrusion in the life of someone so recently dead I shivered a little, then rebuked myself. I was as much doing this for Anna as for any other reason. The noise she heard or thought she heard had troubled her so much. Something had disturbed her and it was up to me to find out what it might be. Whatever it was it might have had nothing to do with her death, but on the other hand it might have been part of the cause.

I looked around the room for a suitable place to settle myself for the night and spied an easy chair by the window piled high with cushions, which I promptly dumped on the floor.

While these rooms in the West wing conformed to a kind of standard, some were more luxuriously equipped than others and this was certainly better than the one I'd been allocated, possibly because it was the latest renovation.

I put my bag beside the chair and took everything out and then went into the ensuite to fill the kettle. Best to start with a cup of coffee and the one thing I hadn't thought to bring from my own room was the kettle.

All I was supposed to be doing was collecting my camera and I'd this terrible dread someone might come along, hear me and my cover story would be blown. There was no reason I should be making coffee in the Burrows' room when I'd perfectly adequate facilities in my own.

Settled at last with a cup of coffee and a biscuit, I sat back in the easy chair and opened my book, snuggling in to my fleece as the heating clicked off with a ping as midnight approached.

Perhaps the stories about this hotel being in difficulties weren't so far-fetched after all, if the heating system was anything to go by.

There was a sudden noise and I put my cup down and strained to hear what it might be, but it was only a couple leaving the lift on the floor below, returning from the Elvis tribute evening and I could hear one of them whistling *Heartbreak Hotel* in a low tone. There was a gurgle of laughter from someone else and then silence as a door slammed shut.

I settled back again, trying to read my book, distracted by the moonlight streaming in through the window where I hadn't dared to pull the curtains for fear of alerting someone to my presence. It was going to be a frosty night. Perhaps I should have brought an extra blanket from my room. There was no way I was going to use any of the bedding here. The very idea gave me an uneasy feeling.

Thoughts came and went as I considered the story Anna had told me and the strange nature of the noise I'd heard that first night with her. I only hoped that whatever the noise might be, I'd hear it soon, could capture it on my recorder and head back to the comfort of my own bed. I'd a busy day ahead and I'd already lost enough sleep on one venture or other.

Freddie came to mind. Where could he possibly be? The only idea I could come up with was that he'd returned to their home in Glasgow, but surely that was one of the first places the police would have checked. Besides Freddie knew the island reasonably well: he'd told me of his visits as a child.

I sipped my now cold coffee. This had been a mad idea. Not only did I have no scheme for dealing with the source of the noise if I did hear it, I'd be giving away my ruse for getting the key under false pretences.

But then, as I waited in the quiet and the stillness and the minutes slowly ticked past, I felt my head fall forward and a few moments later, exhausted by the events of the day, I was sound asleep.

19

I wakened with a start and for a few minutes had no idea where I was. Disorientated, I gazed around aware only that this wasn't my room. Groggy with sleep, I tried to take in the unfamiliar surroundings, the unmade bed and the clothes lying nearby which weren't mine. Then I remembered this was the room belonging to Anna and to Freddie and a swift glance at my watch in the dim light confirmed it was half past two.

Something had disturbed me and I sat up properly, rolling back my shoulders to ease the pain from the crick in my neck, a result of the uncomfortable position I'd been lying in.

I stood up slowly and crept towards the door, an instinctive but useless gesture as any sound was unlikely to be coming from inside the room.

My heart began to race as I realised what had wakened me. There it was again, that same sound I'd heard the night I kept watch with Anna…a sobbing, most certainly coming from outside, somewhere along the corridor and it was louder than before. I cautiously opened the door a fraction and peered out but all was quiet, no sign of anyone in the half light cast by the subdued lighting.

Leaving the door ajar, in case I had to rush back inside, I began a slow, very slow tiptoe along the corridor, listening intently all the while, but there was no further sound of weeping, no noise of any kind.

I stopped at the far end beside the door leading to the fire escape. This was very strange. Could I be imagining it after all? Perhaps in my half-awake state, anticipating the event, I'd only thought I'd heard it. I waited for a few moments, but there was no repetition of the sound.

Admitting this was a waste of time, I'd almost convinced myself any noise was the result of my suggestibility. But as I stood there, about to retrace my steps before heading back to my own room for some well-earned sleep, the sobbing began again, more insistently this time.

As quietly as I could, so as not to disturb whoever or whatever was making this sound, I crept further along the corridor.

As I reached the spot where I'd thought it was coming from, as suddenly as it had begun, it stopped and I was left frustrated, unable to pinpoint the exact source.

Apart from the room allocated to Anna and Freddie there were no other rooms on this floor ready for occupation. As far as I could see some were used for storage, but others appeared not to have been touched for a long time.

None of the guests on other floors seemed to have noticed anything amiss, or if they had, they hadn't mentioned it.

Whatever was going on, I was determined to get to the bottom of it. Anna hadn't been mistaken: there was something strange about this part of the hotel.

As I turned away, something odd caught my eye, something I hadn't registered before - there was the outline of a door immediately beside room 314.

It was very faint, as though it had been papered over, but in the dim light of the corridor, the shape showed up more clearly than it did in daylight.

There was no way to confirm my suspicions, but I'd a conviction this was where the noise had originated.

I put my ear to the hidden door, but in spite of waiting for a good five minutes, listening intently, there was nothing more to be heard.

Inch by inch I crept back to room 302, pausing every few seconds in case the sound started up again, but to my disappointment there was nothing except for the soft hum of the overnight lighting.

I gathered my belongings as quickly as I could from Room 302, almost dropping my camera in the process and once safely back in my own room with the door firmly locked, considered what to do next.

I had heard a noise, of that I was now sure, and it could only be coming from that part of the corridor where there had once been a door.

Could there be someone behind the façade? No, that wasn't in the least likely - the door, if that's indeed what it was, had obviously been wallpapered over, disused for some considerable time.

My plan had been to go back to my room to get some sleep before the busy day ahead, but there was no possibility of that now. I switched on the bedside light and in my usual method for dealing with something I couldn't understand, I rummaged in my bag for a notebook and pen.

I headed a fresh page with the title 'Bute Hydro Hotel - mystery' and began to make a list of what I knew.

Strange sound of sobbing
Heard by Anna, but not by her husband (or not admitted)
Not mentioned by any of the other guests
Heard by me - once with Anna and once on my own
Sound definitely coming from the top corridor-behind wallpapered over door?
The Manager reluctant to discuss/ admit problem

That was as much as there was. Not a lot to go on. Should I approach the Manager? Perhaps my story would be more convincing than Anna's. Or check with some of the other guests? After the increase in volume, possibly I could find a way of asking guests with rooms on this floor if they'd heard anything or noticed anything strange. Or would that cause panic, given so many of them were elderly?

This was ridiculous. I was going round in circles and it wasn't really anything to do with me, except that Anna had asked for my help and I felt a certain loyalty, a certain duty towards her, given her sudden death.

As I read through the list again I realised in all the confusion I'd forgotten to use my recorder. How stupid of me.

Then I had an idea. Kelly knew the place well. She'd worked here since it had re-opened and hadn't her family been employed the old hotel? I was sure she'd said her mother or her grandmother - or perhaps both - had worked in the Hydro. I seemed to remember a discussion one evening when guests had been particularly interested in her tales of those days when the Hydro was at the height of its popularity.

She might have some notion of any stories about the shape of the original building, about the rooms on the third floor. It would surely be worth a try, if I phrased the questions carefully.

Perhaps I could claim to be considering writing a short history of the original Hydro, about its popularity in Victorian times, about its use as a naval base during the Second World War and how money had been found to resurrect it again?

What's more, Kelly was much more approachable than Yvonne. And Yvonne had made it clear when she handed over the key to Room 302 that she didn't believe my story, though she stopped short of accusing me of lying.

The more I thought about it, the more the story of the Hydro seemed a possible idea for my next project. I'd nothing planned after these *Turkey and Tinsel* weeks, nothing firm that is, so there might be some mileage in a history of the building.

I'd had a lot of success with my book about the Rothesay Pavilion and with the story of James Hamilton of Kames - there was good reason to think this idea might not be so far-fetched.

With the decision made, feeling much more positive about everything, I snapped the notebook shut. The details had to be worked out, but after a good night's sleep I was sure I'd be able to come up with some plausible story about why I was so interested in the history of the Hydro. And I'd start with Kelly.

As I drifted off, I suddenly remembered the key to room 302 was in my jacket pocket. Was it a good idea to go down and try to sneak it back on to the board now? Or should I wait and risk returning it in the morning?

In the end sloth won. I was so tired, so very tired and the only desire I had at the moment was to sleep. If there was a problem about returning the key in the morning I'd deal with it. I was surely practised enough in this kind of thing to come up with a plausible excuse.

20

As luck would have it, Kelly wasn't on duty when I
eventually surfaced the next morning, feeling decidedly
muzzy in spite of sleeping right through. I'd forgotten
to set the alarm and thank goodness there was nothing
special lined up for me to do that morning.

'Kelly not here?' I said to a very bored Yvonne,
fingering the key to Room 302 nestling accusingly in
my jacket pocket. Or at least boredom was the
impression she gave, lounging back in her chair reading
some magazine or other.

She gave a guilty start and pushed the magazine
under the desk, before adjusting her glasses and
replying, 'No. She's had to take some time off again.
Her little one is still not well and her mum can't help
out today.'

'So you've no idea when she'll be back on duty.'

'None at all. The Manager is lucky I'm able to help
out at short notice. He made the wrong choice there.'

'Oh, how come?'

Yvonne hesitated, as though unsure how much she
should tell me.

'Well…the truth is there were a number of
applicants for the post of senior Receptionist and Kelly
got it. She made all sorts of promises, but it's obvious
she didn't tell Clive she might have problems in
looking after her child.'

Her tone of voice made it abundantly clear what she
thought of Kelly, in spite of her claim that they 'worked

together' but I was determined not to rise to the bait. Gossip travels fast in a small community and I didn't want to antagonise Kelly or anyone else for that matter. So all I said was, 'Kelly was probably very keen to have the job,' and turned away.

But now it was clear she wasn't going to let me go without some kind of explanation. 'More than that. She applied first for the post of Assistant Manager, but she didn't have the necessary experience for that.' Yvonne sniffed and preened herself, making it clear she thought she was very much superior.

Then she seemed to realise she should have been more discreet. 'Was there some special reason you wanted to talk to Kelly? Is there anything I can help with?'

It was clear she hadn't noticed the key for Room 302 hadn't been returned. Could I distract her sufficiently to sneak it back on to the hook on the board without her noticing? Unfortunately I couldn't think of a single way to lure Yvonne away from her post.

Sometimes the truth is the best option. Taking a deep breath and casting my eyes down in the hope it would make me look suitably shame-faced, I muttered, 'So sorry, but I completely forgot to return the key for Room 302 last night.'

A look of alarm came over Yvonne's face and she turned quickly to examine the key board before leaning forward, hissing, 'Shh. Don't say a word. I could be sacked for lending it to you.'

She looked all around, as did I, but with no one else in sight she quickly regained her composure.

As I pulled the key from my pocket and put it on the desk she slammed her hand over mine.

'Quick, before anyone notices. Thank goodness no one thought to check last night.' She was clearly angry with me, very angry, which was a nuisance, because it meant my chances of another visit to that room were slim.

As she turned her back to slip the key on to the board, I suddenly thought that Yvonne might also be a Brandane and therefore know something about the history of the Kyles Hydro Hotel so I said, 'I'm thinking of writing a short book on the old Hydro. Would you know anything about it?'

Now that the key was safely back she seemed to regain her poise. 'I should say so. So many of my family worked there. They all lived in Port Bannatyne and the Hydro gave employment to most of the village. It was a real blow to the local economy when it eventually closed.'

'Did it cease to be popular?'

The Santa started up again, but this time Yvonne silenced it mid 'Ho, ho, ho' by reaching round the back and switching it off.

She shook her head. 'One of Clive's less bright ideas,' she said before returning to the subject of the Hydro. 'It has a long history. A private house stood on the site originally, then it became a sanatorium (that was in the 1880s, I think) and re-named the Kyles of Bute Hydro.'

'So what was the difference between a Hydro and a hotel?' This conversation was proving more interesting than I'd first thought.

'They were trying to provide holidays or convalescence along the lines of what was on offer in the spa towns. It was all very strict from what my granny said - prayers each morning and no drink of course. Though she did say that this rule wasn't always kept to. There was many a dram smuggled into the bedrooms.'

'It looks very imposing,' I said, pointing to the large sepia photograph of the Hydro on the wall opposite the Reception desk.

Yvonne swivelled round to look at it. 'Oh, good gracious, that's the replacement Hydro. The first building burnt down in the early 1900s. The island didn't have a fire brigade at the time and the new Hydro was built a couple of years later and the West wing was added then.'

'Ah, and that's the only part of that building now left?'

'Yes, it was some place. My granny's mother worked there as one of the Entertainers who organised the Bridge nights, the concerts and the sports events. Table tennis was particularly popular she said.'

'So what happened? How could such a well-liked place fail?'

'As with so many things it was the war years that sounded the death knell. It became the training place for the midget submarines and the human torpedoes. It was renamed as if it was a ship, but I can't quite remember what that was.'

She paused, frowning in concentration.

'What was it called again? It began with a W or a V, I'm sure.'

'I can find that out later,' I said, eager for her not to lose the thread of this story.

'Anyway,' she went on, 'after the war the place was never the same again. It became difficult to make it pay and then the death knell was the arrival of cheap holidays to places like Spain. Who would want to come to Bute, with its unpredictable weather, when you could have guaranteed sunshine for the same price?'

'So that was the only reason?'

She shook her head. 'It was also because the people who finally ran it lacked vision, couldn't see the opportunities the place still presented. That's why we're all so pleased that this hotel,' stopping to wave her arms in a general direction, 'has been built and incorporated the old West wing.'

Finally I could get to the nub of my questions. 'So with all that history, the West wing must have seen quite a few interesting events.'

'I dare say - there was plenty going on here at one time.'

I had to introduce the question I really wanted to ask as delicately as possible, make it sound no more than a casual enquiry. 'And did you ever hear any tales of strange happenings? Of events that might have frightened people?'

For a moment she looked confused, as though she didn't understand. Then light dawned. 'Oh, do you mean are there any ghosts lingering around the old West wing? Not that I've heard about, though with an old building you can never be sure. There might be one or two haunting the place.'

She must have seen the expression on my face change because as quickly she said, 'Don't worry - I'm only teasing. There aren't any ghosts that I've heard about.'

She chuckled as she spoke. 'If you do find one, for goodness sake don't tell the Manager: he's worried enough already.'

'Worried about what?'

She shrugged. 'I know it's silly and I know I've said there are no ghosts, but there's concern the place might be jinxed.'

'Surely that's nonsense.' This comment sounded even more unlikely than there be a ghost stalking the corridor.

'Well, there you are then.'

It might be better to try a different tack. 'I've noticed at the end of the corridor on the floor above my room there's a place where it looks as if there was once a door? But it's been covered up. Do you know anything about that?'

This new topic of conversation seemed to surprise her. 'I've never been in that part of the hotel,' she said, 'but I couldn't possibly imagine why anyone would want to board up one of the rooms.' She said this so determinedly that for a moment I wavered. Perhaps I'd made a mistake and in the half light had imagined a door, but before I could question her further, the phone rang.

She had given me enough information to convince me that there might be some mileage in writing up the history of the Hydro. It certainly sounded as if it had been a magnificent place in its heyday and even what was left of the West wing had a grandeur not found in many hotels these days.

It wasn't hard to imagine how the place must have looked, sitting as it did high above the bay of Port Bannatyne, or envisage the upper middle class guests in their finery sweeping through these wide corridors on their way to dinner or a game of bridge or a party. Yes, there was indeed some possibility here.

But in the meantime I was no further forward with the noises I'd heard during the night. If only I could think of another way to check. Then it came to me in a blinding flash. Of course. I'd seen it in some film or other. I could check the number of rooms in that part of the building, check the number of windows inside and then compare them with what I could see outside.

If there were more windows on the outside then it would be confirmation I was correct, that I hadn't been deceived, that there was indeed another room in that corridor.

Yvonne had finished her phone call and as she turned back to the computer, I had to ask her one last question. 'Those rooms on the top floor of the West wing - are they all alike? Each room has only one large window?'

If she thought this query odd she gave no sign, or perhaps I'd asked so many peculiar questions she was getting used to it.

'Mmm…as far as I know. The rooms were refurbished before the hotel re-opened and the ensuites were carved out of a corner of the room, but none of them has a window. That part of the hotel is listed and you have to be very careful what you do. It can be a real nightmare getting planning permission for any modern changes. I'm not so sure about the top floor though. There is still a lot of work to be done there. If it's ever completed.'

She seemed to have forgiven me for not returning the key, thank goodness. And that was the first part of my question answered, but I was curious about her words "if it's ever completed". I'd have to ask her when she was less busy.

I mouthed 'Thanks,' and hurried up to my room. All I needed now was to find a warm fleece and go out in to the grounds at the side of the West wing to count the number of windows. Then I would know for sure if there was indeed a room in that corridor that for some reason had been covered up.

21

Yvonne had given me food for thought and I wondered if I should now approach Kelly, or take a chance on my guess about the room on the top floor of the West wing. Once back down in the Reception area, suitably clad to brave the chill of the morning, I considered my options. This area of the hotel was full of activity as the last of the guests drifted out from the breakfast room, chattering and greeting friends they'd made during the week.

'Ah, Alison,' said Lily Herrington bustling up beside me. 'We so much enjoyed your last talk, but there were some questions we wanted to ask you.'

'Yes, questions we wanted to ask,' twittered Iris peeping out behind her, tapping her stick to emphasize her point.

I looked around wildly for a reason, any reason, not to be delayed by the sisters. Exhausted after a night of little sleep, I doubted if anything I said would make sense.

'I'd love to chat to you,' I replied, quickly changing a frown to a smile and hoping they wouldn't notice, 'but I've promised Clive Timmons I'd check out with him a few of the details for one of my talks next week. Perhaps,' edging away, 'I could catch up with you later?'

Their faces registered disappointment. 'What a pity. We'd so like to talk to you...' said Lily.

'...about the way this hotel was in the old days,' finished Iris. 'We thought you might be interested...'

'...as we can tell you some stories,' said Lily.

'I'll see you later, I promise,' I called and slipped away before anyone else could detain me.

I zipped up my fleece as I went outside into the chilly morning. There was a mist swirling round the hotel that made it look spooky and the mainland was completely hidden from sight.

It was as though we were adrift on an island within an island and it took me a few moments to orientate myself and find the right spot to start from so seamlessly had the old been grafted on to the new.

After a few wrong guesses I pinpointed the start of the West wing not far from the ruined greenhouses and noticed with surprise that the pond was much larger close up than it appeared from a distance. I craned my neck to locate the top floor before moving further back to get a better view, then forward again as the mist closed in.

I walked slowly along the length of it, taking my time. I didn't want to make a mistake about this. I'd already had too many episodes when I'd jumped to conclusions, often with disastrous consequences. This time I wanted to be sure.

I counted along the windows, one, two three, four...until I reached the total on this side of the building, before retracing my steps and counting yet again, pausing only to remind myself of the order of the rooms on the top floor corridor.

Think, Alison, think, I admonished myself. How many rooms should there be on the top floor? Room 301 to Room 313 should be immediately above me, with 302 to 314 on the opposite side, though I'd have to double check. Few of them were numbered at the moment until the renovation resumed.

A little tingle of excitement went through me. I hadn't made a mistake. My guess had been correct.

There weren't six windows - there were seven on the side of the corridor that started with Room 302. There must be an extra room somewhere on that top floor, unless Yvonne had been mistaken and one of the rooms had more than one window. But was it likely she would make that kind of error? And if all the rooms were identical, surely there was no possibility of one of them being bigger than the others.

Suddenly aware I was shivering from cold as much as from excitement, I pulled my fleece more tightly around me before going back to the beginning of the West wing to start counting again.

It was clear there was an extra window and desperate to check the inside of this wing of the building, I hurried back indoors. All I had to do was go back up to the top floor and double check the number of rooms there.

The lift was busy, a queue snaking almost to the bottom of the stairs, so I decided to walk up. But as I did so the thought struck me - if I was correct and there was a room that had been sealed up, who would I tell? It was unlikely the Manager would be interested or perhaps he knew already and was keeping it quiet for some reason I couldn't come up with at the moment. Whatever, I had to investigate and I needed someone to help.

I considered the Major. He'd expressed an interest in the history of the building, but then again I didn't see him being willing to hammer at the wall where the door might be on my say so.

Pausing only to leave my fleece in my room, frustrated by my inability to solve this puzzle, I went upstairs and took some time walking along the top corridor. There was indeed one fewer door than window.

I stopped outside the faint outline of a door I'd noticed the night before. It was much more difficult to see it in the daylight but I peered closely and traced my finger carefully round the oblong shape, feeling the grooves where the door had once been. It had been skilfully concealed, but from certain angles it was obvious that there was indeed an entrance to another room.

Why would it be wallpapered over? What possible reason could there be for doing this? Wait a minute - some of the rooms still had their old numbers. There was Room 310 but the next room along was 314.

Strange I hadn't noticed that before now. I checked once more to make sure, but indeed Room 312 seemed to be missing.

22

It was most unlike me to refrain from rushing headlong into making a decision, but for some reason on this occasion I decided to wait, to take my time before deciding my next move. What I had to do now was review everything that had happened to date. There must be others I could ask about the strange goings on at this hotel.

In the meantime a foray down to the village for a brisk walk along the shore at Port Bannatyne was in order, something to help clear my head. I popped back briefly to my room, only long enough to pick up the warmest jacket I'd brought with me. Layered up, with a jumper and cardigan and this jacket I should be well enough equipped to ward off the chilly breeze from the bay.

As I pushed open the front door, the Manager came rushing towards me. 'Alison, I'm glad I caught you. Are you going somewhere?'

About to reply, 'I would hardly be dressed like this if I was staying indoors,' I bit my comment back. It was possible he was about to rebuke me for my lack of attention to the guests. Part of my contract had been to mingle with them, to chat about Bute, answer their questions and instead I'd spent most of my time so far avoiding them.

So guilt made me say instead, 'I'm having a quick walk and I won't be long. Was there anything in particular you wanted?'

My heart sank as he said, 'Actually there was something I wanted you to help me with.'

Clive stood shuffling his feet, making me more anxious than ever about what his request might be.

He looked up. 'It's about this evening. There's a little problem. Nothing serious,' he hastened to add seeing the expression on my face. 'We were supposed to be having a *Magic Memories* night - you know, dancing to some of the songs these guests might remember with affection from their time as teenagers, visiting Bute and dancing at the Rothesay Pavilion, but Marty Craymore has let me down. He's phoned to say he's ill, but it's my guess he's had a better offer and doesn't fancy coming over here in November.'

Without allowing me to comment, he went on, 'He's a very popular entertainer and he did express some concern about getting off the island if it became stormy. Though why he couldn't have said so in the first place I don't know - some people are so unreliable. I won't be asking him again, that's for sure ...'

I cut in, dreading his next words. 'And how can I help you?' If he was about to ask me to take Marty Craymore's place as the singer for the evening it was a lost cause. There are some things I won't make a fool of myself doing, even if I did have an open-ended contract.

He took a deep breath. 'Well, it's like this, Alison; Marty has a great knack of getting people involved, encouraging them to participate. He seems to know the kind of songs people remember and love...'

Oh no, I thought, he is about to ask me if I can sing. On this point I'd be very firm indeed. 'Sorry, Clive, I don't know how I can help you with this. I can't sing to save myself and …'

'Sing? I wasn't going to ask you to sing, Alison.' He threw back his head, laughing loudly. 'Marty always has a selection of records and only sings some of the songs. We could make do with someone playing the records and not singing. I'm sure one or two of the guests might volunteer to sing - a kind of karaoke evening.'

This wasn't much better than asking me to sing. I wasn't the kind of person able to jolly people along at this sort of event.

'You can't possibly expect me to do this all on my own?'

'No, Kelly will help you - and Yvonne. It's really that we need a team and I thought, given that you're supposed to be mingling with the guests, you would be willing to help.'

This little barb at my lack of engagement with the guests didn't go unnoticed but just in time I refrained from commenting. What could I say? It didn't sound too difficult and if Kelly and Yvonne were there to help it would make up for the way in which I'd neglected the guests so far.

'As long as you're sure the others will be there. I expect you're using some kind of sophisticated equipment and I'm not the least bit technically minded, if you remember that unfortunate incident with my talk.' That seemed as good an answer as any.

He waved aside my concerns. 'That's great,' he said, a note of relief in his voice, 'and don't worry - the equipment will all be set up and the girls are well able to deal with any problems of that kind. I'll brief you all straight after lunch and we can have a run through.'

What could I do but agree? 'Fine. See you then.' And I hurried out before he could line me up for any more unusual tasks. If Kelly and Yvonne were going to help, perhaps it wouldn't be as bad as I'd feared. I could be the person on the sidelines changing the music.

In spite of this unexpected request for the moment my head was full of the dilemma of the missing room. As I headed down the hill towards the seafront it was all I could think about, any concerns about the evening's entertainment forgotten.

The earlier mist had drifted away, leaving a bright morning of blue skies and the Christmas lights along the shore were still shining out. On top of the bus shelter a giant Santa struggled to keep his reindeer under control, while it seemed as if in every house along the front there were more decorations than before, each trying to outdo the other in the number of fairy lights, illuminated elves and Santas.

All this light lifted my spirits: if only all this gaiety could be kept to see us through till the end of the dark days of January, but we had to enjoy this while it lasted. Many people complained about how early Christmas decorations went up, but for me it couldn't be soon enough.

I walked briskly along the shore, past the slipway, the deserted holiday cottages and the North Bute Primary school where it was break time, judging by the noise coming from the schoolyard behind the high stone wall. Suddenly a football came sailing over and then a little head popped up.

'Can you throw our ball back, please?' said the boy, tottering about as he did so. I suddenly realised he was actually standing on the shoulders of another child and hurried to do as he asked before there was an accident. Even so, in my haste, or perhaps my lack of expertise, and in spite of my willingness to help it took three attempts before I was able to lob the ball over the wall.

At the Boatyard in contrast, all was quiet, the boats snugly locked up for the winter. A few showed signs of ravages of the autumn storms, with peeling paint. Some of the owners would be busy once Spring arrived.

On the crane perched out over the water at the Marina, another Santa swung back and forth, this one having the advantage of height, though it did look rather perilous.

I paused at the railings for a few moments to look out over Kames bay, but on a morning like this of complete stillness there was nothing to see except the reflection of the sky, the light giving the grey and silver waters of the bay an oily sheen. Shivering in spite of my warm clothing I turned back and retraced my steps. That was enough fresh air for the moment and I quickened my pace as I reached the holiday cottages.

As I came near the Coronet Hotel on the corner of Marine Road, I crossed over to take the road up towards the Hydro and as I passed the entrance almost collided with a figure scurrying out, saying to someone unseen, 'I told you there would be no possibility of it working. Wait and see. I'm sure I'm right. We're wasting our time. And now the police are involved.'

'Oops, sorry,' I said, stepping back.

The young woman stopped and raised her head. It was Kelly.

23

We stood staring at each other in silence until 'I didn't expect to see you here,' I finally said.

She avoided my gaze, looked down at the ground. 'My uncle owns this hotel,' she muttered as though reluctant to tell me.

'And yet you work for the Hydro?' I blurted out.

She suddenly became defensive. 'What do you mean by that?' she demanded. 'My uncle has enough staff here. Jobs on the island are scarce and the opportunity to work at the Hydro was one I couldn't pass up.'

'Sorry, sorry,' I said, taken aback by this outburst, regretting my words. 'It was only a friendly enquiry - nothing more.'

This appeared to calm her but she said briskly, 'Well, I must be getting on. I'm on duty soon and I still have a couple of things to do.'

I stood staring after her as she hurried off in the direction of the Hydro, realising I'd no idea where she lived or much else about her, apart from what Yvonne had told me about her having a small child. But whether she had a husband or a partner or more children, I'd no idea.

Still, none of my business and dismissing Kelly from my thoughts, though still feeling uncomfortable at the encounter, I made for the Post Office cum general store a little further along the road. It was about to open and I'd buy a morning paper if they had been delivered from the ferry.

Sammy, who owned the shop, was someone I knew from previous visits to the island and he greeted me with a, 'Lovely morning for a walk,' as he pushed back the red half-gate across the entrance, 'as long as you walk quickly.'

'Mmm, I do feel the better for it,' I said. Which was true. I hadn't come to any decision about what I should do next about that strange room, but I did feel some of the cobwebs had been blown away.

He lifted the bundle of papers lying inside the gate and together we went into the shop.

'Won't keep you a minute,' he said, disappearing into the back shop to put on the lights and start up the coffee machine.

I looked around as I waited, marvelling how much could be crammed into such a small space. One half of the counter was devoted to the Post Office with all the usual posters and paraphernalia, the other had a counter where the chill cabinet was set up for the morning's delivery of fresh sandwiches and cakes, its top crammed with sweets, packets of biscuits, chocolate bars and other goodies. In the far corner, behind the counter, the coffee machine began to hiss and splutter as it started up, the cups and saucers at the side juddering perilously as it did so.

Round the walls a plethora of shelves displayed a cornucopia of goods ranging from essentials such as bags of sugar and tins of soup to luxury items like tinned pate.

As though this wasn't enough, one shelf held brightly coloured buckets and spades and fishing nets and all the other bits and pieces necessary for a holiday by the sea, though Sammy had placed these high up, no doubt realising there would be little call for them at this time of year.

In the middle of all these goods sat a large wooden table surrounded by chairs: the café part of the shop much favoured by local residents.

'You've decided not to use the outside tables and chairs then?' I said as Sammy came back through to the shop, pointing in the direction of the windbreak which was neatly furled at the front beside the door.

He laughed and shook his head. 'A bit optimistic to put them out at this time of year - I don't want to risk them being blown away - far too expensive to replace.'

A wise decision. It was a day for walking, not sitting outside

'Now, what can I get you? The coffee shouldn't be long. And do you want a paper?'

I was about to say, 'Just a paper, thanks,' but the aroma of coffee was tempting and I thought, why not? I was in no rush back and sitting here, enjoying freshly brewed coffee (as opposed to the insipid stuff they served at the Hydro) was very tempting. 'I'll have a cappuccino, thanks,' I said and sat down at the table.

Sammy brought over the coffee and a newspaper. 'I've unwrapped the local paper first,' he said. 'You can read that: the others should be tallied and ready by the time you leave.'

Grateful for this cosseting, I sat back, allowing myself to enjoy the smell of the coffee wafting towards me before taking a long, luxurious sip. 'Gosh, that coffee is good,' I said.

Sammy looked up from cutting through the string that tied the bundles of newspapers together. 'Glad you like it. It's one thing I pride myself on, the coffee.'

Of course I should have known that the opportunity to sit in silence and read the local news in *The Buteman*, while enjoying my coffee was a futile hope. Even this early in the morning, Sammy was looking for someone to chat to.

'Saw you with Kelly a bit earlier,' he said, heaving another bundle of papers on to the rack beside the front door.

'Yes.' I looked up from a most interesting article about the plans to renovate some of the buildings in the town centre. One of the great things about Bute is that it has a real town, Rothesay, at its heart, so while much of the island is as you would expect, rural, having a town gives it a completely different feel to many of the islands round the west coast of Scotland. 'She's working up at the Hydro. That's where I am at the moment.'

'Interesting that. And her uncle owns the Coronet: it's a wonder she doesn't have a job there.'

'She told me there were enough staff at the Coronet, that's why she's at the Hydro.' Now I was intrigued. It was obvious Sammy was leading up to telling me something, but exactly what I'd no idea.

'That's not what I've heard. It's hard to believe a village like Port Bannatyne could support more than one hotel and a lot of money was spent on refurbishing the Coronet a few years back, as you know.'

I did know about it, as I'd spent a lot of time there when I'd had the job of assistant scriptwriter on the film *A Man Alone*. It had been a favourite meeting place for the cast and the film crew.

'But it's not the villagers who use the hotels, surely,' I said, thinking of how Pelias Productions had

138

almost completely taken over the Coronet. 'They bring in people from all over who want a break on the island.'

Sammy raised his eyebrows. 'That's as may be. But I've heard since the Hydro opened, trade at the Coronet has been badly affected and that there are serious problems. The Hydro should never have been allowed to re-open. There isn't enough business for two large hotels in the village, not nowadays. It was different when the original Hydro was built - there were plenty of visitors to the island then.'

He shook his head and appeared about to continue with this theme when the front door opened and another customer came in to the shop.

I sat and stared at *The Buteman*, but not really seeing it. This problem was one I hadn't considered, but it made complete sense. In a small place like Port Bannatyne it was difficult enough to fill one hotel on a regular basis, never mind two. And was this anything to do with what was happening at the Hydro? The cases of food poisoning, the deaths, the strange sounds in the night. Not very likely, yet I couldn't get this nagging doubt out of my head. When you put everything that had happened at the Hydro together it was clear that something was going on, that was for sure.

24

There was no further news of Freddie and the Manager seemed to have dismissed concerns about him, my questions being met with a brusque, 'I'm sure the police have it in hand, Alison.'

I wasn't looking forward to the proposed musical evening one little bit, although Clive had assured me over and over again that it would be easy, there was nothing to be concerned about.

'Everyone is well disposed towards an evening like this,' he'd said airily. 'There's nothing to it. You'll be fine. And Kelly and Yvonne will be here to help.' It was as though having persuaded me to take on this task, he'd moved on to other matters.

I wasn't as optimistic as he was by a long way. For one thing I lacked the breezy style of Marty Craymore and there was no chance I'd be able to imitate it. The guests would be expecting him with his flamboyant suit and quiff hairstyle and charming manner, his easy way with jokes and banter, not the woman who'd been lecturing them on the history of Bute.

There was no option now and after dinner I went straight up to my room to rake through my limited wardrobe and decide what to wear. There wasn't much choice: anticipating two weeks in an overheated hotel, I'd brought a couple of my smarter suits (well, my only suits) in order to look business-like and added some warm jumpers and outdoor clothing for the times I'd be able to escape the stuffy atmosphere of the hotel.

Eventually I decided to put on the most glamorous outfit I'd brought with me, which wasn't saying much. I'd only packed this long dark blue gown, adorned at the neck with pearls, at the very last minute on the off chance it might be suitable for the Welcome dinner. Truth to tell, it was a dress that had been hanging at the back of the wardrobe for several years after one outing to a college event when Simon was head of department and I'd splashed out. I hadn't even thought to try it on again before leaving: I hoped it still fitted me. It did, thank goodness, but only just. If I didn't move about too much it should hold out for the night, but to make sure I added the lightest cardigan I owned. The addition of my single pair of high heels completed the outfit and as I regarded my reflection in the mirror I thought I might pass muster, as long as the lighting was dim.

I was ready far too early, but eager to find out if there had been any developments, I locked my door and walked towards the lift. There was no way I was risking the stairs in these shoes. As I reached it, still thinking about the evening ahead and hoping Kelly and Yvonne would be able to carry things along without too much help, I heard a strange noise from further along the corridor.

For a moment I couldn't think what it might be, then I realised the sound was coming from the floor above and it was a low sobbing, very, very faint as though coming from a long way off, but nonetheless audible.

A chill ran down my spine. This was a new departure. To date the noises had only been heard in the middle of the night and to the best of my knowledge not on this floor. I looked round the corridor but there was no one else in sight: those who hadn't already made

141

their way downstairs to the ballroom to claim the best seats would still be in their rooms getting ready. I was tempted to knock on the nearest door and ask if someone would come along the corridor with me and make sure it wasn't another instance of my imagination at work.

But a moment's hesitation made me realise that wasn't a good idea. Surely if the sound was audible to all, someone else would have investigated by now?

I stopped and listened, straining my ears in the quiet of the corridor. Screwing up my courage, I headed towards the stairs and up to where I'd located the missing door. As I reached it, quite without warning, the sound ceased as abruptly as it had on previous occasions.

This was confirmation of what I'd suspected. The noise had most certainly been coming from that room. I put my ear to the door and listened, scarcely daring to breathe.

There was nothing to be heard, not the slightest noise, not even a whisper. This was nonsense. It was impossible that there should be someone behind the missing door. From all appearances the door had been sealed up for a very long time.

I thought about the way the noise had sounded. As suddenly as it had begun, it had stopped. It didn't die away gradually as you would expect, but ceased very suddenly as though the person making the noise had been cut off.

I waited a few more minutes, but there was no repetition of the noise and a quick glance at my watch told me I'd no option but to head for the lift if I didn't want to be late.

Yet I couldn't leave things like this. I had to tell someone about the incident, about these noises that only Anna and I appeared to be able to hear. The only person I could talk to, had to talk to, was the Manager, Clive. It was only right he should know what was going on and he might even have an answer, a simple explanation for everything.

As luck would have it, he was standing looking around when I came out of the lift and I hurried over to speak to him before I had the chance to change my mind.

'Can I have a word with you?' I hissed, noticing that a couple of the guests were determinedly bearing down on him and it was clear they weren't happy.

'Is it urgent?' He looked perplexed, unhappy at my request. 'There's a lot still to do. We should be starting promptly. Once everyone has had the first free drink, we have to make sure we begin in case...' He meant of course in case most of them decided to stay in the bar rather than participate in the arranged entertainment.

'Yes, I'm aware of that, but I need to ask you something …and we have to go somewhere private.'

'You're not going to back out of this evening's entertainment?' A look of alarm crossed his face and with some difficulty I stifled the laughter I felt bubbling up.

'No, certainly not. Why else would I be dressed like this?'

My reply seemed to pacify him up and he said, sighing audibly, 'Fine, as long as it's a quick word. Come in here.'

He gestured for me to follow him past the Reception desk and into a small back room where there were a couple of easy chairs and a coffee table strewn with popular magazines.

He turned to face me, but there was no invitation to sit down. 'How can I help you Alison?' He began to shuffle from foot to foot almost as if he was practising for the evening's dancing.

Now that I had his full attention, I began to wonder if this had been a terrible mistake, if I should keep my worries to myself until I had some more concrete evidence. Too late now. I had to say something.

I took a deep breath. 'It's about the missing room on the top floor of the old West wing, 'I said then, seeing the bewildered look on his face, I went on, 'What I mean is there should be another room before that last room at the end of the corridor, but the door's been sealed up for some reason.'

He looked astonished at this suggestion then shrugged. 'Is this a problem? I'm sure it was something the architect decided during one of the hotel's many earlier renovations.' He hesitated as though seeking a plausible answer then said, 'Probably it was a way to increase the size of the adjoining rooms. We'll sort it out when we continue refurbishing that floor. Why would you be interested in that?'

'Because,' I almost shouted, becoming increasingly annoyed by his off-hand manner, 'I've heard noises coming from the room that no longer exists. Sounds as if someone is sobbing.'

The Manager turned deadly pale and without a word he sank in to one of the chairs, all his bluster gone.

Seizing the advantage, I said, 'I'm not trying to alarm anyone, but I'm absolutely sure I've heard it on more than one occasion.'

144

'Have you told anyone about this?' His voice was no more than a whisper. Then with a note of alarm in his voice, 'Does anyone else know?'

'It was Anna who alerted me to the noise,' I said. Now that I'd started, I might as well tell him the truth, tell him the whole story.

'Anna? When did she tell you?'

'The night before she died. She asked me to keep watch with her because she was concerned about it. She heard it the first couple of nights they were here. Anna might have been elderly, but there was nothing wrong with her hearing, I can assure you.'

'And did you hear it that night - the night with Anna.'

I nodded. 'Most certainly. And I am sure there is another room, hidden behind a false wall. I checked it out. If you walk along the West wing outside you can see that there are more windows than rooms.'

There was a silence and for a moment I began to wonder what had happened, if he'd fallen asleep as he sat there immobile, with his eyes tightly shut.

When he opened them, there was fear written all over his face. 'I hope you won't mention this to anyone else, Alison. Not till I've had the chance to check it out. I wouldn't want the guests to be upset or alarmed. Most of them are elderly and this kind of thing would cause panic. There must be a simple explanation.'

'Anna told me she'd already tried to talk to you about it.'

He shifted uncomfortably in his seat, looking shame-faced. 'Yes, yes, but I dismissed it as the wanderings of an elderly lady who was imagining things. And why upset the other guests with wild stories?'

145

'Fine,' I said, relieved at last to have passed the problem on to someone else. 'I'm not elderly and I most certainly heard it. It may be nothing, but if you assure me you're going to investigate, then I'll say no more about it.'

He nodded and I turned to leave the room. But as I closed the door he was still sitting there and the expression on his face told me there was much more to this than he was prepared to admit. And I strongly suspected that, in spite of his protestations, he knew exactly what I was talking about.

25

The evening passed off pleasantly in spite of my fears. It was all down to Kelly and Yvonne and very little to do with me. They selected the music; they complied with the many requests and deftly avoided a problem when the song asked for wasn't available.

It was a masterstroke to announce to the eager crowd, all dressed in their finery in expectation of being in the same room as Marty, that the evening would be one where they could choose exactly what they wanted.

There were some strange choices and many of those selected I didn't recognise, but Kelly and Yvonne jollied everyone along, kept up the happy atmosphere. Of course some of that might have been to do with the fact that, anticipating a possible mutiny at the non-appearance of Marty, the Manager had decreed at the last minute that the first couple of drinks would be on the house.

I skulked in the background, well understanding my limitations as a disc jockey, but I was able to mingle with the guests, to chat to those whose stamina didn't allow them to take the floor for every tune.

And Kelly and Yvonne had come up with another great idea, showing how well they understood the client group. As the break approached (sandwiches, cakes and yet more 'refreshments'), Kelly took the microphone. 'If I could have your attention for a moment, everyone.'

Those who'd made the front of the queue for the buffet turned round, unwilling to give up their places while those slowly approaching stopped in their tracks and I'd no idea what she was about to say, not having been briefed beforehand.

'We've had a great first part of the evening,' said Kelly, 'and I hope you've all been happy with the choice of music. You've been most receptive and most understanding that Marty couldn't make it this evening much as he regretted it.' A downright lie, but one carried off with confidence.

A round of applause broke out from several tables where the guests hadn't yet got to their feet. 'Hear, hear,' shouted Norman and 'Bravo,' in unison was the response from the Herrington sisters.

Kelly acknowledged this with a wave of her hand. 'But to make the evening a little different, we're going to have...' a pause for maximum effect... 'a karaoke session immediately after the interval. So make sure you're in good voice. We'll be wanting plenty of volunteers.'

My immediate thought was, this will never work, but Kelly knew the group better than I did and as soon as the break was over and everyone was back in the ballroom, suitably refreshed by a more abundant buffet than usual and a couple of glasses of wine (in the larger glasses) she launched straight into the session.

She took the microphone from its stand and came down from the stage to wander among the audience. 'Now who will be brave enough to start us off? I'm sure there are some good singers among you: don't keep your talent to yourself.' She hovered behind one chair after another, placing an arm on one or two, smiling encouragingly all the time.

There was a lack of response for the first few minutes, an uncomfortable silence and suddenly Norman got to his feet. 'I don't mind having a go,' he said.

Calla grabbed at his jacket, but he shook her off as she hissed, 'Don't go making a fool of yourself, Norman.'

But there was no stopping him now and to the sound of cheers from the rest of the audience the usually meek Norman seemed to be possessed of an extraordinary vigour as he followed Kelly towards the stage where Yvonne was poised to start up the music.

'So what would you like to sing then, Norman?' Yvonne asked.

'*When we Meet Again* is what I'd like,' he said and there was a ripple of applause at his choice.

As soon as he started, it became clear Calla's attempts to hold him back were nothing to do with her desire to be boss and more to do with her respect for the other guests. Whatever other talents Norman possessed, singing wasn't one of them. Or perhaps he'd been a good singer once upon a time, but lost his voice as he grew older. Thank goodness it was karaoke.

No one in the audience seemed to notice and as he was half way through the fourth verse (there seemed to be lots of them) some of the other guests began to join in and he eventually left the stage to thunderous applause.

Pink faced with delight, Norman walked back to his seat, waving to acknowledge the kind comments of those he passed. Marty himself couldn't have carried it off with more grace.

And now it was as though a dam had burst and one after another the guests clamoured to take the stage. Some were indeed in fine voice, but others had less talent than Norman.

There was little else for me to do except sit back and enjoy the evening, but as it drew to an end, I began to feel guilty about how little I'd contributed to the event and in spite of several shouts of encouragement, I determinedly shook my head every time the suggestion that I take the stage was made, pleading I didn't know any of the songs. This was an excuse which was far from plausible given that both Kelly and Yvonne participated with gusto.

In an attempt to make some kind of positive contribution to the evening, I decided the best I could do was seek out those guests who appeared to be on their own and chat to them. A quick glance round the room showed there weren't many who hadn't made a friend or two during this first *Tinsel and Turkey* week, but eventually I went over to one of the tables in the far corner where I'd spied a very elderly lady sitting by herself.

She might have been old and rather stooped, with a clear sign of a dowager's hump, but my first thought was that she was the picture of elegance, dressed as she was in a pale rose dress of some soft, silky material which beautifully set off her carefully styled silver hair. Up close, I saw she was wearing a little too much make-up and the powder had settled into the lines of her face. But her brown eyes still sparkled with life and she greeted me warmly as I approached the table.

'Hello, I'm Alison Cameron,' I said by way of introduction, sitting down in the empty chair beside her.

I had to repeat what I said in a louder voice and then she replied, 'Ah, yes I know, Mrs Cameron. I'm so pleased to be able to tell you how much I enjoyed your talks this week. They were as entertaining as they were informative. And you spoke in a nice loud clear voice, unlike many of these youngsters who seem to mumble all the time.'

That was the most likely explanation for her solitary state. My mother suffers increasingly from deafness and it is often easier to be on your own than try to follow the conversation or keep asking people to repeat what they've said.

'I'm glad you enjoyed them,' I said, deliberately keeping my voice at a loud pitch.

She smiled. 'I'm very interested in the history of Bute and you've made me want to find out more. I'm Effie MacDonald.'

'That's always good to hear, someone who has an interest in the history of the island. When you agree to give these talks you're always a bit concerned about keeping it at the right level.'

'Well, you needn't have worried,' she said, leaning towards me. 'Your talks were excellent.'

'Do you know Bute well?' I was doing no more than making polite conversation, but her answer surprised me.

'I haven't been back for many years, but when I saw this advertised in my local bookshop in Milngavie, I thought it was such a good opportunity to return to a place where I'd spent many happy summers in my youth.'

'Which part of Bute did you holiday in?' This wasn't unusual: with its proximity to the large city of Glasgow,

Bute had been for many years a favourite holiday destination.

She narrowed her eyes and regarded me shrewdly as though this was a strange question. 'Why here, of course, at the old Hydro. That's why, when I heard the West wing had been refurbished and the new building added, I absolutely had to come back, even though I'm not as able to travel as I once was.'

'And you're in the West wing?' I didn't recollect seeing her about the corridor at any point.

She gave a shudder. 'No, I'm in the new part. I wouldn't want to be in the West wing at any price. It was bad enough then.'

'But I thought the old hotel closed many, many years ago?' She was certainly old, but not as old as that surely. A quick reckoning and if what she said was correct that would make her over a hundred – not likely.

She chuckled as though she'd read my mind. 'Ah, some of my family were regulars here before the war - my grandmother spent many summers here and then after the war we came for a few years before the Hydro closed for good in the late sixties after the terrible fire.'

This was an interesting conversation and thinking once more about my idea to write a history of the place, I was keen to pursue it. 'But you also came before the war?'

Her eyes misted over as though she was remembering those days long ago. 'Ah, indeed. I was a young girl then and thought the place was like a fairytale palace. But then who wouldn't be impressed by the magnificent hall with its staircase of specially imported Italian marble? There were two lounges as I

152

recall, and a well stocked library where I spent many a wet afternoon. We were more able to entertain ourselves in those days. We didn't always have to look to others for amusement.' She chuckled again and patted her hair. 'Even in those days it rained on Bute, though many people would like to tell you otherwise. Nostalgia is a great eraser of unpleasant experiences.'

'It sounds marvellous. I'd no idea the facilities were so good.' This was true. I'd done some research before coming to the island to take up this post, but it had been sketchy.

'Oh, there was more.' Effie was now in full flow as she recalled the pleasures of the past. 'There was a large billiards room (not that I was allowed in there) and a writing room. I remember my mother sitting at one of the little desks writing postcards to her friends. Then of course there was the main lounge, the tearoom and the ballroom with a proper stage and footlights. I recollect seeing a performance of the *Mikado* there - the summer months were particularly good because there was a resident orchestra.'

She paused. 'I think they also played during the Christmas and New Year period, but we were never here at that time of year. My mother preferred to have the festive season in her own house, but I would have loved to experience even one Christmas here. It must have been marvellous.'

'What a shame it closed. Still,' I said brightly not wanting to see her sunk in gloomy reminiscences much longer, 'it's great that it's been renovated like this.'

She sighed. 'I suppose so, but it's not the same. This is no more than a shadow of the original.' She leaned over. 'I suspect it's all been done as cheaply as possible and there's a lot they haven't restored. The old Hydro had tennis courts and badminton courts - all sorts of outdoor activities. And the greenhouses where so much of the food we had was grown. I heard there's some talk of restoring the pond. It's so overgrown, but it would be good if it could be used for boating once again.' She chuckled again. 'Not all of the outdoor activities were on the standard list of activities on offer. But that was because the grounds were so extensive it wasn't hard to find a secluded spot for a bit of a cuddle.'

'It sounds idyllic,' I said.

To my great surprise, over on the stage Iris and Lily Herrington were performing a duet, though the words were a little unclear. From the way they were swaying, I suspected they'd continued with the glasses of wine.

'Silly women,' said Effie, sniffing. 'People like Iris are a real problem - I've told her sister so. She'd be better off in a Care Home.'

Not wishing to comment, I realised I should be making my way round, speaking to other guests, interesting as Effie's stories were.

'It's been a great pleasure to meet you,' I said standing up. 'I hope I'll see you again before you leave. I'd better go and speak to some of the others,' and I started to move away.

'Yes, I suppose it was a wonderful time.' Her eyes took on a dreamy look as though she was gazing back into the past, remembering happier times, almost unaware of my presence.

But before I left I had one more question for her. 'And you stopped coming because it became run down after the war? You preferred to remember it as it was in the pre-war days?'

She came to with a start and stared at me, as though trying to recollect who I was. 'What did you say? Sorry, I was miles away.'

I smiled. 'I was asking if you stopped coming to the Hydro because it became run down, an uncomfortable place to stay?'

For a moment she was silent as though weighing up how she should reply and it struck me that perhaps she was forgetful in her old age, couldn't remember our recent conversation.

But that wasn't the reason she'd hesitated to answer my question as I discovered when finally she said, turning away so that I wouldn't see the expression on her face.

'No, no, dear. It wasn't because the place gradually became run down that we stopped coming, though that was the excuse my mother gave. It was because of that girl who went missing.'

26

In response to my complaints about lack of contact, Simon had phoned regularly. 'I'm coming down at the weekend,' he'd said on Wednesday. 'I miss you...and so does Motley. It's not the same without you.'

I very much doubted if Motley, our cat, did miss me. As long as there's someone to feed him, like most cats he's very independent.

'You've surely plenty to occupy you working for Scottish Alignment, not to mention trips to London to work with the team in Head Office.'

There was another reason for Simon's discontent, I suspected. He was suffering from a lack of being able to play golf. Even had he not been working, with the weather we'd had over the previous few days even the most determined of golfers wouldn't have ventured out.

In spite of my reservations, I would be glad to see him. The weekend was the changeover period when one set of guests departed and the other arrived and I was due some time free on Saturday as they settled in. If the weather changed, improved even slightly, there would be an opportunity for some proper walking. I was beginning to feel stifled with being indoors so much in an over-heated atmosphere as well as from too many cups of tea, cakes and stodgy meals. The chance to head out to Ettrick Bay and walk along the shore was appealing; though ending up at the Ettrick Bay tearoom with its fine selection of goodies might be equally appealing.

'I'll come down on Saturday about lunchtime,' he said, 'and go back on Sunday evening.'

'Fine, but remember I have to attend the first night Welcome dinner and you'll have to join us. One more shouldn't cause the chef any difficulties.' I wasn't too sure about that, judging by the fuss that was made if anyone requested anything out of the ordinary. 'Not that it's Haute Cuisine,' I warned him.

He laughed. 'Don't worry. I won't starve for one night.'

'Have you seen Maura?' One of the downsides of being away for two weeks was missing seeing Connor. Two weeks is a long time in a baby's life.

He chuckled. 'Yes, I went through to Edinburgh yesterday evening in time for his bath. Had great fun.'

I stifled a pang of jealousy, saying, 'I'm so looking forward to seeing them soon,' as I rang off.

In the meantime I was both intrigued and surprised by what Effie had told me, but as I'd been about to ask her for more information, the others at her table came back from the dance floor and our conversation abruptly ended.

Confident there was time yet before she left, I resolved to catch her at breakfast the next day. Possibly I could persuade her to join me for coffee in the small Reception room that was seldom used, being north facing and gloomy, although the hotel was trying to maximise space to squeeze every penny out of the facilities. Without conferences, weddings and weeks like *Tinsel and Turkey*, many hotels would be in dire straits.

The text from Simon on Friday evening confirmed his plans.

'Decided to come on the ten fifteen ferry tomorrow instead of the lunchtime one. Won't bring the car. Can you meet me?'

One car on the island was fine, but it did mean I'd have to make arrangements to be off the premises for a while.

I hurried to find the Manager, to let him know I wouldn't be around for part of the morning and to explain Simon would be sharing my room.

He was surprisingly gracious about it. 'Good idea, Alison. There's no problem about one extra - it's a double room you're booked into anyway.'

But the reason for his magnanimity soon became clear as he added, gazing at me thoughtfully, 'What exactly does your husband do? Would he be able to help out at all? It looks as if Marty might be unavailable next week and I can't ask Kelly and Yvonne to cope two weeks in a row. They've plenty to do.'

'He wouldn't be keen on that,' I said firmly, imagining the look on Simon's face if he was asked to fill in as a DJ. 'He's only coming for the weekend.' I hurried off before the Manager could come up with any other bright suggestions. What's more, I had to think of a way of avoiding being involved in the *Magic Memories* night myself. Once was more than enough.

After sending Simon a text to confirm arrangements for meeting him and, exhausted from the evening's activities (though I hadn't actually done much), I headed for bed and was asleep within a few minutes of my head touching the pillow.

But any hopes of a peaceful night's sleep soon vanished. In the middle of the night I was suddenly wakened from a deep sleep and sat up in bed, groggily reaching for the clock on the bedside table. Two a.m. I sat still, listening intently, but the only sound was my heart beating a bit too fast for my liking.

Nothing, no noise. I must have been dreaming. That was it. I'd been wakened out of a nightmare, though I'd no recollection of what it had been. I slid down the bed, punched the pillow to make a comfortable position and closed my eyes, hoping to be fast asleep again in a few minutes.

Thank goodness Simon would be joining me, even for a short time. His presence is always very reassuring - something to do with his considerable bulk perhaps. Recently he's piled on the pounds in an alarming way and the only advantage is that it makes me feel positively sylph-like in comparison.

As I began to doze off again, I heard a faint noise outside the room. This time there was no doubt. It was fainter in this corridor, but it was certainly a sound, and nothing to do with late night revellers. Even the most determined of guests would be safely snug in bed by this time of the morning.

My first instinct was to put the pillow over my head, blot out the noise but, berating myself for being so cowardly, I grabbed my dressing gown and opened the room door before my courage failed me.

The noise was louder out in the hallway and as I slowly made my way to the bottom of the stairs, moving on tiptoe, it increased in volume. There was only one explanation. It was that same sorrowful sobbing and it was coming from the floor above.

I crept up the stairs, pausing on every tread, willing the noise to cease but it continued, low and soft. As I climbed, it became louder. Yes, it was coming from behind the door that had been sealed off. Then, as suddenly as it had begun, it stopped.

I waited, scarcely daring to take a breath, thinking it would start up again. But there was nothing to be heard.

Why was I the only person, now that poor Anna was dead, who was able to perceive it? Unless, unless. My room was right at the end of the corridor on the second floor – was the sobbing funnelled in some way so that it wasn't easy to hear on the rest of my floor? Plenty of questions, but no answers.

I shivered and drew my dressing gown tightly round my shoulders. The sensible thing to do would be to go straight back to my cosy bed and forget all about it. How could it possibly be real? It must all be a figment of my imagination.

But this was no longer an option and slowly I made towards the hidden door, my footfalls making no sound on the carpet. As I reached it, all was silent. I stopped, waited, walked forward a few paces and put my ear to the spot where the door had once been. No sobbing, not even a whimper.

Then suddenly it started up again, low and insistent. I felt all round the door frame, but there was no way of opening it that I could establish. There was one possibility. The room next door, if indeed it was a room, might not be locked. If I could get in, there might be a connecting door and I'd at last find the source of the persistent weeping.

I leaned against the wall, willing my thudding heart to slow down. Had I imagined it? Was it part of a waking dream? I pinched myself hard a couple of times, hoping this was some kind of nightmare, in spite of the evidence that Anna had also heard it.

Decision made, I took a deep breath and pushed hard at the door of the next room, almost losing my balance as it yielded easily to my touch.

At first I couldn't make much sense of my surroundings, then a closer look revealed I was in some kind of huge cupboard, one wall entirely covered with shelves, all of them empty. This must be part of the original building; the store cupboards sited beside accommodation for the servants for ease of access.

There was dust everywhere, the sour smell and musty odour of a place long disused. One of the panes in the large window was broken, the bird droppings on the sill a sign it had been like this for some time. It was freezing cold and I sneezed violently several times.

There was nothing here to help me, no sign of a connecting door. That had been a wild guess. This was no more than an old store room, one of the many on this floor ripe for renovation.

Time to head back to bed, but as I turned I spotted something unusual in the far corner and went over for a closer look. The shelving wasn't, as I first thought, screwed permanently to the wall but was a free standing structure. Not that this discovery took me much further forward: it was far too heavy for me to attempt lifting it on my own.

Shivering again in the chill of the night, I was about to head for my own room when the moon sailed from behind a cloud and light spilled in, showing up faint traces of footprints in the dust, footprints that appeared to be recent. Straightening up, I reasoned they could belong to anyone. Some one might have been here to conduct a preliminary survey prior to the next stage of renovation.

With only a short time available in the morning before I had to collect Simon, I was determined to speak to Effie and find out what more she knew about the missing girl.

27

As it happened, I was luckier than anticipated about catching Effie the next morning. After a restless night, peopled by strange creatures, I awoke with a rapidly beating heart, drenched in sweat, out of a dream where I was surrounded by huge ghostly figures all wailing loudly as they crept closer and closer. In spite of leaving my door slightly ajar and waking every hour to listen carefully, there had been no repetition of the sobbing.

In the stillness, watching the grey dawn creep in through the chink in the curtains where they didn't close properly, I went over the events of the previous night, then reached out to turn on the radio. Listening to the news was one way to banish the thoughts crowding in, but if anything it only made me feel worse. Stories of fighting, death and destruction weren't guaranteed to cheer me up, even before the weather report with its dire warnings of snow and ice and road closures and accidents.

The seven o'clock news came on, but tired as I was, there was no hope of going back to sleep. I slipped out of bed, showered and dressed and was down in the dining room by seven thirty, expecting to be first there, to have a few minutes of quiet to think about how to find out more about Effie's story of the missing girl – or whether it would be better to forget all about it. That's what I might have done had I also been leaving that day, but with another week ahead of me, coupled with my inability to let something like this go, I knew what my decision would be in spite of my attempts to fight against it.

To my amazement when I opened the door to the dining room it was almost full. Either the guests were poor sleepers or they were trying to make the most of what little time was left of their *Turkey and Tinsel* week.

Yvonne was running about, shepherding guests into line, looking more harassed than ever, while Clive Timmons appeared to be counting the number of eggs each person was taking, as if to make sure no one had more than their fair share.

At the front of the queue Effie was laughing and joking with one of her companions from the previous night as she helped herself to a large portion of porridge from the enormous black cooking pot bubbling on the hotplate at the far end of the buffet table.

I waited until she turned to make her way to one of the tables and moved forward to intercept her, earning myself a glare from a couple of women clearly under the impression I was attempting to jump the queue.

'Some people are very rude,' said one of them pointedly staring at me, but I'd concerns other than explaining to them.

'Effie,' I said, touching her lightly on the arm, 'is there any chance I could have a word with you after breakfast?'

She turned round, startled by my action and staggered, almost dropping her plate of porridge in the process. She frowned, as though failing to recognise me and then she smiled and said, 'Oh, it's you, Alison. You gave me a fright.'

'So sorry, Effie.'

She waved away my apology. 'What was it you said you wanted?'

I whispered my request, avoiding the interested gaze of the others in the queue, but she replied, 'You'll have to speak up. What do you want to talk to me about?'

Knowing she was a woman whose sharpness belied her years I'd thought of a plausible explanation for catching up with her so early in the day.

'I was intrigued about what you were telling me about the old Hydro,' I said. 'As you know, I've written a couple of short books related to Bute: one about the Pavilion and one about James Hamilton of Kames. I think the Hydro would make a really interesting subject for another book. I'm a freelance writer and it's exactly the kind of item that would sell well on the island and beyond. I might even be able to sell copies here.' Aware I was starting to gabble on, I stopped, telling myself, Don't overegg the pudding, Alison, though it appeared that what had been no more than a kernel of an idea was beginning to become a reality.

She regarded me keenly as though weighing up this request, then shrugged. 'I'm not sure how much I can help you, but if you want…'

'That would be fine,' I butted in, before she could change her mind.

'I'll see you in the conservatory in about an hour,' she said in a voice that brooked no argument and went over to join her companions who had been observing this exchange very keenly.

As soon as she sat down, they began to question her, but from the set of her shoulders and her pursed lips it was clear she wasn't going to satisfy their curiosity.

165

I returned to the end of the queue to collect some fruit juice and toast and put in an order for a large pot of coffee. I'd the feeling it was going to be one of those days where I was going to need the caffeine kick.

Allowing for interruptions, this plan gave me a good hour to chat to Effie before I had to collect Simon from the ferry in Rothesay. The changeover of guests didn't take place until early afternoon. In deference to the age of most of the guests it allowed them a leisurely breakfast and a snack lunch after vacating their rooms.

I found a seat in the far corner of the dining room, hoping no one would decide to join me and glancing over towards Effie from time to time. She seemed to be engaged in an altercation of some kind with the Manager, an argument that became increasingly heated before she dismissed him with a regal wave of her hand and he stood up, turned on his heel and almost ran out of the room.

What was that all about? I wondered, though whether it would be worthwhile asking her later was doubtful. I'd more important matters on my mind.

I pulled out my notebook and began to make a list of questions. It was clear from our truncated conversation the previous night that if I asked Effie directly about the missing girl, she'd clam up completely. I had to convince her I really was interested in writing up the story of the old Hydro and as I considered a series of questions I began to think, well, why not? There would be interest in the history of this hotel and it was a story worth recording. And with no other work in view at this moment, it would be something to pitch to an editor.

I drank the coffee and the orange juice, but could only nibble at the toast, knowing when I met Simon we could always head for one of the coffee shops in town for a late breakfast.

Once out of the dining room, I went immediately to the conservatory. A number of final activities had been arranged for the morning: I hoped Effie hadn't signed up for any of them and might forget about our arrangement.

The conservatory, situated at the far end of the old West Wing to catch the best of the light, was as you would expect, a large airy room, filled with plants only some of which I recognised, a nod to the Victorian origins of the hotel. They'd been hugely fond of plants, especially those from foreign countries and the Victorian Fernery at Ascog was one of the still popular tourist venues on the island, the place lovingly restored by the owners.

The furniture was large and comfortable, much more comfy than it appeared at first glance and I settled myself into a squashy armchair overlooking the bay. From this height you could see how the trees along the High Road had grown unchecked in the intervening years and the view wasn't as unrestricted as it had once been.

Even so, it was magnificent and on a day like today when the early greyness had given way to a sky of clear, bright blue and the waters in the bay were calm you could understand why the Victorians loved coming to this place.

My daydream was interrupted as the door was pushed open and Effie came in slowly, carefully carrying a glass of orange juice.

'My, you're early,' she said.

I stood up but she motioned me to sit down again. 'I'll have that chair right beside you if it's all right. My hearing isn't as good as it once was, that's why I wanted to meet you here, away from the noise.'

'I'm surprised that more people don't use this place,' I said, pointing to the view.

'Ah, they're all far too busy.' A strange remark, but not to be pursued at the moment.

She took a few moments to settle herself, then said briskly, 'Now what do you want to know about the old Hydro?'

Although I'd spent time preparing a list of questions I was tongue tied, couldn't think where to begin.

'Suppose I tell you my story, from the beginning and you can interrupt with anything you want to know,' she said, in an attempt to put me out of my misery.

'Sounds good,' I said, wondering how I could get her on to the track of the missing girl without sitting through a lot of personal reminiscences. After about twenty minutes of her stories about her early visits, how she'd learned to swim in the small pool, the difference between the Turkish and the Russian baths on offer, how her aunt had always preferred the Russian, my mind began to wander so I came to with a start as she said, 'I always thought the business with that missing girl was one of the problems. Oh, I know they said that it was the war years. They gave the place the name of a ship, you know. HMS …something beginning with a W…or was it a V? Yes, HMS Varbel, that was it. It became the training base for the midget submarines and the human torpedoes and of course they weren't too careful with the place. But I think it would have been in trouble anyway after what happened.'

Now was my opportunity to find out the details of the story. 'Was she one of the guests?'

'Who?' Effie looked puzzled. She drank the rest of her orange juice and put the glass on the table in front of her and shuddered. 'All the food is of such poor quality here now. Awful.'

'The missing girl,' I prompted her.

'Oh, yes, that's why there was a great huge hue and cry.' She stopped and gazed out of the window, down past the denuded trees to the bay far below. This was going to be a lot trickier than first anticipated. Any information would have to be on a piece by piece basis and I was rapidly running out of time. Even so, best to take it slowly, not alarm her.

'So she was one of the guests?' I repeated.

Effie nodded. 'She was so young and one night she disappeared. She hadn't been long at the Hydro. I saw her round the place once or twice. I particularly noticed her, because she was about the same age as my elder sister and I remember thinking how constrained she was. Here we were enjoying all the benefits of a holiday at this wonderful hotel and a newfound freedom and she was kept close by her parents all the time.'

'But was she never found?'

'No, that was the point.'

'What happened to her?' I was conscious of time slipping away and we seemed to be getting no nearer the crux of the story.

Effie sighed. 'I don't know all the details. Remember I was young and didn't pay much attention to adults. And my sister was more interested in the handsome boy who'd come with one of the families we knew slightly back in Glasgow. We heard later

169

Gertrude had gone to bed early on Christmas Eve, pleading a headache.'

'But there must have been an investigation?'

'Yes, there was …of a kind. But one of the other staff claimed to have seen her at the back door talking to a man he didn't recognise. The rumour was that she'd run off with him, he was someone from the mainland who'd been on holiday in the village and he and she had clicked.'

This was no clearer, no help in solving the problem. 'But why did they block up that room on the second floor of the West wing? Was that to do with her?'

Effie sniffed and gave a low chuckle. 'I've no idea. Is one of the rooms blocked up?'

My feeling was one of bitter disappointment: the noises I'd heard, the sealed room on the top floor were nothing to do with this story of the missing girl. I was no nearer an explanation for the sobbing Anna and I had heard. And the account of the missing girl had turned out to be no story at all.

28

Simon was one of the first off the MV Bute, bustling
down the skywalk that takes foot passengers from the
ferry into the terminal building, stopping once or twice
to adjust the large bag of golf clubs slung over his
shoulder. I'd arrived a good ten minutes before it
docked and sat in the car listening to the radio and
postponing going out in the cold as long as possible.

As soon as I saw him, I jumped out, ran forward and
we hugged. 'Good to see you, Alison,' he said planting
a kiss on top of my head. He looked well.

'And you,' I replied, a feeling of relief sweeping
over me. Simon's solid presence usually helps dispel
some of my more extravagant fancies, though on this
occasion I wasn't too sure. He would try to put me off,
to encourage me to forget all about the 'noises' as no
more than the product of an overactive imagination,
assuring me the door to the room on the top floor had
been covered over for a good reason. I'd have to choose
my moment carefully.

So I didn't mention it, kept the story to myself,
although part of me was itching to tell someone,
anyone, about what was going on at the Hydro hotel.

'Hungry?' Best to start with the practicalities.

'Yes, I could do with some breakfast,' he said,
rubbing his hands. 'I'd only time for a cup of coffee
before I left. When I looked at the timetable I realised
I'd have to hurry to catch the train from Central Station
to link with this ferry.'

'Then let's make for the Kettledrum,' I said, linking my arm with his. 'I hear they do a good breakfast and another cup of coffee wouldn't go amiss. I started very early this morning.'

After stowing his golf clubs in the boot of the car, we crossed arm-in-arm over to the Kettledrum, the large café on the corner of the road opposite the Albert Pier. Even at this time of year the parking area was full, several of the spaces being taken up by a large tour bus labelled *Highland Delights Tours*. Partly true, as the line dividing the lowlands from the highlands of Scotland runs through the pavement outside the Discovery Centre tourist office in Rothesay.

'So what have you been up to?' said Simon as we waited in the cosy fug of the café amid the savoury smells of bacon and coffee for our order to be delivered. He raised his hand as he saw the look on my face. 'No, stop. Perhaps you'd better not answer that. Let me put it this way - how are the talks going?'

'Very well,' I smiled. 'Both seem to have been well received. And I had a starring role at the *Magic Memories* evening.'

'What?'

'It was fine,' I said and told him the story of filling in for Marty.

He drew back, laughing heartily, almost upsetting the tray with our order as the waitress approached the table.

Now might be the time to confess. He'd have to be warned before we headed for the Hydro. Better to come from me rather than from someone else, so I added in a low voice, leaning in towards him, 'There have been a few problems at the hotel.'

172

He put his head in his hands and groaned. 'What on earth have you got yourself involved in now, Alison? You've only been away a week - no less than a week.'

I sat back and crossed my arms defensively. 'It's nothing to do with me, Simon. It's partly because a number of the guests are elderly. One of them has died,' I said, adding in a low voice, 'as well as the events Manager.'

He lifted his head, a look of horror on his face. 'Two dead…and you call that nothing. Oh, Alison!'

'Yes, but there were reasons,' I protested. 'I'm sure there was nothing sinister in what happened. It was a coincidence that there were two in the same week.'

He didn't reply, but started to eat his breakfast in silence. I know what that means - it's a sign he's not convinced by my version of events. And who could blame him. Perhaps it's because he's had too many experiences of my visits to the island ending in disaster.

'Let's not discuss this, Simon. It's honestly nothing to do with me, believe me.' I didn't dare mention the strange noises in the corridor. If I had he might have insisted we turn and go back to the mainland on the next ferry. Then brightly, making an attempt to change the subject, 'Anyway, enough of the Hydro, what's been happening back home?'

'Not a lot. I told you about Maura on the phone: I'm glad to say all is going well there and Alan's mother has come up from Kent to help out for the week. Oh, and Deborah is talking about changing career. She came over for dinner last Wednesday and told me of her plans.'

'You cooked dinner for her?'

'Well, not actually. It was a bit short notice, so we sent out for a pizza.'

I said, 'What's she planning to do now?'

As the youngest of three children, Deborah is the most unpredictable. Our elder daughter Maura is very organised and sensible and although Alastair, the middle child, is a rather vague academic, he is wedded to his work. Deborah, on the other hand has had more changes of career than I can count and my heart sank at the thought she might be contemplating yet another move. 'So has she given you any indication of what she might do?'

He shrugged. 'She's thinking about training as a teacher - an Art teacher.'

'Well, at least her time at Art college won't have been wasted then,' I said.

Fortunately at that point the waitress came over again. 'Anything else I can get you?'

'No, thanks,' Simon said as I added, looking at my watch, 'Gosh, we'd better be heading back to the hotel. There's a lunchtime quiz that I have to help with, one of the last events to keep everyone busy until the coach comes to pick up this week's guests before the next group arrives.'

'So there's a complete change every week?'

'Not sure. I think some of the guests are planning on staying for another week – the Herrington sisters and Mrs Openshaw, who apparently spends a lot of time in the hotel.'

I had to explain briefly who these people were as we paid the bill and walked over to collect the car from the Albert Pier. The town was crowded with shoppers, tempted by the glittering displays in the Print Point bookshop, the Bute Jewellery company and the other small shops in town.

I intended to do most of my Christmas shopping before leaving the island. With no large stores, the island was a treasure trove of unusual gifts in the many small independent craft shops, some of them 'pop ups' for the festive period. I'd even made a list of who would get what, though it wouldn't be a good idea to mention Christmas shopping to my husband.

Simon had brought little luggage apart from his golf clubs - only a small holdall - 'in case the weather's good enough for a game' - so there was no problem about settling him into our room in the Hydro before I headed off to help out with the lunchtime quiz.

'Gosh, it's a terrific view from here,' he said, gazing out of the window.

'Yes, this is part of the original hotel. I think I've been told some eighty one of the eighty nine rooms in the old Hydro had sea views. And though it's not as high up as this, the conservatory has spectacular views. I'll take you down before I join the guests for the quiz. I met one of the guests, Effie, there earlier this morning. She was able to give me a lot of information about the place in its heyday. Might make the subject for a new book.'

'Great, I'll take my camera. It will be good to get some shots of Bute at this time of year as well as in the summer.'

Downstairs I introduced Simon to Yvonne, who was currently on Reception duty. 'Is Kelly not in today?' I said by way of conversation.

'No, she's off again. Another crisis. I can't go on filling in for her like this. I've told the Manager, I've commitments too. The job of Assistant Manager isn't as easy as he seems to think.'

I hadn't expected this explosion of criticism and to distract her I said, 'This is my husband, Simon. He's staying over the weekend.'

Yvonne acknowledged his presence a trifle ungraciously, which was not at all like her. Perhaps there were other problems she hadn't mentioned.

Clive Timmons was nowhere to be seen and increasingly Yvonne appeared to be running the hotel and doing most of the jobs. If the chef left (something he was threatening to do yet again) poor Yvonne might have to help out there.

The staffing levels in the hotel were almost at crisis point: the hotel might have been resurrected, but by all accounts it was nothing like it had been in the old days.

'This way,' I said to him, nodding briefly to Yvonne, but she deliberately or otherwise ignored me and Simon followed me down the corridor to the conservatory at the far end.

'It's not much used at the moment,' I said pushing open the door. 'It's lovely if the sun is shining but the heating isn't great so it's too chilly for most of the guests. They prefer the comfort of the lounge – I'll take you in there later. There are great views from that room as well.'

As I put my hand on the door, I hesitated. 'The views might be better from outside. The windows will distort and I don't think it would be advisable to open them.'

I noticed a shadow pass over Simon's face and joked, 'It's not as bad as that. You won't get chilled through taking a few photos.'

Then I turned to follow the direction of his gaze, looking into the conservatory.

Effie was still there, sitting in the chair exactly as I'd left her, the empty glass fallen on the floor beside her. Surely she should have been preparing to leave by now, but perhaps I'd misunderstood and she was staying on for another week.

I went over and touched her lightly on the shoulder. 'Effie,' I said, 'are you okay?'

There was no response and then I noticed she was so still, so immobile there could only be one reason. She was dead.

Simon came up behind me as I said, 'Oh, no, not another one.'

'Now are you still telling me there's nothing strange about all these deaths, Alison?' he said.

29

Another ambulance, another visit from the local police, Clive Timmons ashen-faced as the police officer said, 'You'll have to stop killing off the guests like this. Your hotel will be getting some reputation.'

'I know exactly what you mean,' said Sylvia Openshaw, sweeping across the foyer to join him. 'It would appear no one is safe.' Today she was carrying a large yellow handbag with gilt clasps and Jasper was manifestly returned to full health judging by the amount of yapping he was doing.

Clive didn't appreciate this attempt at black humour and said curtly, wringing his hands, 'It's nothing to do with me. It's merely a coincidence that we've had three deaths in such a short space of time.'

The police officer shook his head. 'Even so,' he said, more seriously this time, 'There will have to be a full investigation.'

'These are elderly guests,' said Sylvia, ignoring the fact she wasn't in the first flush of youth herself. 'You have to expect there will be a few problems. Anyway,' putting her face up close to Jasper, 'you are too sensitive for this, my darling. Mummy will take you away from all this.'

'Not too far away,' said the police officer. 'We'll want to question everyone.'

'Of course I won't be far away – I'm booked in for at least another week,' she sniffed and deliberately turned her back on him to head for the lounge.

'It always seems to happen when I'm on duty,' grumbled Yvonne, but no one paid her the slightest attention.

'It's all my fault,' wailed Mina, one of the women who'd been in Effie's party.

'Why is that,' said the police officer, turning to face her. 'What could you possibly have had to do with the lady's death?'

Mina sobbed loudly. 'I should have noticed she hadn't come in to the lounge for the game of cards. We always play a hand of whist after breakfast. She really looks - I mean looked - forward to it. Especially as this was our last day. She wouldn't have missed it unless there was a very good reason.'

'You didn't notice she hadn't turned up?'

Mina stopped sobbing for a moment. 'Yes, I did notice, but…'

Her voice tailed off as one of the other women beside her came forward saying, 'The truth is that Effie was very good at the game…and almost always won. Without her there the rest of us felt we stood a better chance. What's more she became very cross if she didn't win. So although we noticed, none of us went to look for her.'

So the little group of friends had had their differences, I thought, as Mina resumed, 'If only we'd gone to look for her, we might have managed to save her, called an ambulance in time.'

Lily Herrington came bustling over and put her arm round Mina. 'Don't blame yourself, my dear, she was very elderly. And she could be very annoying.' Which would have been a funny remark coming from Lily, had the situation not been so serious.

'Yes,' added Iris, appearing like a shadow behind her sister. 'None of this is to do with you.'

'Even so,' Mina was not to be pacified. 'She was in good health as far as any of us knew. Never a day's illness in her life, except for that time...'

'I very much doubt it,' said the police officer, cutting into what promised to be a long explanation, 'because …'

But before he could finish his sentence, the sergeant came back in and called him over.

There was a heated conversation and the expression on the police officer's face showed that whatever was going on he was both shocked and surprised.

'Are we sure?' I heard him say and then saw the sergeant shake his head to indicate he should say no more.

Without another word, they hurried out with the Manager.

'What was that all about?' said Mina.

I didn't know, but I could make a good guess. And so I suspected could Simon who was standing in the far corner of the room, looking less than pleased to be caught up in this.

I waited in silence as Mina was helped out by Iris, though it wasn't clear who was supporting whom, swallowing hard to get rid of the terrible dryness in my mouth.

Of course Effie was old, but Mina was right. She was one of those women who seemed destined to go on for ever.

If I was being honest, I'd had enough experience of deaths in recent years to be able to guess what was so disturbing the police officers.

There was only one reason they might be so concerned: they suspected Effie's death, in spite of her age, hadn't been due to natural causes.

30

Yvonne was grumbling again when I saw her later. 'Kelly should be here,' she said. 'I can't stay on much longer. I do have a life as well.'

I'd wandered into the foyer with Simon, hoping to head for the kitchen and beg a cup of coffee, but my instinct told me this would not be a good idea.

There was a gloomy feel about the place - understandable with three deaths within the space of a week. The conservatory had been sealed off for the SOCO and the departing group of guests had been delayed while the police took statements. With so many of them and so few police, this was taking longer than anyone wanted. Once released from questioning, many were jostling for position at the Reception desk to pay any outstanding bills, eager to leave as soon as possible.

I heard Clive Timmons mutter to Yvonne, 'Try not to let any of the new arrivals know there might be a problem.' Rather optimistic in the circumstances.

Clive moved away and was hovering round the entrance, wringing his hands, talking to every police officer who passed his way with a pleading look on his face.

'He's worried they'll close the place down,' said Yvonne in response to my query.

'Surely they won't do that?'

She shrugged, 'Who knows,' then turned her attention to one of the guests who'd mislaid his case.

In the meantime the next group of guests had started to roll up in their coaches.

The lunchtime Quiz had been cancelled of course, a decision which didn't please several of the guests, making me reflect how concerned people were with their own little world, to the exclusion of others.

'I mean, I know it's a great sadness, but we've all paid good money for this week and there have been enough interruptions already. I hope the management will be prepared to give us all some kind of discount.' This from the Major whose increasingly florid complexion confirmed his fondness during his stay for the many varieties of whisky on offer in the bar.

Calla was standing beside him, a roll of flesh round her waist showing in the tight jumper she was wearing, today revealing what was clearly her own over-permed hair. 'You're right, Major. People shouldn't come on these holidays if they're not in the best of health.'

Iris and Lily Herrington were hovering about in the lounge, still in their indoor clothes. Neither looked particularly disturbed by events, but perhaps if you'd lived as long as they had and had buried three of your sisters, death wasn't such a big deal.

'All packed and ready to go home when this is over?' I said, moving over towards them.

'Oh, dear me, no,' said Lily. 'Why would you think that?'

'We're not quite ready yet,' said Iris.

I didn't want to seem to be interfering, but I was officially one of the staff and in the circumstances, Clive needed all the help he could get. Possibly Iris and Lily were a little forgetful.

'The bus will be here soon: I think it's waiting at the far end of the car park,' I urged them.

Lily chuckled. 'We're not going, dear. Not today.'

'No,' added Iris, 'we're staying on for another week, aren't we, Lily?'

'You'll be here for both weeks?' I would have thought a week would have been enough for anyone.

'We're having a lovely time. This is such a good idea, this kind of entertainment. And we're not the only people staying on. Several of the guests are booked in for two weeks.' The deaths in the hotel didn't appear to be troubling Iris.

'Yes, Effie was one of them. She decided at the last minute she would like to be here for both weeks. Such a shame when she'd paid her deposit'. Lily frowned as she considered this, though it wasn't likely to be a high priority.

'I suppose it's non-returnable,' Iris picked up the theme.

'Though it's a pity about that Sylvia Openshaw. Her dog, if you could call it that, is horrible. She's getting on everyone's nerves.' Iris nodded vigorously in agreement with her sister's comment.

I merely smiled, seeing an opportunity to move off. 'She is a regular customer,' I said, 'so I suspect she will be here more often than not.'

Almost together Lily and Iris made a snorting sound.

Enough of this conversation. I didn't want to become embroiled in gossip about the other guests.

I walked over to join Simon who had positioned himself on one of the sofas in the far corner. 'This is a fine mess, Alison. Are you sure it was nothing to do with you?'

184

'How could it be?' I said, with more confidence than I felt. It was certainly strange, given my previous record, that there had been three deaths at this hotel. The first two could have been natural, but what about Effie's? Was it possible there had been someone who had overheard what she was telling me? Not wanting to alarm her, to make her suspect there was more to my questions than a passing interest, I hadn't made any notes.

Of course I'd meant to do so as soon as we'd finished chatting, but I'd had to rush off to meet Simon. Now I racked my brains to remember exactly what she'd said, though it was hard to imagine what bearing that might have on her death.

She did tell me about the missing girl, but that was so long ago surely there wouldn't be anyone interested in that, even if it was an unsolved mystery? I made a mental note to look to my usual source of information for everything to do with island life: to check out the relevant back copies of *The Buteman* for that period kept on microfiche in the local library in Rothesay.

How I wished I'd asked Effie to be more specific, had asked for more detail. How was I to know there wouldn't be another opportunity?

And she'd been certain she knew nothing about the missing room, though to be fair I hadn't pursued this question, in case it alarmed her. Or was it possible she did know something, but had decided not to tell me?

Simon interrupted my train of thought, saying, 'I might go over to the Port Bannatyne Golf course - fit in a game while the weather's still reasonable.'

He gestured to the large picture window. The day still looked cold, but the grey skies of the morning had given way to a crisp bright afternoon.

'Fine, fine,' I said. It would be better if he was out of the way for a while. I might find out more about what was going on without my husband hovering round, disapproving of my every action.

'I'll see you later.' He jumped up, perhaps worried I might try to detain him and after giving me a quick peck on the cheek he went to collect his clubs. I sighed, then changed it to a cough in case anyone in the group heard me, but they were all too engrossed in their own conversations to be worried about mine.

I couldn't blame Simon for wanting to escape. Every time I came onto the island there was some disaster or other and I always seemed to become involved, no matter how hard I tried to stay on the sidelines.

No sooner had Simon left than the main door swung open and a very breathless Kelly came rushing in, her usually immaculate hair windblown and dishevelled. 'Sorry, sorry I'm late,' she said rushing over to Yvonne.

'Well, at least you're here, which is something,' said Yvonne in a grudging tone of voice. 'I've had to close Reception meantime and it's chaos here.' She waved vaguely in the direction of the foyer where both departing and arriving guests were milling about in a state of confusion.

'Sorry, sorry,' said Kelly again.

'Though trust you to be out of the way and miss all the excitement, if it could be called that.'

Kelly raised her eyebrows. 'Has something happened here as well? Is that why there are all those people in Reception? Why you closed it?'

'There was nothing else we could do,' said Yvonne defensively. 'There was no way to cope with so many...and I'd no answers to their questions.'

Intrigued by this conversation, I moved a little closer.

'What do you mean?' said Kelly.

'We've had another death. Poor Effie was found dead in the conservatory only a short time ago.'

Kelly visibly paled and held on to the desk for support. 'Effie's dead? How could that have happened?'

Yvonne made a face. 'She was elderly. Suspected heart attack. It's unfortunate there have been another two deaths, but I'm sure it's no more than coincidence. Believe me, as soon as I find another job, I'm leaving. Elderly or not, I don't want to be around a place where people are dropping like flies.'

But this didn't register with Kelly. She kept shaking her head and saying, 'It can't be, it can't be.'

It looked as if she would go on in this vein for some time, so to sidetrack her I said, 'What was your news, Kelly? You said something had happened. Your reason for being late?' It would serve me right if she told me to mind my own business.

If she thought I was being nosey she gave no hint, merely stared at me.

'Yes, yes, there was some news in the village. I met Donald as I came up the road. He'd been in to the Post Office and word is that Freddie's been found at last.'

For a moment my heart began to beat faster and I felt almost faint. What did she mean 'Freddie found at last'? Surely she wasn't going to tell us that he was also dead?

31

'He's not dead?' The note of horror in Yvonne's voice echoed my feelings.

Kelly shook her head. 'No, thankfully he's alive, though it was touch and go. He's in the Victoria hospital suffering from exposure.'

'Exposure? Why was he out in this weather? A man of his age?' This news distracted Yvonne from her concerns about the current situation in the hotel.

'It looks as if he was much more distressed by Anna's death than anyone thought. With so much going on, no one thought to keep an eye on him. It appears he wandered off and couldn't remember where he was living. He was found sound asleep in the Bogany wood by an early morning dog walker. He must have found shelter, but he's no idea where.'

'He'll be okay?' A wave of remorse hit me. I'd been responsible for organising his accommodation in Port Bannatyne and hadn't considered how an elderly man like Freddie might not be able to cope with a strange environment, following the shock of his wife's death.

'Yes, they think so, but they're keeping him in for a couple of days for observation. Thankfully he seems to be made of strong stuff and the doctor anticipates he'll make a good recovery.'

'I'll have to go and see him.' I'd been so obsessed with finding out about the room on the top floor I'd completely forgotten about him, or even that he'd been missing. I tried to convince myself Freddie wasn't entirely my responsibility, but a niggle of guilt gnawed at me.

Kelly and Yvonne were deep in conversation and didn't notice my departure, but I could tell by the set of Yvonne's face that she was determined not to tolerate Kelly's cavalier attitude to their agreed shifts.

Although it was still early afternoon, the clouds had gathered, obscuring the sunshine of earlier and the wind had turned decidedly chilly. Hopefully Simon was well wrapped up, had remembered the golf course at Port Bannatyne is on the side of a steep hill. It might have extensive views across the bay, but it's subject to the vagaries of the weather on this Atlantic coast.

Pausing only to run upstairs and collect my coat from my room, I drove to the cottage hospital on the High Street in Rothesay, reaching it within fifteen minutes. It never ceases to amaze me how quickly you can get around Bute - none of the traffic jams, road works and hold-ups of the city.

The police station was busy, not a single car parking space remaining in front of the low rise building. It had to be a sign the C.I.D had arrived from the mainland.

The hospital has the appearance of a once grand Victorian house and stands on the opposite side of the road from the King George's Field Recreation ground where the annual Highland Games are held. I slid into a parking space at the main door.

Inside the entrance hall of the hospital it was warm and quiet, my shoes making no sound on the rubber floor as I headed for the Reception desk.

'I'm looking for Freddie Burrows,' I said to the smartly dressed middle aged woman behind the desk.

'Oh, Freddie? He's in Ward Three. He'll be pleased to have a visitor.'

'How is he?'

She smiled, her eyes twinkling. 'He's doing really well, I'm glad to say. Certainly complaining enough - always a good sign.'

The room was easy to find: any really serious cases have to go to the main hospital on the mainland at Inverclyde, so this was evidence Freddie wasn't seriously ill.

Before I saw him, I heard him. '…and I tell you I'm fit enough to leave. I won't stay here a moment longer among all these sick people.'

I peeped round the door. Freddie was sitting up in a bed beside the door, remonstrating with a young nurse who was doing her best to soothe him, with little success.

His face lit up as he saw me. 'Ah, Alison, come in, come in. Am I glad to see you. Perhaps you'll tell this young lady I'm perfectly fit and don't need to be taking up a bed in this place a moment longer. And I certainly don't want any of these pills they keep trying to make me swallow.'

The young nurse turned to me and raised her eyebrows.

'I saw that,' shouted Freddie, 'there's no need to treat me as though I'm stupid.'

'Oh, Freddie, what have you been doing?' I said, pulling out the chair near the bed and sitting down as the young nurse moved away to attend to another patient, clearly delighted to be reprieved for a short time. 'You have to realise everyone is only concerned for your welfare. They want you to get better as soon as possible and you're in the best place for that.'

'Am better,' said Freddie, in the tone of a sulky child. 'It's being kept in here that's making me ill.'

I shouldn't have laughed, but the expression on his face was so cross. 'Yes, that's fine while you're in a nice warm bed, being looked after. How will you manage when you get out?'

The young nurse, pleased to have passed the problem of Freddie on to someone else, had slipped quietly out of the room.

Whether it was because he knew he was making a fuss about nothing, or whether he was ashamed of his outburst, Freddie sniffed and lay back on his pillows, saying, 'I don't want to stay here a moment longer.'

'And no one wants you to be here, taking up a bed, if you are well.'

'Suppose so.'

'What will you do when you get out? Are you going back to the flat in Port Bannatyne?'

'No, no way. I'm going back to the mainland. I'll go and stay with my daughter.'

'I thought you were going to stay on the island, make the funeral arrangements. Didn't you tell me Anna had fallen in love with the island, wanted to be buried here?'

'That's as may be.' A tear glistened in his eye and slowly trickled down his cheek. 'But it's not as simple as I first thought. It seems there will have to be an inquest.'

'Isn't that always the case with a sudden death? I expect it will be a formality.'

'A formality? I don't think so, Alison. You haven't heard then?'

'Heard what?' My heart sank.

'There's some concern about the way she died. The police suspect it may not have been the heart attack everyone thought.'

32

Simon had stayed overnight, but headed off on the late morning ferry, mindful of the Cal Mac alerts about strong south westerlies which might affect the crossing. Before he left he made it clear he wasn't happy about my decision to remain at the Hydro for another week.

'I have to get back to the mainland,' he'd said as we lingered over the Welcome meal in the hotel the previous evening. He'd tried to persuade me to head for one of the restaurants in town, but I pointed out I was on duty, though he grumbled in a low voice about the quality of the meal, a Christmas dinner, of course.

'This turkey is like leather,' he said, prodding at it with his knife.

'I did warn you,' I said, then hastily changed the subject before he could start complaining about the soggy potatoes, saying, 'At least you managed a game of golf.'

As I dropped him off at the ferry terminal, he appeared more cheerful. On a previous trip he'd become friendly with someone who lived in the Port, and although he'd assured me they'd had a full round, given the weather it was more than likely they'd spent most of the time at the nineteenth hole.

Last minute doubts as he said, 'I'm not sure I should be going and leaving you here, Alison. You always seem to end up in trouble. If I didn't have to meet that chap from Scottish Alignment Limited about a possible new contract, I would stay and...'

I cut him short. 'Nonsense. There won't be any more problems. It happened to be a coincidence that three people died.' Even as I said it, I realised I shouldn't have reminded him of the number of deaths at the Hydro.

He hesitated for a moment, but only a moment, at the bottom of the Skywalk. 'Are you absolutely sure...don't you...'

'No, go. You have to take this opportunity. I'll keep in touch and I promise not to become involved in anything I shouldn't.'

Whether this reassured him or not was hard to tell, but after he kissed me and turned to head up the ramp, I didn't wait to see if he would change his mind. Best to go while I could.

But what made me go into the Coronet Hotel on the corner of Marine Road? I've no idea, it was one of those spur of the moment decisions with unforeseen consequences.

Once I'd dropped Simon at the ferry, I'd offered to go along to the flat in Port Bannatyne and collect some bits and pieces for Freddie. His reading glasses for one thing. 'Can't even read the paper to pass the time,' he'd said, looking decidedly unhappy.

He had little information about the inquest on Anna, only that it was likely to be some time before her body was released for burial. He would be better back on the mainland, I thought, well away from where it had happened. He might even decide it would be more appropriate for the funeral to take place there. 'That's what my daughter keeps nagging me to do,' he'd said. 'She wanted to come over at once, but I told her to hold off, she'd be more help later once we knew what was to happen.'

It seemed rather callous of his daughter but it wasn't my place to make comment on matters concerning his family.

He noticed the expression that passed fleetingly across my face and said, 'She lives in Aberdeen and has four young children and a husband who works on the oil rigs. It's not easy for her.'

I didn't reply and he added in a low voice, 'They didn't get on, Anna and our daughter.'

When I came out of the Victoria hospital the wind was beginning to whip up, sending scurries of waves crashing against the seawall at Ardbeg as I drove towards Port Bannatyne.

About to take the high road towards the holiday flats, I spied the friendly lights of the Coronet Hotel and suddenly realised I'd had no lunch. I wouldn't be missed for a while yet and I was decidedly hungry, so the decision was made. I'd have a quick bite to eat and then collect Freddie's belongings.

I hadn't been in the hotel for some time, not since my involvement with the film company, Pelias Productions and the filming of the story of James Hamilton and as it was under new ownership, I was unlikely to run into anyone I knew.

Anticipating a better lunch than would have been served at the Hydro, I parked the car on the seafront and crossed the road to enter the hotel. The inside was much as I remembered, except that new tables and chairs had been added, much more modern than before and the flooring now boasted sparkly tiles of black and silver. The overall effect was rather odd as many of the original features had been retained, but it was comfortable enough and the smell of fresh-brewed coffee very inviting.

After giving my order for some homemade pumpkin soup and a cheese sandwich, I settled for a table at the window, tucked out of sight of the main room, wishing I'd stopped off somewhere in town to buy a paper. Too late now, as the bartender came over with my order saying, 'That should keep the cold out.'

I leaned forward to savour the hot spicy smell. This was better fare than was available at the Hydro and I set to, eating it with gusto, scarcely registering that it was hot enough to burn my mouth.

I'd only managed a few spoonfuls when I heard a voice I recognised, but couldn't put a name to and craned my neck to look round to the back of the room and the source of the noise.

To my surprise I saw Kelly, engaged in a heated discussion with a man of about my age. He was looking very cross and her head was bowed.

'It's not my fault,' she was saying, unaware that I was able to hear every word.

'Of course it is. We have an agreement. Nothing will come of this unless you make more of it, raise some doubts. You have to go on with it.'

'It's not as easy as you think.' Now Kelly's voice was raised in anger. 'You come up with the ideas and expect me to carry them out. It's not on. It's a lot more difficult than you imagine. I'm not getting the reaction we expected and I'm not happy about the deaths at the Hydro.'

Now it was the turn of the man to raise a hand and say, 'Don't speak so loudly. Let's go into the back room and we can discuss it there.'

'There's nothing to discuss,' Kelly said and turned on her heel to storm out.

As she passed me, I was about to call out to her, but as quickly thought the better of it and lowered my head as though the pumpkin soup was the most interesting thing in the world.

Now I was consumed with curiosity. What on earth had they been talking about? And why was Kelly here in the Coronet hotel when she should have been on duty at the Hydro?

33

Still pondering the strange encounter between Kelly
and the Manager of the Coronet Hotel, I made my way
back along the Shore Road, past the War memorial still
garlanded with wreaths of poppies in remembrance of
local men who had died in both world wars and headed
for the road leading up to the hotel.

There was no one around, the streets deserted and
silent and I guessed Kelly had headed up to the Hydro a
few minutes before me, so I took my time. I didn't want
to meet up with her, not before I'd decided what
questions to ask. Her conversation had probably been
entirely innocent, but I couldn't understand why she'd
been in the Coronet, while claiming she had family
problems that meant Yvonne had to take over her shift.

I was half way up the hill when I suddenly realised
that, absorbed in my thoughts about Kelly, I'd
completely forgotten the purpose of my visit to the
village and made my way back down to the holiday
flats to collect Freddie's belongings. Fortunately Mrs
Underwood lived in the first of the cottages and she'd
told me, "Knock at any time. I'm not out much in the
winter."

This was true, but it meant she was also keen on
having company, someone to talk to and she was indeed
pleased to see me. 'Come away in,' she said. 'I've had
the kettle on and off for the past hour, not quite sure
when to expect you.'

The aroma of fresh baking drifted towards me as she ushered me through the tiny lobby and into the overheated lounge, crammed with bulky old-fashioned furniture.

Heavily patterned red wallpaper clashed disturbingly with a dark green carpet and a pair of large tapestry covered sofas. Elaborately carved coffee tables (I counted three) and the standard lamp with its frilled shade were an indication she had once lived in a much larger house and couldn't bring herself to buy furniture more scaled to the size of her current home.

My guess had been correct. She was anticipating my visit as an opportunity to chat.

Resigned to my fate and having to add some of her home baking to my already substantial lunch I took a seat in one of the armchairs at the side of a blazing coal fire.

'Make yourself comfortable. Give me your coat,' she said.

The room was cosy to the point of suffocation and I took off my heavy coat before realising this condemned me to spending even more time here.

Best to get the ground rules sorted at once. 'I don't mean to be rude, but I have to take these bits and pieces to Freddie and then head back to the hotel,' I said. 'They need every member of staff after what's happened.'

'How is the poor soul? Are they going to keep him in hospital long?'

'Not if he can help it. I think he's doing well, but they want to make sure he's completely fit before they discharge him.'

'Och, you'll have time for a cup of tea and a bit of cake. The kettle's already boiled.'

There was no way to refuse without seeming rude so I nodded. 'Yes, a cuppa is always welcome.'

She bustled off into the kitchen and returned a few moments later, as I was about to nod off, suffocated by the heat, with a tray laden with cups, tea and a cake stand groaning with scones, fruit cake and highly coloured cup cakes.

She must have seen the look on my face and said defiantly, 'You don't have to eat it all. But you can try some of it.'

Although the niceties had to be observed, I wondered if it would be possible to sneak a cake or two into my handbag without her noticing.

She was too eagle-eyed for this strategy to work and I made a valiant effort as she pressed cake after cake on me together with several cups of tea till I began to feel ill with the surfeit of sugar and the cloying heat of the room. We chatted about the village, about Christmas plans. 'I'll be off to my daughter in London on the 14th, providing the ferries aren't disrupted by the weather.'

I made sympathetic noises. One of the problems of living on an island is that the weather rules at all times and plans have to be flexible.

Finally, when we had exhausted all possible topics of conversation, conscious I was already very late, 'I really have to be going,' I said, standing up and looking round for my coat.

'Oh, must you go so soon?' She looked disappointed. 'You've hardly eaten a thing. Never mind. I'll fetch the spare key. You can return it at any time.'

That wasn't how I felt. Quite the opposite. I felt I'd grossly overeaten and I'd have to stop off at the Post Office general store for something to calm the overfull feeling in my stomach.

As I reached the door she said, handing me my coat, 'I expect you've heard about the plans for the Hydro. There's been a lot of talk about it.'

'No.' I wasn't sure if this was no more than a delaying tactic, but if so it was one that worked.

'Yes,' she said putting on her coat to accompany me and taking down the correct key from the large key rack in the hallway. 'The application has been in for some time, but most people are unhappy about it, say it will spoil the character of the village.'

'So what are they planning to do?'

'They want to open a casino and make use of that enormous ballroom in the old West wing.'

'A casino!' My voice came out as a squeak. Anything less likely than a casino in the sleepy village of Port Bannatyne, even though the hotel was up on the hill some distance away, was so unexpected that for a moment I was lost for words.

She chuckled. 'Took you by surprise, did it? That's the effect it's had on most people, I've got to say. It's not likely however, though the rumour is that's why the Hydro was refurbished in the first place, but why they haven't completed it.'

'I should think not. Apart from anything else surely the road isn't good enough? There are problems already with some of the delivery lorries from what the kitchen staff say.'

She chuckled. 'The planning application includes a massive upgrade of the road …and that's what's likely

201

to cause the biggest problem. Still you never know.'
She sighed. 'Stranger things have happened. We never
thought we'd see a major supermarket come into that
gap site in Montague Street.'

'Even so. A supermarket isn't anywhere in the same
league as a casino.' I found it hard to think she wasn't
giving me a tale, one of those 'Chinese whispers'
rumours that sweep the village from time to time,
although it would explain why the ballroom had only
had the skimpiest of makeovers.

Mrs Underwood went on as though I wasn't there.
'Of course the difficulty is that something like that will
give the Hydro an even bigger pull. The owner of the
Coronet Hotel isn't happy: he's trying hard to lobby for
planning permission to be refused.'

'I'm not surprised. I expect he's found business
difficult enough since the hotel reopened - having a
casino would be the end of the place.'

'Exactly. It's providing opportunities for lots of
gossip in the village. As you would expect some people
are completely opposed to the idea, but others think it
would reinvigorate the Port, bring lots more people in,
people with real money and might even restore the
village to its heyday.'

We walked over to the flat Freddie had rented. Mrs
Underwood continued to chatter about other subjects,
the new Christmas lights in the village, the plans to
extend the Marina, the assurances that the village
school would continue to stay open, but my mind was
firmly fixed on this astonishing news about the proposal
for a casino. If true, the Coronet would find it difficult
to continue in business. Poor Kelly must be torn

between her good job up at the Hydro and family loyalty to her uncle.

It didn't take long to gather Freddie's few possessions into a carrier bag and with promises of returning soon for 'another chat and a cuppa' I left Mrs Underwood at the door to her cottage.

After depositing the bag at the front desk in the hospital I drove to the Hydro as fast as I could. I'd been away much longer than intended and it would soon be time for afternoon tea and my duty of welcoming new guests.

My head was so full of this proposal for a casino and my resolve to ask the Manager if there was any truth in the story, I thought the break for tea would be a welcome relief, though I certainly wouldn't be eating anything. An even bigger problem awaited me when I finally opened the door into the hotel. There was an air of tension about the place that was evident as soon as I walked in.

Yvonne and Phyllis were at the Reception desk, their heads close together, poring over something and I could hear their animated chat. They looked up as I approached.

'Something wrong?' I said, puzzled by their almost guilty manner.

'You'd better ask the Manager,' said Yvonne, casting a nervous glance over her shoulder to where Clive Timmons stood talking animatedly into the house phone. He banged it down as he finished his conversation.

'That's it! We're really in trouble now.' His face was almost purple with rage.

203

With my head full of the plans for the casino, I immediately thought he could only mean one thing. The application had been refused.

'Trouble about your plans for the building?' I ventured, hoping he would tell me the truth about the possible casino.

A look of surprise crossed his face. 'No, it's nothing to do with the building. What would make you think it was anything to do with the hotel? It's Hamish.'

He turned as though to leave and I caught him by the elbow, eager to find out what had so disturbed him. 'The funeral's been arranged then?'

He stopped and stared at me, as though considering whether he should answer me or not. Finally he said, 'It's nothing to do with the funeral. It's news about the post mortem. Preliminary findings suggest it wasn't a natural death. He didn't die of a heart attack after all. It looks as if he was deliberately poisoned.'

34

My first thought wasn't for poor Hamish, nor for the hotel Manager and staff, nor even for the guests who would be alarmed by the idea that there might be a murderer on the loose, but how Simon would react when he found out I was involved in yet another suspicious death.

With some trepidation I answered his next call, guessing he would once more try to persuade me to leave.

'Don't you think you'd have been better to come home with me? You've had enough problems with this kind of thing, surely you don't want to be involved in yet another? I'm sure you can come up with some excuse.'

It was no consolation to know he was right and the notion of abandoning it all, heading for home on the next ferry, made me pause, sorely tempted. But then duty got the better of me. 'But I've agreed to do this next week,' I said. 'I can't let them down - they won't be able to find a replacement at such short notice.'

'Don't you think many of the guests are likely to call off once they find out what's happened?'

'Perhaps, but that's not my problem. If the rest of the week is to be cancelled then I can come home straight away, but at least I'm not letting them down.'

I could imagine him shaking his head in sorrow. 'Have it your own way, Alison, you never do take my advice.'

About to protest this wasn't strictly true, I bit back my comment. No point in getting into an argument with Simon. He'd come to my rescue often enough. Trouble was, he knew me too well, understood part of my reason for staying on was to find out what had happened to Hamish and I wouldn't be able to let it rest.

'I'll cancel my meeting for tomorrow and that way I can be around if you need help at short notice. Surely a decision will be made soon.'

This was a supreme sacrifice and I was duly appreciative. Whatever was going on in this hotel, Simon's offer of support was reassuring.

We tried hard to carry on as normal: afternoon tea was served, I chatted to many of the guests and Yvonne and even Clive Timmons helped with this, making their way from table to table and listening intently to the most trivial of stories.

There was no indication the news about Hamish had upset the guests, but then only those who had booked in for the two weeks would have known him. In that case perhaps it wasn't surprising no one mentioned it. I suspected the Manager was determined to keep it quiet for as long as he could. A notion confirmed when I confronted him later.

'No, we haven't made the information public,' he said, his pinched white face betraying his anxiety. 'There's no point in alarming everyone at this stage. It is only a preliminary finding. You know that they can sometimes get these things wrong and why would we frighten people if it turns out to be a mistake.'

I didn't think this likely: he was trying hard to convince himself Hamish had died of natural causes.

He stood in silence for a moment or two. 'However, I guess I should tell Mrs Openshaw and the Herrington sisters. They did know Hamish. Or would it upset them?'

It was easy to understand why he might not relish this task and by the way Yvonne raised her eyebrows behind his back as he spoke, it was clear she didn't believe him either.

I resolved to try to get her on her own later, find out what she knew. I suspected there might be more to the death of Hamish than the Manager was willing to admit.

35

When I went back to Reception, Yvonne had left. Kelly
wasn't there either so wherever she'd been heading
when I spied her in the Port, it wasn't to the hotel. In
their place was Phyllis.

'I expected Yvonne or Kelly would be here?' I said
as I approached her.

'No, only me, filling in. Yvonne should be back
later. I sometimes help out when it's the changeover
weekend - that way both of them get a proper break. It's
pretty hectic here with people coming and going, lost
luggage, people missing the bus to the ferry, others
turning up thinking they've booked in when they
haven't…we've had every crisis you care to name.'

'I'm glad you're so cheerful about it. I find it
difficult enough dealing with my own problems.'

She grinned and her face lit up. 'When you're a
student you're glad to work when you can. This suits
me fine at weekends and during my vacations. Means I
can stay at home here on the island. A lot cheaper than
staying in Glasgow. Mind you, there might be plenty of
work coming my way if everything goes according to
plan.'

Ah, she could only mean this business about the
proposed casino, but I pretended ignorance saying,
'And what's that?'

She frowned and put her hand over her mouth.
'Ooops, I've said too much. It's not official yet of
course, but there may be opportunities for extra work if

the Hydro becomes even more popular and…' she blustered on in this vein for a few minutes but I wasn't taken in. Probably lots of people knew about the casino proposal but few were saying anything about it and I could have a good guess at their reasons for silence on the subject.

'Anyway I must get on,' she said, turning to the computer to hide the fact she had turned a shade of bright red. 'Do you want to leave a message for Kelly or for Yvonne?'

'No, it's nothing important. I'll catch up later.' I headed for the lounge and, as I had reckoned, in spite of the Manager's decision, the news about Hamish had spread quickly judging by the groups engaged in low whispering. There's no way to keep anything secret in a small community, that's for sure, in spite of all Clive's efforts.

Out of curiosity I went through the double doors at the end of the dining room leading into the old ballroom where the main events of the *Turkey and Tinsel* weeks were held.

It was still resplendent with the elaborate cornicing of the old hotel, though if you looked closely you could see the renovation in this part of the building had been a hasty job. However the huge marble fireplace had been properly restored and a log fire crackled invitingly at its heart.

Even with a stretch of the imagination it was hard to imagine this might be given over to some kind of casino. I thought about a trip Simon and I had made a number of years back to Las Vegas when we were in America visiting Susie Littlejohn. A friend since college, Susie had met and married an American and

209

had persuaded us to visit her for several weeks. Though she lives in California, nothing would do but we would join her on a trip to Las Vegas, though her husband Dwayne declined to come with us. 'Not my scene, folks,' he'd said with a firmness I didn't think he possessed, at least where a request from Susie was concerned.

While we'd enjoyed the trip across the Mojave desert, the experience of Las Vegas with its wonderful mock ups of Paris and Venice, its lavishly appointed hotels and its exuberant entertainment, it was hard to imagine this magnificent ballroom full of slot machines. Perhaps it would be more upmarket than that, more like one of the casinos on the French Riviera. Not that I'd been there, but I'd seen plenty of films where they featured.

Duty called and with a sigh I closed the ballroom doors and went back and resumed talking to the guests in the lounge, heading first for the group in the farthest corner.

'So what do you think of the news about Hamish?' Lily leaned over from the group at the next table and tapped me on the shoulder, catching me as I was asking a rather morose man beside me, 'Are you enjoying your stay?

I turned to face her, to see she was grinning from ear to ear, not quite what I expected.

'Who knows?' I shrugged. 'There's only been a preliminary post mortem - the full report won't be available for some time.'

'We suspect,' she gestured to Iris sitting on the other side of the table, 'that he might have been poisoned by the food.'

Several heads nodded in acknowledgement of this pronouncement.

'Oh, let's not exaggerate,' I said, looking round anxiously. 'Whatever happened I'm sure the food wasn't to blame.' I didn't want to encourage gossip, nor be quoted as a source of authoritative information about the cause of Hamish's sudden death.

'Word is they buy out of date food and disguise it with all sorts of strange sauces,' said Iris. 'It's a wonder more of us haven't suffered.'

At this I couldn't help but burst out laughing. 'I'm sure the police wouldn't let us continue to eat here if they thought the food was the least bit suspect. They would have closed the hotel down. Health and Safety would have been down on the place like a ton of bricks. You're mistaken, I'm sure.'

'He wasn't a very nice person,' said Lily. 'He even upset you, Alison.'

She was not to be swayed from her opinion, no matter what I said and I tried to change the subject.

It was clearly going to be more difficult than I imagined during the second week. I'd thought that having had the practice run of the first week, the second would be a lot easier. But with the news of the reason for Hamish's death and the death of Effie, not to mention the strange noises in the night and Anna's sudden demise, this was shaping up to be a horrendous few days.

And those guests who had stayed on were beginning to annoy the new arrivals by insisting on talking knowledgeably about the events planned for the week ahead.

I had this horrible sinking feeling that wouldn't go away, no matter how I tried to dismiss my concerns. It was my own fault – I should have abandoned the contract and headed home when I'd had the opportunity.

Oh dear, what would happen next? In spite of my assurances to Simon, I had this awful feeling that we weren't out of the woods yet. Meanwhile I had to change and steel myself to be merry and bright at the next event.

36

Once dressed and made up, I wandered down into the foyer, thinking I'd head for the kitchen and beg a cup of coffee from someone there. I certainly didn't want to join the guests enjoying a pre-prandial drink in the bar. But as I came into the foyer my instinct told me something wasn't right. The police were swarming everywhere, interviewing everyone again, scouring the public rooms, examining the kitchen.

The Manager was hovering around the entrance, wringing his hands, talking to anyone who would listen with a look of desperation on his face.

'He's worried they'll shut down the kitchens, which means closing the hotel,' said Kelly who was back on duty, much to the relief of most of us who'd found the student's casual attitude to our needs difficult to deal with. Yvonne was also there: this was the busiest part of the week and they were both required to deal with the problems that seemed to arise, no matter how much preparation had been done.

'Surely they won't do that?' I said. 'I thought it was all sorted.'

Kelly didn't reply, her attention taken by yet another flustered guest concerned she was too late for the free pre-dinner drink.

'Not at all,' smiled Kelly in a patient voice. 'If you follow that gentleman in the black velvet jacket you'll find the others in the bar.'

The woman hesitated, fingering her heavy jewelled necklace and Kelly urged, 'Go on. One of the ideas of this week is to make new friends.'

Somewhat reluctantly the guest moved slowly towards the bar and as Kelly leaned over to me, I caught a whiff of her perfume, one I recognised. *Valle D'Or* was also a favourite of Maura and though my sense of smell isn't great, its distinctive musky, woody aroma is one that makes it easy to identify.

The sound of yapping heralded the arrival of Sylvia Openshaw, her dog's head peeping out of yet another bag: this one encrusted with sequins which glittered and sparkled in the light.

'I hate this part of the week,' she said. 'Absolutely loathe it.'

'You're not going to enjoy it?' Why had she stayed on then?

'Oh, my dear, it's not that. I mean that it's all so busy, the usual air of calm about the place disappears while guests forge friendships.' She shuddered. 'It quite upsets poor Jasper.'

I was lost for words. How could she possibly describe the past week as 'calm'?

She called over to Kelly, well hidden behind a sea of heads as more of the guests clustered round the Reception desk seeking advice on what to do next. 'I'm off into the conservatory for some peace and quiet till it's time for dinner. Now that we can use it again, I may as well take advantage of it. Poor Jasper's nerves are quite frayed with all that's been going on.'

'I'm sure that dog's no more than a talking head,' muttered Yvonne coming up beside me. 'I've never actually seen it out of one of her many bags.'

214

It was hard not to laugh. 'If Mrs Openshaw is staying on for a second week Jasper can't be suffering that much.'

'It's worse than that. She's decided to book in from now until New Year is over. How we'll manage, I've no idea.' Then suddenly aware she shouldn't be making these disloyal comments about guests, she said, 'Though I'm sure she's lonely, poor soul and enjoys the company. Even complaining is part of the fun for her.'

With that she turned to serve the next guest who seemed to be disputing loudly the number of tea bags on the hospitality tray in his room.

But I wasn't to escape so easily. As I passed the conservatory, the main door was wide open and Mrs Openshaw called out to me. 'Ah, Alison, my dear. Do come and chat if you've nothing else to do. We'd welcome some company, some interesting company away from all those old dears I'm going to have to put up with all week.'

As Sylvia Openshaw must have been at least eighty, in spite of her efforts to disguise it with several face lifts, I suspected, it was rather odd to be calling the other guests "old dears". Some of them were younger than I am.

This was the last thing I felt like doing, but mindful as ever of my duties I joined her in the conservatory; though I made sure to keep well away from the snappy Jasper.

'I don't know what to do. I need some advice,' she fluttered. 'I'm booked in here till after New Year. I thought it would be a good idea: the Hydro re-opened, such a happy place once upon a time. Even in the 50s the place had an air of gaiety about it. I understand it was empty for much of the year but at Christmas and New Year it was such a jolly place. The brochure I received gave every indication it would return to its former glory. Instead,' she clutched at her chest in a melodramatic fashion, 'instead we've had one death after another. And one of those might not have been due to natural causes. It's all too distressing. And Jasper and I have had to put on a good face, not alarm the guests. No easy task let me tell you. I keep sensing the aura of the dear departed who once frequented the Hydro.'

'I'm sure in the circumstances if you wanted to leave, you'd be perfectly entitled to do so,' I said, trying to sound understanding of her predicament, but apparently that was the wrong thing to say.

'Leave?' she said in astonishment. 'Where would I go? Everywhere worthwhile was booked up long ago. There would be no possibility of a decent hotel now. Besides I'm not going to leave them in the lurch. They need all the support they can get.'

'Perhaps you'd be better off having a family Christmas this year,' I said, attempting to make things better and only succeeding in digging myself deeper into another hole.

A tear glistened in her eye. 'Jasper is all the family I have,' she whimpered, 'since my dear husband Tristan passed away. I can still feel his presence.' She nuzzled the dog, who repaid her attention by making to bite her.

'Now, now, Jasper,' she said, 'that's very naughty to do that to Mummy. You'll make Mummy very cross.'

I couldn't stand much more of this, but had no idea how to extricate myself without appearing rude.

216

'Yes,' she said, turning her attention once more to me. 'I do have a son, but he lives in Australia and there's no way Jasper could travel there with me.'

I'll bet your son's glad about that, I thought but aloud I said, 'That's a pity. It's always difficult when your children live so far away.'

I thought about Alastair, who works at the University of Maple Ridge in British Columbia and who hasn't managed back for Christmas for the past couple of years. At least Deborah lives close enough to come home and Maura, my eldest daughter even when she lived in London made the effort to journey north with her husband, Alan.

So although Mrs Openshaw was an extremely annoying person, I did feel sorry for her being so alone over the festive period. So alone she had to make do with the company of strangers and the forced jollity involved.

I stood up. 'I have to be going. There are several things to check with the Manager. Some adjustments may have to be made to my talks this week and the sooner the better. I should be giving the first one tonight, but Clive has decided it would be better to start tomorrow.'

But she wasn't going to let me go. 'I might come along with you and sit beside you at dinner.' She shivered and wrapped her cardigan round her more tightly. 'I'm not sure if I'm cold or nervous. It wasn't such a good idea to come in here after all. Even the view isn't very good.'

She was right. A fine mist of rain obscured the bay and darkness was rapidly encroaching on the bare and empty gardens.

'Or,' she went on, 'it might be because this is where it happened.'

'Where it happened?' I echoed. 'Oh, you mean where poor Effie was found.'

'Yes. There's so much been going on in this place, it would make a person with a less strong constitution very nervous indeed. I have this ability to link with those who have passed over.'

Ignoring her claim she was able to communicate with the dead, 'I'm sure there's no need to worry. We know they are saying Hamish didn't die of natural causes,' I said, trying to choose my words as carefully as possible, 'but that may have been a mistake. Even the experts can get things wrong.'

She looked at me, a puzzled expression on her face. 'How absolutely dreadful! Hamish as well?'

'Sorry?' I wasn't following this part of the conversation. 'Wasn't that what you meant when you talked about the news about someone who hadn't died of natural causes?'

'Dear me, no.' She looked stunned. 'That's not what I meant at all. I was talking about poor Effie.'

'Effie?' I said and my voice came out as a squeak. 'What on earth makes you think she was murdered? She was very old and not in the best of health.' She bristled visibly as I said 'very old' and I attempted to divert her as quickly as possible. 'What makes you think there was anything suspicious about Effie's death?'

For a moment I thought she was going to refuse to answer me, as she looked away and began to pet Jasper. When she did reply, she didn't lift her head.

'She thought some one was after her. Some one was stalking her.'

This was so unlike anything that might happen to Effie: it sounded more like something out of a spy novel and if the subject hadn't been so serious I'd have been tempted to laugh.

'Surely no one would have been after Effie? I can't think of a single reason.'

'It was **your** fault, Alison. It was because of you and your questions about the old Hydro.'

'But all I wanted to know was what Effie remembered about the early days when the hotel was in its heyday. She told me her family were regular visitors to the place, how much they enjoyed it.'

'Yes, but there was more to it than that, wasn't there?'

She lifted her head and I was surprised to see her face suffused with anger. 'You go around asking all kinds of questions without the slightest regard for the effect they might have.'

This was so preposterous I found it difficult to disguise my annoyance. 'I've no idea what you mean. I told her I was considering writing a book about the old Hydro. I'm a freelance writer and I'm always on the lookout for new projects. It seemed to me this was a subject that would sell well to tourists and there would be a natural market for it here at the hotel.'

I stopped, aware I was rattling on, talking too much.

She made a face. 'Oh, I know all about you, Alison. I've seen your books for sale in the town - about the Rothesay Pavilion and that one about James Hamilton. I suppose it's fine if you like that kind of thing.'

Her tone of voice made it perfectly clear that she didn't like "that kind of thing", but I ignored this and decided to push her for an answer to my question about Effie. 'What makes you think there was a problem? That it wasn't simply old age?'

She visibly softened. 'I spoke to her after you left. She was very distressed she'd been persuaded to tell you so much. All she'd intended to do was give you a few stories about the old days, but somehow she said it all came out.'

Light was beginning to dawn but even yet I wasn't sure if I was right. I decided to play for time, not give her any leading information. 'Was there anything in particular she was concerned about?'

I fished in my bag for my notebook and pretended to consult it, turning over several pages slowly and frowning in concentration. 'There doesn't seem to be anything here that might be a problem.' I kept the notebook carefully turned away from her line of sight so she wouldn't realise the pages were almost empty.

'Oh, but there was and I can imagine it was exactly the kind of story that would have intrigued anyone, especially you, Alison.'

'Well, I haven't any idea,' I said. 'What did she say to you?' Was she going to tell me, or would I have to disclose what Effie had said to me?

There was a moment's hesitation and she started to stroke Jasper. Unfortunately by now he was sound asleep and didn't welcome this intrusion and made his feelings known by growling. It was amazing how such a deep growl could come from such a tiny dog.

Sylvia looked up. 'She told you about the girl that went missing, that's what the problem was.'

'So? That was all she said. She didn't give me any details. I'd have been interested in the story - you're right - but all she said was that a girl had gone missing. I don't know when it happened or who it was or anything more about it, so I can hardly see why you would think Effie's death would be anything to do with me, or the stories she told me.' I hoped that sounded suitably vague.

'But that's the whole point. Someone wanted to make sure she didn't tell you any more. That the rest of the story wasn't made accessible to someone who might write about it, stir things up after all these years.'

'Well, I'm sorry, but I think you have it wrong. If Effie didn't tell me much, it could hardly have been my fault she died - if it wasn't a natural death.'

'But you would have wanted to meet up with her again, find out more?'

A reluctant, 'I guess so.'

'Aha, exactly as I thought. You would have pestered her until she told you the whole story.'

'Look, Mrs Openshaw,' I said, becoming increasingly tired of this conversation and slurs on my merits as a writer, 'it wouldn't have mattered if she told me or not. It's perfectly simple to look up something like that in the past copies of *The Buteman* at the local library.'

'Yes, the event would have been recorded for sure, but only Effie knew the whole story and someone wanted to make sure she didn't reveal it.'

I stared at her. How come she knew so much? Did she know the 'whole story?' If she was right someone had wanted to make sure Effie didn't have the opportunity to talk to me again, reveal what she knew.

221

Yet the only person who seemed concerned by this was Mrs Openshaw. No one else had mentioned this story of the missing girl and some of the guests who had visited the old Hydro, people like Iris and Lily, must surely know about it? She had her failings, but somehow I didn't see Sylvia as a murderer. Or was she?

37

Whatever the truth of the matter, I was now intrigued. Part of me thought Mrs Openshaw's comments were more likely to be the product of a tendency to be over-dramatic, the other part thought there might be something in what she said, given the recent deaths. For a moment I was tempted to tell her about the sobbing, test her so-called powers, but as quickly dismissed that idea.

As I mulled over the possibilities, a further suggestion came to mind. Hamish's death was at the very least suspect and Sylvia believed Effie's death was also suspicious: did that mean there was also something odd about Anna's death? Or was it no more than a coincidence she had died when she did?

I needed to talk to someone about this, someone I could trust. Simon was back on the mainland and even if he had been here, he would have dismissed my concerns, urged me not to become involved or worse, insisted I go back home with him, contract or no contract.

What about Kelly? This time I abandoned the plan almost as soon as I came up with it. There was a problem there also, given what I had witnessed at the Coronet hotel.

Then I remembered Mrs Underwood: she had lived on Bute all her life and her family before her for many generations. She'd been particularly eager to stress her proud heritage to me, 'We're true Brandanes, people born on the island, not incomers claiming to be Brandanes.' She'd said to drop in any time.

Did I have time to pay her a visit before dinner? I scrabbled in my bag for the piece of paper where she'd written down her phone number and after discarding old receipts, sweet wrappers, a broken comb and a ticket for the Guildford Square car park, I found it scrunched up at the bottom. I smoothed it out as I considered what to do, then thinking, what the heck she can only refuse to see me, I dialled the number.

At first it looked as if my call was going to be picked up by her answering machine and I had no notion what kind of message to leave, what to say without giving too much away, but at the very last ring, or so it seemed, she picked it up.

'Hello, Mrs Underwood, it's Alison Cameron here.'

'Oh, hello, Alison, I didn't hear the phone at first - I have to have the television turned up really loud. I must think about getting one of those amplifiers for the phone. You see them advertised in the newspapers, though my late husband was always wary of that kind of advert in case it was some kind of con...'

I interrupted this digression, but she didn't seem to notice. 'I know it's short notice, but could I come over and have a chat to you?'

'You're always welcome, Alison,' she replied but there was a puzzled tone in her voice and I had to do some explaining. Luckily I'd mentioned to her that possibility of writing a book so was able to say, 'I'd like to follow up the information about the old Hydro. I'm now very keen to write about it and I've a limited time on the island.'

'Oh, that's no problem. I go to bed late. I'm a poor sleeper. The doctor gave me some sleeping pills, but I don't like taking them too often because the next morning I feel so wretched. Mind you, sometimes there's no alternative. If I've had a few bad nights the only option is to take them. Though I do try to take only one instead of the two he prescribed...'

'Thanks, I'm very grateful. But perhaps I could come along now?' I said, cutting her off again. Was this a good idea? It was going to be difficult to keep her on track. 'I'll be with you in about ten minutes,' I said and rang off.

I decided to walk down to see Mrs Underwood, in spite of my finery. There was almost an hour before dinner started - plenty of time even for a conversation with Mrs Underwood.

At this time of the evening the Christmas lights were all switched on and they illuminated the village, dispelling the gloom of a winter's night and a brisk walk was exactly what I needed. Unfortunately my shoes weren't designed for walking any distance and I hadn't gone far before realising I should have changed them for a pair less crippling.

It was cold and frosty, the pavements glistening in the streetlights as the temperature fell. I could see my breath make little wraiths of mist in the chilly air, reminding me of the reason for my visit.

A warm welcome awaited me in more ways than one. I needn't have worried about my abrupt ending of our phone call.

'Come in, come in,' said Mrs Underwood, opening the door and letting a pool of light spill out into the darkness at this end of the village where there were no festive lights. 'The kettle's on.'

And sure enough, I could smell the aroma of baking. 'You haven't been baking for me, have you?' I said, suddenly feeling guilty about this sudden visit.

'No, no,' she chuckled. 'It's the church fair tomorrow and I have to take my contribution over very early so I thought I'd get ahead and make some of the cakes tonight. But,' a twinkle in her eye, 'I've put one aside for you.'

Oh dear, was my liking for sweet stuff so obvious? Hopefully her hospitality wouldn't be as lavish as last time, else there'd be no possibility of my doing justice to the Hydro dinner.

Once settled beside a roaring coal fire with a cup of tea and the smallest cake I could select, we chatted for a few minutes about this and that: the village fair, the price of goods on the island, the problems about the CalMac ferry in winter until I managed to steer the conversation round to the reason for my visit.

'Thanks for giving me the opportunity to chat about the old Kyles Hydro,' I said, conscious of the minutes ticking away. 'I'm keen now to write about it and perhaps you could help fill in some background information?'

'Of course,' she said, settling herself back in the chair. 'Ask what you want and I'll try to fill in as best I can.'

'I suppose your family have known about the old Hydro for some generations back if you've always lived on the island?'

'Most certainly,' she said. 'Look at these.' She stood up and went over to the display case in the corner of the room to bring out a set of silver egg cups on a little stand with a handle. She gave them a rub with the edge of her sleeve before holding them up for my inspection. 'These were from the old Hydro when it was finally closed. My mother worked there and members of staff were allowed to buy some of the goods that were being sold off.'

She smiled. 'Or at least that was the story. Whatever, these have been in the family for years.'

'Did you ever hear any tales about strange goings on at there?'

This was the wrong tack to take as she launched into a series of reminiscences about people she'd heard about, the eccentric habits of some of the guests, the bizarre musicians who'd come along one Christmas and refused to play anything except Beethoven. Once she'd started I found it difficult to make her to stop, in spite of several attempts to steer the conversation in the direction I wanted.

I pretended to make some notes as a way of feigning interest. Even if I did eventually write something about the Hydro there was no way I'd be able to use most of this material.

Finally as the time wore on I had to come clean about my real reason for the visit, tell her what I wanted to know.

'Did you ever hear a story about a girl going missing?'

'What sort of story? One of the staff? Or one of the guests?' I felt guilty. She was anxious to help me and had no idea of the real motive behind my questions.

'I heard a vague rumour there had been a great to-do many years ago about a girl who'd gone missing. It

227

must have been when the hotel was in its heyday, but more than that I don't know. Not when, not her age, nothing else.' It seemed prudent to give her as little information as possible, let her tell me what she remembered.

Mrs Underwood wrinkled her brow in concentration. 'Mmm…you don't think that's the kind of story you'd forget. Unless of course you've only had half the story and she went missing but was then found. Have you checked that out?'

This solution hadn't occurred to me, so sure had I been that the missing girl and the missing door on the top floor were somehow connected.

Before I'd the chance to reply she said, gazing at the wall behind my head as though seeing something there, some distant memory, 'I do seem to remember my mother saying something about a girl. She was a guest, but it was something to do with one of the staff…one of the young men.'

She paused. 'Have I got that right?' She shook her head. 'Sorry, Alison, I don't really remember the details. My mother told so many stories about the place and I only half listened. You know what it's like when you're young and then when you get older you wish you'd paid more attention.'

She sat back and raised her feet to toast them at the fire. 'Oh, dear, I don't think I've been much help to you.'

'Of course you have,' I lied, 'you've given me some ideas I can follow up.'

I stood up. 'I think I'd better be going, dinner will be starting soon and it won't look good if I'm late.'

'Oh, must you go so soon? It's been great to have your company. Are you sure you wouldn't like another cup of tea? It's no bother. It won't take me a minute to put the kettle on again.'

She saw me to the door, still chatting away and it was a good few minutes before I was able to extricate myself and then had to hobble back to the hotel as quickly as my uncomfortable shoes permitted.

At this time of night, the village was silent but light from the windows of the Coronet Hotel made patterns on the frosty pavements and I could hear the sounds of laughter as I passed the front door.

I wouldn't say my trip to see Mrs Underwood had been a waste of time and if I ever did decide to write something about the old Hydro, I had some possible material, or source of material, but I was no further forward in finding out about the 'missing girl' if indeed she had been missing. Old stories often became muddled in the telling.

And it was more than likely Mrs Underwood was correct. If a girl had gone missing, had run off with one of the men working at the hotel, it was likely the ending to the story was that she had been found by her family and taken home in disgrace. There was no connection between this story and the room on the top floor.

But on Tuesday, after I'd fulfilled at least part of my duties with the newly arrived guests, I'd slip off to the library and search through the back copies of *The Buteman*. Perhaps there might be a clue to the real story there.

But even if I found out what had happened to that missing girl, there still remained the question - why had the room on the top floor been wallpapered over?

I didn't believe in ghosts, didn't agree with Anna's idea that the West wing was haunted, but there was something strange going on in the Hydro.

38

Monday passed in a flurry of activity: helping the new guests settle in, giving my first talk of the week, fielding questions, most of them nothing to do with me and generally being on hand to help out.

When I awoke on Tuesday morning my first thought was that I must have overslept. The room was filled with a strange light and the usual sounds of activity outside were muffled, distant.

I leapt out of bed, but a swift glance at the clock told me it was still early and on opening the curtains I looked out on a world gone white. During the night heavy snow had fallen, shrouding all the familiar landmarks, making eerie shapes of the bushes. Two of the porters were already hard at work clearing the long curving driveway, a fruitless task as snow continued to fall in thick white flakes from a leaden sky.

Shivering a little I grabbed my dressing gown, pulling it tightly around me as I set about making coffee to help kick start me into the day.

Once showered and dressed I hurried down to the dining room, forcing a smile as I passed the tables, greeting guests.

There was more to do than anticipated: today a small party of young people had arrived from Edinburgh, most of them with an interest in the island as their ancestors had originally come from Bute. They clustered round me as soon as breakfast was over like a flock of little starlings, chattering and asking questions without waiting for the answer.

'Whoa,' I said, holding up my hand. 'I'll be covering several of these topics in my next talk,' and I made my excuses as I left, worn out by this onslaught. They moved away towards the lounge, still chattering nineteen to the dozen. It looked like being a busy week.

I managed to escape soon after eleven o'clock and drove to the library in Moat Street, luckily finding a parking place outside the Community Centre. The roads had been gritted, but even so there were a few treacherous patches where ice had formed and the journey was slower than usual.

A blast of hot air hit me as I pushed open the door and to my surprise the library was already crowded and most of the computers in the front room occupied. Fortunately there was one in the far corner still free, possibly because it was a bit of a squeeze to manoeuvre into the seat and after ordering the microfiche from the librarian on duty I settled down to scroll through the back copies of the original newspapers. There had been a number of attempts to provide a newspaper for the island: some short-lived like the *Rothesay Advertiser and Literary Journal* which managed only four issues.

I flicked through my notebook to check when the Hydro had opened - the 11th June 1879. At that time there were two main newspapers - *The Buteman* and the *Rothesay Express* - and I concentrated my efforts on these.

Almost immediately I found a report covering several columns about the special steamer, adorned with bunting, that was laid on to take people from Weymss Bay to the Swanstonhill Sanatorium as the

Kyles of Bute Hydro and Spa was originally called. This was a promising start.

One after another I scanned the later copies: weeks would go past with no mention of the place and then a long article about some event or other would suddenly pop up. Many of these made the front page: in a small place like Bute such incidents were worth a detailed report. But nothing took me any further forward in my search for the story about the missing girl.

It was probably a futile search. I'd no real evidence the incident had ever happened and, even if the story was true, there was no more to it than that someone had run off and been found soon after. So many tales become exaggerated over time.

My eyes were becoming bleary through focussing for so long on the screen and I sat back and rubbed them as I reached the 1909 report of the fire responsible for the destruction of the original Hydro building. There was no fire brigade on the island at that time and only some of the West wing survived to become part of the hotel when it was rebuilt in 1911.

So far there was no report of any missing girl, nothing worth a front page spread.

The librarian came over. 'Hello, Alison, good to see you again. What are you researching this time?' She peered over my shoulder at the screen. 'Ah, the Kyles Hydro. Yes, that would make an interesting subject for a book.'

'Do you know anything about a story of some girl who went missing from the Hydro?'

She shook her head. 'When would that be?'

'I've no idea,' I sighed, 'that's the problem. I've got as far as 1911 and the rebuilding but there's nothing about a girl going missing.'

'You've a fair bit to go then,' she said. 'Sorry I can't help. But if you can't find anything leave me a contact number and I'll ask Tina. I'm sure she told me once that her grandmother worked at the old Hydro. She might have heard something.'

'That would be very helpful,' I said with feeling as she went back into the main library to deal with the queue of people waiting at the counter to have their books stamped. Ideal weather to be snug indoors with a good book and a cup of tea, I thought wistfully, remembering I had to go over the details for my next talk.

Aware it was almost lunchtime, I quickly scanned through the next few editions, trying hard not to be distracted by the stories of life on the island and the multitude of advertisements for all kinds of products so familiar at one time, but now weird and wonderful to modern eyes.

I stood up and stretched to relieve the crick in my neck then scribbled my contact details on a bit of paper torn from my notebook. One day I must get round to having proper business cards printed as Simon was always advising me to do.

'If Tina has any information, I'd be very grateful. Even a steer in the right direction. When you look at so many of these it's easy to miss something and I've no idea if she went missing of her own accord, or if she went missing and was then found. In fact I know nothing about her except the story I heard.'

If she thought my quest odd, she didn't show it, merely saying, 'I'll tell Tina when she comes in and ask her to call you.'

With that I had to be content. If I didn't hurry, I'd be late for lunch and I was determined to see this week through, no matter what Simon's reservations about my time on the island.

When I came out of the library it had stopped snowing and the temperature must have risen, because by the side of the roads snow had turned to slush and I drove back through Ardbeg towards Port Bannatyne, my head full of the various stories I'd read about the old Hydro, with more than a glimmer of hope that I could write an interesting book about the place. Even so my main concern was to find out something, anything about the missing girl or if she'd even existed. The more I thought about it, the more likely became that explanation. It was no more than a story, muddled and mixed up with some other tale and quite possibly nothing to do with the Hydro.

And that door on the top floor would have a simple explanation. I had to get rid of these concerns. It was all to do with my imagination, nothing more.

I could only hope that Tina would have some news for me…and soon.

39

I made it back in time for lunch with only a few minutes to spare and had to abandon my coat in the cloakroom by the main door. There was no time to change my boots and conscious of the way they were making little puddles of water on the deep pile carpet, I headed for the table I'd been allocated in the dining room.

The Manager had had the bright idea of organising a member of staff to 'host' a table at lunchtime. It wasn't always possible to do this in the evening – there weren't enough members of staff, but it made for a good atmosphere over lunch. Fortunately he'd been persuaded to allow a change of table each day.

The result of this way of organising meals was unpredictable. On some occasions guests were friendly, chatty; on other occasions they were silent, shy and persuading them to contribute to the conversation involved enormous effort.

This time I breathed a sigh of relief. With Sylvia Openshaw, the Herrington sisters and Major Revere at my table, I'd be lucky to get a word in.

As I sat down, Major Revere was as usual holding forth, his booming voice carrying across the dining room, causing other diners to look round, curious to hear more.

'Yes, it's not the relaxing place you would think, this hotel, eh?' he said. 'And even the food isn't up to standard. Why, when I was in the army we thought the stuff they served up then was pretty bad, but here there are so many problems.'

'So why did you decide to stay on another week,' said Lily a little tartly.

'Had booked two weeks, m'dear. Thought it would be a good way to pass this time of year when the garden doesn't need much attention.'

'Ah, so you're a gardener, then? We love gardening, don't we, Iris?'

Iris nodded in agreement as Lily continued, 'We always find Hellbora Sempens does very well in our climate.'

'Yes, yes,' blustered the Major. 'Couldn't agree more. Ideal for Scotland.'

Lily and Iris exchanged a look which the others didn't catch as Sylvia made it clear she had been out of the limelight long enough. Here were people having an interesting conversation in which she couldn't participate and she didn't like having her nose put out of joint.

'I no longer have a garden and when my dear husband was alive the gardener did all the work. I'm so terribly ignorant of matters horticultural.' She made it sound like a virtue. She went on rapidly in case anyone else jumped in. 'I'm an only child,' she sighed, dabbing at her eyes with a handkerchief. 'That's why I'm so fond of little Jasper. He's my constant companion.'

'I'm not sure we approve of dogs in the dining room, do we,' said Lily. 'Most unhygienic.'

'I suppose Jasper is very small,' I said, trying to avoid a social disaster, but Lily was having none of it. 'That's as may be,' she said, peering into Sylvia's bag. 'And yes, I suppose it looks more like a rat than a dog.'

237

'You'll upset him,' shrieked Sylvia. 'He's very sensitive.'

This was not going well, but fortunately at that moment the waitress came over to take our order. In the aftermath of this spate, no matter how hard I tried to keep the conversation going through lunch, there was little response.

Mrs Openshaw sat in stony silence, deliberately provoking the sisters by feeding titbits to Jasper, while Lily and Iris tutted their way through the meal and the Major droned on about his time in the army.

Finally, as coffee arrived, I made my escape saying, 'Good to see you all again.'

As I left I heard Lily say in a tone of voice designed to be heard, 'We're going straight to the Manager to ask for a change of table. There's no way I want to share any more meals with a dog.' I guessed Iris would agree with her, meekly follow on. That wasn't my concern: it was something else for the Manager to sort out.

But they weren't finished yet. As I stood at the Reception desk, the sisters came twittering towards me. Lily grabbed me by the elbow. 'He's nothing but a fraud, that man.'

For a moment, my mind on other matters, I was baffled.

'That story about the garden - there's no such plant. He knows nothing about it. And I suspect he's no more a Major than I am. A complete fraud.' She shuddered. 'Nasty man.'

Under my breath I swore I'd never become involved in anything like this again. Though I wouldn't admit it to Simon, I wasn't cut out for all this socialising with the guests, especially when their expectations were so high. These *Turkey and Tinsel* weeks were being offered at a rock bottom price, but even so it didn't stop the complaints coming thick and fast.

As I walked through the foyer my mobile rang and I stepped into the lounge to answer it. It was Tina from the library. 'Alison? Tina here. You were making enquiries about an episode at the old Hydro? About a missing girl.'

'Yes, I was interested in the story.' I felt my heart skip a beat. Perhaps Tina would be able to solve the puzzle for me?

'I've managed to find the article in *The Buteman*. It was quite a sensation at the time. If you want to come along to the library this afternoon I could show it to you.'

'How did I miss it? If it was a major event?'

'You probably stopped before it happened. The girl went missing in the 1930s.'

'Ah, you're right. I stopped at 1911 when it was rebuilt.'

'I don't go off shift until five o'clock so any time before that would be fine.'

I did a quick calculation. 'I've one or two things to sort out here,' I said, 'and then I'll be along. Thanks for getting back to me so quickly.'

'A pleasure. See you later.'

She rang off and I stood for a moment, then sat down in the nearest chair to gather my thoughts. So the story was true: it wasn't a myth or something misremembered. A girl had gone missing from the old Hydro. In spite of my curiosity I'd deliberately not asked for any more information over the phone - better to go and read the stuff for myself and not be

239

influenced by the story being filtered through a third person yet again. I'd have to clear my head of all previous versions.

I hurried out into the hall where Yvonne was on the Reception desk. 'Have you seen Clive?' I said. 'I need to speak to him.'

'He was here a minute ago,' she said, gazing around as though he might suddenly pop up from under the desk. 'He muttered something about having to reorganise seating arrangements for dinner tonight.'

Oh dear, that would be the complaints about Sylvia's dog, I thought, so I didn't enquire too closely. 'Could you tell him when he comes back that I've had to go out for an hour or so?'

Yvonne clearly found it difficult to disguise her curiosity about where I was going, but I was determined I wasn't telling her. There was enough rumour and gossip around at the moment.

Indeed, there was no need to give her any excuse. We were supposed to be on duty in the hotel for most of the week - that was part of the contract. Even so, we were entitled to some time off.

A quick trip to the cloakroom to collect my coat then I headed for the library to meet with Tina. I felt a tingle of excitement, though I couldn't say why. The story might turn out to be a non-event, the usual thing about someone going missing and being found again almost as quickly. Or it might be something to do with that door on the top floor of the West wing.

Whatever the truth, I was convinced the story in *The Buteman* would reveal what had really happened in the Hydro many years ago.

40

Tina was waiting for me, standing guard over the microfiche, but I ignored her unspoken questions. The tale might amount to nothing. Best to wait till I'd had a chance to examine the article.

'Thanks for doing this, Tina,' I said, taking my place at the desk.

Of course her first words were, 'Any reason you're interested in this particular story,' as she began to scroll through the microfiche. I'd have preferred to be left on my own, but didn't want to appear rude, not after the trouble she'd taken. I made a quick decision to give her the explanation of my interest in writing a book about the old Hydro. 'Stories like this appeal to readers,' I said, 'rather than bare facts.'

She nodded in agreement. 'Yes, there's plenty of material. Most of what's been written to date has been piecemeal, snippets in books about Bute or short articles.'

She seemed eager to linger as I started my research, but luckily at that very moment one of the other librarians came out of the main library. 'Telephone call for you, Tina,' she said. 'I think it's something to do with the new order. You'd be best to take it.'

'Don't worry about me,' I said, waving her away and bending my head to the screen. 'I've used the microfiche lots of times.'

With no option but to take the phone call, she went off reluctantly into the main library and I watched her go before turning back to the screen.

I didn't have to search for long as the relevant article suddenly appeared on the screen headed by a small and very blurry photo of the missing girl.

The story was a simple one, and at least some elements of the story I'd heard were correct. The girl, Gertrude Fitzroy, was a sixteen year old who'd come to stay at the hotel over the Christmas period with her family. On Christmas morning her mother had awakened to find she wasn't in the adjoining room she shared with her parents. Thinking she might have gone down early to breakfast, her mother didn't worry too much, though she did think it strange Gertrude hadn't waited to open her presents before going off.

Once she and her husband were dressed they went down to the dining room, but there was no sign of their daughter, nor had anyone seen her since the previous evening.

With a mounting sense of panic the parents instigated a search of the hotel and when there was no trace of her, the Head Porter suggested they search the grounds. According to the report the grounds in those days were extensive with acres of shrubs and a rockery surrounding the large pond and, fearing the worst, her parents and as many of the staff as could be spared trudged through the snow, searching every nook and cranny.

There was no sign of her anywhere and, in spite of a brief fear she might have wandered off and fallen into the pond, a quick inspection revealed it was unlikely as the pond was almost frozen over.

It had been snowing hard through the night and any footprints would have been covered up. With no other options the searchers returned to the hotel where a further search of her room revealed her new winter coat and scarf and gloves were also missing.

During a second search of the grounds her father found one of her gloves tangled in the shrubbery near the pond. Everyone feared the worst. For some reason she'd decided to go for a walk the previous night, had fallen into the pond before it had frozen, but dredging it revealed no trace of her. The police admitted they were baffled by the case and no one could shed any light on why she might have decided to go out on her own.

'That's some story,' said a voice behind me and I turned to find Tina looking over my shoulder. I'd been so absorbed in the newspaper article I hadn't noticed her come up beside me.

She leaned over and began to fiddle with the microfiche control. 'There's more news a bit later on,' she said, scooting through the papers for the following year and stopping suddenly at a story on a page in the middle of the paper.

'There it is,' she said, pointing to the headline *No News of Missing Girl*.

The update suggested Gertrude was 'of a nervous disposition' and had to be carefully watched over by her parents - hence the adjoining bedroom. She apparently had had a couple of what were referred to as 'episodes' and the belief was that something had upset her and she'd gone off, become disorientated in the snow (the grounds were extensive) and ended up drowned in the pond late the previous evening.

I looked up at Tina. 'But surely they would dredge the pond carefully?'

Tina shrugged. 'I daresay they did, but I believe it was pretty deep and at that time of year with all the ice and the tangled vegetation they could find no sign of her.'

'So they gave up really easily?'

'Yes. There's a little piece further on,' and she whisked through the next few pages and pointed to a paragraph at the bottom. 'There. The parents went back home, the incident was forgotten and that was the end of it. There might be more information in the Glasgow papers.'

'It all seems very callous,' I said.

She shrugged. 'Perhaps, but the hotel wanted it taken care of as soon as possible. It wouldn't be good for their reputation if there was too much publicity. And there was the story that she was of 'unbalanced mind' whether that was actually true or not.'

She stood up. 'I'll leave you to have another look through the articles, but there's not much more than what I've shown you. I daresay it seems heartless to our modern way of thinking but back then they didn't have the resources to deal with that kind of problem and as I said, the hotel would want the story hushed up.'

I turned back to the machine and scrolled back to the beginning of the articles about poor Gertrude. I looked closely at the photo on the front page of the first article. While it was of poor quality, dark and grainy, it was easy to see she'd been very pretty.

An hour later and I was none the wiser. All the reports assumed Gertrude had somehow wandered out into the grounds late at night and for some reason had ended up drowned in the pond. That no one would think to pursue this, even with the more limited facilities at their disposal in those days, seemed incredibly strange.

And what about the story Effie had told me about the girl running off with a young man? In spite of rereading every word of every article, there wasn't the slightest reference to this possibility.

I sat back and stared at the screen. None of this made any sense and I was no further forward.

I had an option – I could accept this version of events and conclude that the business of the missing door was nothing to do with this story.

Or I could go back to the hotel and try to think of a way of getting in to the room that had been wallpapered over.

Whatever the truth of this story, there was no doubt in my mind that the sobbing had been real, very real. If Gertrude had been proving as troublesome as rumours suggested, had truly been 'of a nervous disposition' was it possible she'd never left her room at the hotel?

41

The police had returned to the hotel and while they were busy questioning everyone again a sudden thought occurred to me. Was this the chef having his revenge for all the aggravation he'd had to take? He'd made it clear he believed it almost amounted to persecution. I dismissed it as unlikely. If he was responsible, surely more of the guests would have displayed symptoms of poisoning. Then I recalled the episode with Clive. The chef's reaction had been out of proportion to the occasion.

'We might as well have rooms here,' the sergeant said as he came in accompanied by several officers, but it was said with a grim humour. Clive was wandering about hollow-eyed, wringing his hands incessantly. There was a good reason for his behaviour: he was worried the hotel would have to be closed down as soon as this group of guests had departed, if not before.

The Herrington sisters and a couple of the other guests who'd stayed on were being shepherded towards the Manager's office for further questioning. Poor Lily and Iris – their second week was turning out to be far less restful than they'd anticipated. In spite of their twittering and their habit of finishing each other's sentences, I'd grown rather fond of them.

There was nothing I could do to help at the moment and I made for the conservatory. The rain was drumming hard on the roof so I could be sure of having the place to myself to read through the articles about

Gertrude. I'd had them copied the better to study them, but there was little progress as I'd no idea if there was any relevance between what I knew about the hotel and this story. And it took me not a step further forward in the mystery of the missing door and the sobbing I'd heard.

Perhaps I should forget the whole business and ignore the insinuation made by Mrs Openshaw that Effie's death hadn't been natural. If I kept my head down, jollied along the guests, tried to survive the remaining few days and gave my talks as my contract demanded, the week would soon be over and I could get on with my life, forget all about this. I'd even gone off the notion of writing a book about the old Hydro.

Dinner that evening was a much easier affair. Perhaps Clive had taken pity on me, had decided I'd done my penance as far as the guests were concerned because when I arrived the waiter stopped me as I headed for my table.

'The Manager has suggested you might like to go to table six tonight,' he said and I was delighted to find myself in the company of a group of Australians on their first visit to Bute as part of a round Scotland tour. They were friendly and chatty and while interested in what I had to tell them about Bute, were more interested in the latest death about which I could tell them nothing, so I had to have very little input to the conversation, which suited me fine and allowed me to make the odd comment as I mentally rehearsed my talk which had been put back to later in the evening.

In the light of the previous week, I'd made one or two adjustments, allowed more time for questions, but I needn't have worried. This was a receptive audience and the questions were much more sensible than the ones I'd had to deal with the previous week. Perhaps a contract for these *Turkey and Tinsel* weeks wasn't such a bad idea after all.

Even so, after a couple of drinks in the lounge at the end, I suddenly felt exhausted and made my excuses to head for bed. How some of these older people had the stamina to sit up drinking half the night and then be up at the crack of dawn was a mystery to me.

Before I headed upstairs I decided I'd speak to the Manager about the missing room on the top floor. No matter how often I went over the information I'd gleaned from various sources, there was no satisfactory solution. It would be easy to ask Clive to come with me to examine that section of the wall where it appeared there had once been a door, but more difficult to decide if I should mention the strange noises to him.

As luck would have it, he was sitting in the lounge with Iris and Lily, looking less than pleased by this part of his duty. When I approached he greeted me warmly, springing to his feet. 'Ah, Alison, how are you? I was saying I'll have to attend to several things for tomorrow.'

'Oh, must you go?' said Lily. 'We were so enjoying our little chat.'

'Yes, it's not often we have the opportunity of such entertaining male company,' said Iris, smiling in a coquettish that was decidedly unnerving.

If Clive expected me to take his place he was very much mistaken - I'd no intention of doing so, although I'd assist by giving him an excuse to leave.

'I wondered if you could help me,' I said, adding hastily as his face fell, 'nothing serious, just a query.'

He put his arm round my shoulders and rushed me out of the room. 'Good night, ladies, I hope you'll enjoy the rest of the evening. Duty calls and all that.' He gave a grin which could only be described as wolfish as he hurried me into the foyer where he dropped his arm saying, 'Phew. Thanks for that, Alison. I thought I'd never get away from those two. I'm so glad you noticed the hole I was in. They seemed to want a rundown on each and every guest staying this week. Incredibly nosey if you ask me. And I'm not the only one who thinks so. They've been poking around at Reception, disturbing the chef in the kitchen. As if I haven't enough to do with the police swarming all over the place.'

'I'm glad to help,' I said, 'but I really do want to talk to you.' I glanced around at the busy foyer. 'Not here. It's not private.'

'Now you've really caught my attention,' he grinned, 'come into my office.' And he ushered me behind the desk and into his office at the back of the Reception desk.

The jolly Santa had disappeared and I suspected Yvonne might be the culprit.

'Sit down, sit down,' he said indicating a large chair. This was the first time I'd been in the office and I looked around with interest: the Manager certainly wasn't stinting himself in this part of the hotel. Everything was of the best quality from the thick pile carpet on the floor to the luxurious leather chairs, the antique wooden desk, the soft lighting and the barely concealed drinks cabinet in the far corner.

'Gosh, this is lovely,' I said, unable to stop myself passing a comment.

249

'Yes, one of the perks of the job.' He made no apology for the luxury. 'I wouldn't have it any other way. This is a difficult job and I need some kind of escape route. Now, what was it you wanted to talk to me about Alison?' A look of alarm suddenly crossed his face. 'You're not thinking of leaving are you? These recent deaths haven't caused you a problem? They were nothing to do with you.'

'No,' I reassured him quickly and smiled at the look of relief that crossed his face. 'I wanted to ask you something about the old part of the Hydro, the West wing.'

He leaned back in his leather swivel chair; so far back he appeared to be in danger of falling over. 'Ask away, Alison. I don't guarantee I can answer all your questions, but I might be able to tell you where you can find information about the history of the place.' He stopped, waiting for me to continue.

Now that I had the opportunity I wasn't sure where to begin. There were two questions nagging away at me: the mystery of that missing room on the top floor and the story of Gertrude. Once again I decided on the same course of action as I'd adopted with others - to tell him I was thinking about writing a book about the old Hydro. If I told many more people this story they'd be starting to pre-order copies and I'd be compelled to write it, but that was a worry for later.

'Great idea,' he enthused, leaning forward across the desk. 'It would sell well. In fact we could include it in the packs we give to visitors,' a momentary frown, 'as long as it wasn't too expensive, that is. Yes, that's a brilliant suggestion.'

Delighted to be on a firm footing, if somewhat bemused by the enthusiastic reception of my idea, I plunged in before he could start trying to negotiate a discount for a bulk order. 'There are one or two things I'd like to clear up before I start. I've been doing some preliminary research, talking to a few people and one of the stories that intrigues me is the story of the girl who went missing in the 1930s. I gather she was never found and that there was never an explanation about what happened to her.'

He paused, the expression on his face indicating he was trying to recall what he'd been told about this particular episode.

'Gertrude, her name was Gertrude,' I prompted him.

'Ah, yes, now I remember hearing something about it when they rebuilt the hotel. It was a very long time ago. She was staying here with her parents over Christmas and the consensus was she'd wandered off late one night. They didn't find a body in spite of extensive searches of the grounds. The weather was bitterly cold, exceptionally cold for Bute and it might all have been a tragic accident. It was very strange, but anything could have happened. I seem to recall she was rather unstable - 'hysterical' - they called it in those days. She'd been in an asylum for a time, but they took her out for Christmas.'

So his story was the same as I'd read in the articles in the library, with this additional information that she'd been in an asylum for a time, not an unusual way of treating difficult people. I wondered if she fell into that category of what we now call 'learning difficulties'. In those days such conditions were scarcely understood. But there was no mention of

251

Gertrude running off with one of the staff. Effie had it wrong, another example of how stories become confused over time.

'I believe she was with her parents in a linked Suite on the top floor of the West wing, but apart from the room Anna and Freddie had, the rest of the rooms seem to be store rooms as far as I can see.' I waited, wondering if he would say anything about the door that had been covered over.

If Clive thought it odd that I was wandering about inspecting the store rooms in the hotel, he gave no sign. 'Ah, although the West wing is the only remaining part of the original building, the room numbers on all the floors there were changed when it was refurbished and we re-opened.'

'That seems a bizarre thing to do.'

'Health and Safety regulations have changed a bit since the 1930s. We had to make sure there were enough cupboards for housekeeping, had to obey fire regulations and of course everyone expects an ensuite nowadays. No one is going to come to a hotel where they have to trudge down the corridor to the bathroom as they did in the old days.'

'Oh, yes indeed. And how are the rooms numbered now?'

'This is great attention to detail, at this stage in your research,' he said, clearly puzzled, but nevertheless he swivelled round to where his computer sat on another desk behind him. 'Let's have a look if you think it's important.'

He opened a folder on his computer headed *Hydro Building Renovations* and scrolled through what appeared to be a floor plan. 'That's strange. There is no

Room equivalent for those linked rooms. I can't even see where they used to be. The architect isn't due till early in the New Year so I haven't paid much attention to that part if I'm honest.'

A chill ran down my spine. 'Perhaps there's a reason for that,' I whispered.

Still preoccupied with the dilemma of the room numbers, he muttered to himself as he scrolled through one page after another and it was a moment or two before he turned back to me.

'Sorry, Alison, you were saying? I can't understand why this should be. I've checked the new rooms with the old and they're all accounted for except for that one. I must have made a mistake somewhere.'

But now I'd decided that having started I had to continue, had to pursue it.

'I'd like you to come up with me to the top floor,' I said. There's something I want to show you.' Best to catch him while he was in a receptive mood.

I thought at first he was going to refuse. 'Must I? There's probably a good reason why that room seems to have disappeared. It'll have been some kind of administrative thing. Yes, that's what it'll be. Much easier to start with 301 and continue from there.'

'I'd still like to check it out,' I said stubbornly. If I couldn't get him to come with me now, there was unlikely to be another opportunity.

Having come this far, I was determined not to depart meekly, had to show him where I thought the door had once been. I was now sure the room that had been wallpapered over was none other than one of the original rooms where Gertrude and her parents had been staying.

Sighing in resignation, he closed down his computer and heaved himself out of his chair. 'If it'll make you happy, I'll come with you, but I'm sure there's a simple explanation. But we'd better make it snappy,' he warned. 'There's so much to do, I can't afford to be wasting time.'

'It won't take a minute,' and I rushed out the door before he could change his mind, looking back to make sure he was following me.

We took the lift to the top floor in silence and came out into the empty corridor.

'Now what is it you want to show me?' he said in a resigned tone of voice, pointedly looking at his watch.

'I want you to check all these rooms along the corridor,' I said, 'and tell me if you notice anything odd.'

If he thought this an exceedingly strange request he decided to comply with it. Possibly he thought the sooner he could do this, the sooner he could return to his cosy office, though he must be increasingly wondering what kind of book about the old Hydro I had in mind.

I waited at the corner as he slowly made his way down the corridor from room to room, counting aloud as he went. It was clear he was only interested in humouring me, probably worried if he didn't I might decide to quit, the last thing he needed at the moment.

My only concern was to have a resolution to this enigma and persuade him there was a need to open the missing door, so I watched impatiently as he retraced his steps to where I was standing, shaking his head. 'I'm not sure what the problem is, Alison. Everything seems to be in order. It's obviously been a mistake on the plan.'

'Nonsense,' I replied. 'Of course it isn't. The room that should be at the end of the corridor, next to the stairs, is missing, but if you look closely you can see one of the doors has been wallpapered over.'

'What?' He moved back as though to distance himself from me. 'I've no idea what you're talking about.'

'You're wrong,' I shouted at him. 'One of the doors has been covered up.'

Clearly startled by this reaction, he took my arm gently. 'Come and see for yourself, Alison.'

He led me slowly along the corridor, counting off the rooms as we went. He was right. Beside the stairs where I had seen the wallpapered over door and the missing number there was now quite clearly a room marked 312.

I stared at it, uncomprehending, unable to make sense of what I was seeing. It was impossible I'd made a mistake and yet here, clearly evident to both of us, was the missing room.

'I'll have a look if it'll keep you happy,' said the Manager. 'There's nothing there – it's a store room, that's all.'

Too astonished to protest, I could only stand silently by as he fumbled through his set of keys, but as he lifted one saying, 'I haven't been in this part of the building for a very long time but this master key should do it,' there was a noise and a kind of scuffling. We looked at each other and then it came again, louder this time. It was coming from behind the door to Room 312.

I could feel my heart begin to pound as it grew louder, seemed to come nearer. The door, creaking as though in protest, opened very slowly. With my nerves taut, terrified of what would happen next, I felt myself go dizzy.

Then I fainted.

42

When I came to I was back in my own room with several people hovering anxiously over me, including the Manager and Kelly.

'I've called the doctor,' said Clive in a voice full of concern.

'I'm perfectly fine,' I said, struggling to sit up, though I certainly wasn't. 'There's no need to make a fuss.'

'You had a bit of a fright,' said Clive. 'Kelly was assessing the room for the next stage of development. Over and above the call of duty, of course, but it's good to see employees have the welfare of the hotel at heart.'

He glanced over to where Kelly was standing by the window, not saying a word.

Of course it was possible I'd been mistaken, so overcome by the idea that the room was no longer missing. If it had ever been wallpapered over. Was it all in my imagination? Was I seeing things? I now bitterly regretted I hadn't decided to do as Simon had suggested and gone home with him, contract or no contract. Memories surfaced of the health problems I'd had many years ago, after Simon and I had been involved in a car crash. Surely this wasn't some kind of relapse?

The Manager shook his head. 'You'd better stay here meantime. You might have banged your head when you fainted and we can't take any chances.'

This might not be so much concern for me as fear he might be sued for my 'accident' and I couldn't blame him for being extra careful.

'Fine,' I said, lying back on the pillow. 'But perhaps we don't need so many people here.'

The Manager saw this as his opportunity to escape. 'I'll stay with her until the doctor comes,' said Kelly and the small crowd melted away to their own pursuits.

'The doctor won't be long,' said Kelly, 'we'll have you checked out to make sure there's nothing wrong.'

What could I do now? There were more questions than answers and I'd no idea who to trust. Could I tell Kelly what had happened, ask her what she knew? In spite of the Manager's threats Anna might have confided in Kelly. Or was that why she'd mentioned it to me? I had to do something, I couldn't ignore it. I had heard the noise from that missing room and so had Anna. And now Anna was dead. It made it all the more likely that Mrs Openshaw's story about Effie's death had more than a bit of truth to it. Two deaths, without counting poor Hamish. Perhaps there was something, some thread linking them all. But if there was, I couldn't imagine what it might be.

Suddenly I realised Kelly was talking to me. 'What caused you to faint?' she said.

Her voice was soft, solicitous and so weary was I of carrying this burden all on my own that, in spite of my reservations, I felt I had to give her some explanation for my fainting fit. At least I guess that was why I started to talk to her.

She listened in silence as I went through the details: the story of Gertrude, the problem of the room that seemed to be missing, arriving with Clive to find Room 312 was there after all.

'I don't think that's possible, a missing room, do you? Not really. You have such an imagination; no doubt you've become confused.' She laughed, but it wasn't a genuine laugh and she avoided my gaze. Perhaps she was regretting her offer to stay with me.

Any further discussion was cut short by a knock on the door heralding the arrival of the doctor, someone I recognised him from previous visits to the island. As the police surgeon who attends in the case of a sudden death he also remembered me.

'Good gracious, what have you become mixed up in now?' he said, but his voice was jovial. Unfortunately I was feeling decidedly weak, too feeble to rise to his joke.

He examined me thoroughly. 'You don't remember bumping your head?' he said feeling it all over for any lumps.

'No, I fainted, that was all. Perhaps I didn't have enough to eat at dinner time.'

He regarded me sceptically though he refrained from saying what was probably in his mind - I'd enough fat to live on for a good number of days without worrying about food.

He stood up. 'Well, all seems to be in order. I suggest you rest for the remainder of the evening. If there's any problem, call me at once.' He grinned. 'You should be grateful the carpets in these corridors are thick - they broke your fall, saved any real damage.'

He left with a cheery, 'Hope I don't see you again any time soon,' and I said to Kelly, 'Please don't feel you have to stay with me. I'll be fine. I think I might even sleep and I'll be fit and well by tomorrow, I'm sure. I won't let you down. I'll be able to do my talk.'

'If you're certain,' she said doubtfully. I could see her wrestle with her feeling she should stay to look after me and her desire to get back to her normal life.

'Yes, yes, go. I'll be fine.'

'I'll look in later and I'll ask the kitchen staff to bring you up some supper in case it was indeed hunger that made you faint.'

'That's kind of you,' I said, more to get rid of her than any desire for food. Eating was the last thing on my mind at the moment. I needed to be alone to reflect on the latest sequence of events.

As she reached the door she turned to me and said, 'Do try to get some rest, Alison. I'm sure there's a perfectly reasonable explanation for everything that's happened. The noise you and Anna heard coming from that room you thought was concealed was probably no more than imagination. One thing can suggest another. It's only a storeroom and I don't think anyone would be in there sobbing night after night, do you?'

She closed the door softly behind her and I lay there in the half light, drowsing a little, letting the thoughts come and go, glad to be on my own at last. Perhaps after I'd had a good sleep I'd feel better. Thankfully Clive had postponed the talk I was due to give the following evening and organised a 'go-as-you-please' with free drinks for anyone who participated. At this rate he'd be well out of pocket.

The room was quiet, only the soft purring of a car drawing up outside disturbed the calm and I felt sleepy, so sleepy.

Suddenly I was wide awake. What was it Kelly had said? Something about the noises that Anna and I had heard in the corridor? I'd told her most of the story, but I certainly hadn't told her that. How did she know about the sobbing?

43

Was there anyone who could help me with information about Gertrude? Anyone who knew the story first hand? That was unlikely. Even if any of the current guests had been no more than a toddler they would have to be pretty old by now.

Then I thought about Iris and Lily. What age were they exactly? It was difficult to tell. But hadn't they mentioned something about 'stories' of the Hydro?

Only one way to find out and I crawled out of bed, a little lightheaded as I stood up. After a quick shower and a change of clothes I felt much better, ready to head downstairs to find them. Hopefully it wasn't too late and they hadn't already gone to bed.

I was in luck and they were both still in the lounge, with Lily holding forth to a group of less than entranced companions.

'It's so difficult to find anyone who really knows about these things now,' Lily was saying as Iris nodded vigorously in agreement.

'Sorry to interrupt you,' I said hastening over, 'but I wonder if I could have a word.'

'Of course, come and join us,' said Lily, waving me to an empty chair.

'No, I'd like to have a word in private, if that's okay.'

The wrong thing to say as everyone in the group perked up, scenting something exciting.

'Sounds very intriguing,' said Iris with a giggle, standing up and catching the back of her chair unsteadily as she lifted her walking stick. 'You'll have to excuse us, everyone, we're wanted on important business.'

'Yes, we hope to come back soon,' said Lily.

'Oh, don't hurry,' said one of the men in the group, but neither of the sisters picked up on the sarcastic tone in his voice as they followed me out of the room.

'This all sounds very fascinating, Alison. What on earth have you to ask us that has to be kept secret?'

I considered taking them into the conservatory, but decided against it, in case it wakened memories of what had happened to Effie and steered them towards the deserted dining room, switching on the overhead light as we entered. The place looked spooky in the harsh glare, set with white tablecloths and crockery for the morning. We pulled out a chair each.

'Now, Alison, fire away. We're agog to find out how we can help you.' Lily sat up very straight as though about to be interrogated.

'I only hope we can help,' added Iris with a giggle, carefully placing her walking stick on the floor beside her.

Briefly I explained what information I was looking for, spinning yet again the story about writing a short history of the Hydro. I'd told this story so often I was beginning to believe it myself.

For a few minutes there was silence as I finished telling them what I'd discovered, then Lily let out a sigh. 'We'd like to help you, Alison, truly we would, but...'

Oh, no – the sisters were my last hope. The chances of tracking anyone else down would mean an exhaustive search of records, and once I was back on the mainland I would have other matters to occupy me. I had to have everything done and dusted before I left the island.

Almost immediately I discovered I'd been too hasty as Lily went on, '...I do remember Gertrude, or rather a little about her. I was here with my aunt. Our youngest sister Poppy was about to be born and the rest of us were farmed out to various relations. Mother had been ill, very ill and there was a worry something might go badly wrong with the birth.' She turned to her sister. 'I think you went to Grandma's, didn't you Iris?'

'I don't remember. I'm not sure what I recall and what I was told later.'

'Anyway,' said Lily, ignoring this comment, 'it was decided that I should come here with Aunt Orpah. She was a spinster, my father's sister and well off compared with the rest of us. It was sold to me as a great treat, but in truth Aunt Orpah wasn't the easiest of people and had absolutely no idea how to look after a five year old. I was very much left to my own devices as long as I was on time for meals and didn't cause any fuss.'

'Oh, Lily,' said Iris, 'and to think that all these years I believed you had had the best of the bargain while I was stuck at Grandma's.'

'Far from it,' said Lily fiercely. 'Aunt Orpah regarded me as an unwelcome interruption to playing whist with her cronies. She came here every year.'

This was very interesting, but nothing to do with my present enquiry and I racked my brains for a way to steer Lily back on to the subject.

'And that's how you got to know Gertrude?'

'No, no, of course not. She was much older than I was. But that's what I'm trying to tell you. I was allowed to wander at will as long as I didn't get into any trouble. That's how I came to see what happened.'

She paused and 'And what did you see?' I said, attempting to jolt her back into the present.

'What? Oh, what did I see? I was allowed to go wherever I wanted and I was on the top floor, looking out of the window. We had rooms on the same floor as her family. That's how I came to see her leave.'

'Ah,' this was the same story. 'She went off into the grounds of the hotel on her own?'

'Of course not. She went off with that young man, one of the gardeners.'

44

It as all so much nonsense then. There was nothing to the story of Gertrude: it was a simple tale of two lovers fleeing together and either the family didn't want the truth to come out or else rumour had overlaid the original tale. Lily was adamant about what she had seen.

'It was clear from the beginning that the family felt they had a reputation to protect. She was only sixteen and a bit of a handful from what people said. Bad enough she'd run off, but to have run off with one of the **assistant** gardeners.' Lily sniffed, perhaps trying to make me aware of the distinction between a lowly assistant gardener and one with more status.

'So the police search, the worry about her drowning in the pond...?' I left the question hanging in the air.

Lily shrugged. 'It was all a cover story, though I'm sure the police didn't know that at the time.'

'But they found out eventually?' This explained why the story in *The Buteman* had petered out. Once back in Glasgow the family had no doubt realised the mess they'd got into with so many lies. Whatever the outcome, it hadn't been reported, least not on the island.

'I daresay they did, but I've no idea if Gertrude and her lover were found. Mother had the baby and we all went home, everything else forgotten in the excitement of being back in our own place with the new arrival.'

And there the story might have ended, but there was still the problem of that sobbing I'd heard in the corridor. Though to be honest, I was now beginning to think it might be a product of my imagination, constructed out of sympathy for Anna.

A doubt increased by a phone call later that day from Freddie.

'Alison,' he said, 'I wanted to let you know the result of the post-mortem on Anna.'

He stopped for a moment and I heard the tremor in his voice as he tried to continue. 'There was nothing suspicious about her death after all. Apparently she had a heart problem – it could have happened at any time. We're having the funeral next week, on the mainland, though I'll understand if you can't manage. You were so kind to her, so considerate of her imagining those noises in the corridor of the hotel.' He broke off and there was a long silence.

'Freddie, I'm so sorry about Anna,' I said, 'but you must be relieved it was a natural death. Let me know about the funeral arrangements and I'll try to be there if I can.'

I rang off muttering more words of condolence and sat staring into space as I went through all the possibilities.

No matter which way I considered the evidence, the outcome was the same. Anna's death might have been natural, the result of a heart problem, but that was no help in finding out the truth about what happened to Hamish and to Effie.

45

My time at the Hydro was almost over. Only this evening and Friday to go and then the second group of guests would depart on the Saturday and I'd be free.

Most unusually, I hadn't heard from Simon for a couple of days, so during a lull in proceedings before dinner, I called him.

'You've been strangely quiet. Everything okay?'

'Of course, of course,' he said, but he sounded distracted.

'Simon, is something bothering you? You haven't been in touch.'

There was a silence then he came back with, 'I intended to wait till you came home to tell you, but there have been developments.'

'What kind of developments?' My heart lurched. What was he going to say?

'Thing is, I've been offered a permanent position with the parent company of Scottish Alignment Limited.'

'That's great news. Why didn't you want to let me know immediately?' This was good news, though we'd have to work out the logistics of Simon working in Inverness.

'You could rent a more permanent flat in Inverness and commute at the weekends,' I said eagerly, anxious to show my support. 'It's not that far.'

Another silence. 'That's the problem, Alison. It's not in Inverness; it's with U.K. Alignment Limited in London.'

Now it was my turn to fall silent. 'London?' I finally managed to say. 'You want to take a job back in London?'

'I knew that's what you'd say,' he replied, finding it difficult to hide his disappointment. 'Yes, I do want to take it.' A note of defensiveness crept into his voice. 'I've a good few years of working life left and being freelance doesn't suit me.'

'No, no, I understand that,' I said, torn between supporting him and being appalled at the idea of going back to London.

'Well, yes, it's not ideal in many ways, but...'

This was an impossible conversation. 'Why don't we wait and discuss it when I come home? I'll be back on Saturday evening.'

'Fine.' There was an edge to his agreement. 'But I have to let them know by the middle of next week.'

'We have time, then,' I said curtly, suddenly realising this job offer must have been brewing for some time, wavering between feeling annoyed and feeling hurt he hadn't thought to tell me before now.

I rang off with a feeling of dissatisfaction and sat still for a good half hour, mulling over what this job offer meant for us. I had a choice. I could give up everything here and move to London with Simon, or I could stay in Glasgow and let him go on his own. But what would that do for our relationship, at last back on firm ground after so many shaky episodes? End it, that's what would happen.

Somehow the problems at the Hydro, the strange noises in the night and even the suspicious deaths of Hamish and Effie paled into insignificance after hearing this unexpected news. There were more important matters closer to home.

46

There was no more time to consider this opportunity for Simon. Whatever decision I might eventually make, the priority at the moment was to complete my contract at the Hydro. And the main concern now was to go down to dinner, to try to put any personal troubles behind me and act the part of hostess with the guests.

Given I'd taken so long after Simon's phone call, I had to rush to dress for dinner in something less casual than the trousers and thick jumper I was currently wearing.

My wardrobe options were limited and I settled on a dark blue skirt I'd already worn on several occasions teamed with a cream blouse. On pulling it from the wardrobe I realised the blouse was rather crumpled and hoped slinging a cardigan over my shoulders would disguise its creased state.

The lift was on the ground floor when I arrived, so I almost ran down the stairs and into the dining room, casting around for a spare seat. My heart sank as I saw the only possibility was a table in the far corner where Sylvia and the Major were sitting. Well, nothing else for it, and putting on my brightest smile I headed in their direction.

'Is Lily not here?' I said, sitting down beside Iris.

She turned her head to whisper to me. 'She won't be long. She had something to do.'

The Major was leaning in close to Sylvia, unaware his booming voice was carrying across the room. 'You look particularly lovely tonight, my dear. And now you've got rid of that dog of yours...'

'I didn't get rid of poor Jasper,' Sylvia interrupted him frostily, drawing back. 'Several people complained about my darling being where they were eating and I've had to leave him with Yvonne in Reception meantime.'

Spurned by Sylvia, the Major turned his attention to Iris. 'And where is your dear twin sister, eh?'

Iris tried to ignore him, shaking off his hand which he'd placed on her arm.

At that moment, Clive came bustling in and clapped his hands to gain attention.

'It's a buffet night tonight, everyone, so if you'd make your way up to the counter....starting with table one,' he added as it became clear there was about to be a wholesale rush.

Lily appeared at our table. 'I can get yours, Major, save you the trouble.'

'That's what I like, a little woman who knows what a man wants.' He accompanied this remark with an inappropriate leer and a wink and I had to turn away to hide my laughter.

'I'll help,' I said and together we took orders for the first course which seemed to be soup or fruit juice. Having had experience of the chef's soup I wasn't surprised when everyone opted for juice.

Lily bustled in front of me. 'I'll get Iris's and the Major's,' she said, elbowing me out of the way.

She seemed to take an inordinate amount of time putting three glasses of juice on to a tray. 'I could take them all,' I said, but she refused my offer abruptly with, 'I'm fine, I'm fine.'

Together we threaded our way through the other tables and set out the juice.

'This isn't for me, surely?' said the Major. 'Never drink grapefruit juice. Gives me indigestion.' And as though to prove his point he belched loudly.

'I'll have the grapefruit and you can have my orange juice,' I said, passing it across the table to him.

'No, that's not fair. I can switch,' said Lily, putting out her hand to stop me.

'It's not a problem; I can drink grapefruit.' Anything to keep the peace at this table.

Lily watched as I sipped at my juice while the others drank theirs in record time. It was extremely bitter, no doubt the result of being of the cheapest kind. 'You go on up and have your next course,' I said and sipped again, wincing at the taste.

One by one, they left the table to head for the buffet, but Lily hung back. 'Don't drink that if you don't like it. He's such a bully, that man.'

'It's fine, it's fine,' I said, taking a gulp.

As she headed off to queue with the others, the waitress came round and I hastily deposited the half-full glass on her tray with a sigh of relief.

The rest of the meal was the most uncomfortable one I'd had so far, the Major blustering and making so many inappropriate remarks that eventually I excused myself. I'd better things to do, though I could see Lily and Iris were torn between following me out and having dessert. Thank goodness in the end dessert won and I headed for my room for a brief respite before the next part of the evening.

Now that I was back in that part of the hotel, with a little time to spare, I had a sudden urge to check out the

273

top floor again, to convince myself about recent events. Stopping only to collect a torch from my room in the expectation that now the floor was unoccupied the lighting would have been dimmed or even switched off, I headed upstairs.

I crept along the top corridor towards the room that had been missing, feeling the tension mount with every step. What would I find? Would the door again be concealed, or would I find everything that had happened previously had been imagined?

Step by step I went nearer, my pace slowing with every movement until I reached the end. I closed my eyes briefly as I stopped, then willed myself to open them as I stood in front of Room 312.

I switched on my torch and let the light play round the outer edge of the doorframe. It was almost impossible to detect, so carefully had it been done, but there was clear evidence I'd been correct and this door had been papered over and what's more, had recently been cut away to reveal the original.

I tried the handle. To my surprise it was unlocked, but I hesitated, trying to decide if I should go in. My heart started to pound as I turned the doorknob very, very slowly, all the while keeping my torch firmly focussed. If I did enter, would I find a solution to the mystery or would I put myself in danger?

Eventually I made the decision. I had to find out and telling myself I most certainly didn't believe in ghosts, I opened the door and went in.

47

At first I could see very little. It was completely dark
outside and this room faced away from any lighting
around the hotel. I swung my torch backwards and
forwards, not knowing what to expect, then experienced
a surge of disappointment. The room was dusty,
unused, much like the storeroom next door.

Edging my way round the walls, it was easier to see
that this had once been a bedroom. The wallpaper was
faded and torn, the floor had long since lost any carpet
or rugs it might once have had, but the old grandeur
was still evident in the ornate plasterwork. There were a
couple of pieces of ancient furniture stacked up in the
corner: a battered sofa, several bookshelves and small
side tables, probably overlooked when the original
fittings had been sold off.

On the side wall there was another door. This must
be the one leading into the other storeroom, the one I'd
first explored. I tugged hard at the handle, pushed and
pulled, but it refused to budge. I moved back a little
way, frustrated, uncertain what to do next. As I stood
there I became increasingly aware of another smell
overlaying that of the dust and decay. It was strongest
in the far corner of the room and I crept over, sniffing
the air like a bloodhound.

It was a perfume I recognised, strong as though the
owner had recently left the room. Where had I smelled
it recently? For the life of me I couldn't remember, no

matter how much I sniffed the air. It probably wasn't important.

As I stood there pondering my next move, the moon sailed out from behind a cloud and a shaft of moonlight pierced the gloom, casting ghostly shadows. I shivered a little. There was nothing here for me to see, no answer to my questions.

The only thing I now knew for sure was that the room had been concealed, the door wallpapered over and someone had recently opened it up, but for what purpose I'd no idea. And it didn't explain the sound of sobbing.

At the doorway I turned for one last look before heading for my room. I'd only time for a quick freshen up before I had to head down to join the others.

What's more, I was feeling decidedly queasy. I shouldn't have had the chicken casserole. Goodness knows where the chicken had come from, but I had to eat something.

I took a deep breath to control the rising sickness and held on to the door handle for support. It was then I saw it, in the far corner, perched on one of the side tables. Something that certainly wasn't part of the original furniture and in spite of my increasing feelings of nausea, I had to have a look.

It was a music speaker of some kind, fairly modern, but there was nothing beside it to give any clue as to why it was here. I looked around, bent down and checked under the sofa, pushed aside the shelving, but this was the only strange item in the room.

What was it for and why was it here? Nausea made me feel muddled, unable to concentrate. I had to get back to my room before I was violently sick and I stumbled back to the door.

As I carelessly slammed it behind me, I had another sudden whiff of that perfume. But now I realised where I'd smelled it before. It was *Valle d'Or* - the perfume Kelly used.

48

It was difficult to remember when I'd last felt so ill. I spent the next hour alternating between lying on the bed and staggering into the toilet to be sick. There wasn't the slightest possibility I'd be able to join the guests any time soon. I'd be lucky if I was able to summon up the energy to lift the phone and tell Clive what was happening.

Finally it was clear whatever poison had been in my system had been thoroughly rooted out and I stayed as still as possible, mainly because every time I moved the room whirled around at an alarming rate. Eventually, after several tries, I managed to phone down to Reception where Yvonne was on duty.

'Are you sure you're okay? I could call the doctor.'

'No, no,' I said as strongly as my present state would allow. I didn't want another telling off. 'I'll be fine if I stay here quietly and drink plenty of water.'

'I could send Kelly up.'

'No, certainly not.' I'd no wish to encounter Kelly, not until I'd thought through the discovery in the room on the top floor and in my current state that was going to take longer than usual.

I must have dozed, because the next thing I remembered was coming to with a start. I sat up cautiously, but the dizziness had passed and I felt almost human again.

Very slowly and carefully I swung my legs out of bed. So far, so good. As I stood up, I stumbled a little, but it was only a momentary lapse and after a bracing shower and a change of clothes I was almost back to normal.

As I was contemplating my next move, there was a soft rap on the door. At first I was tempted to ignore it. It might be Kelly, sent up by Yvonne in spite of my refusal. But if I didn't answer the door they might think I was ill or worse, dead, and as the knocking became louder I reluctantly went over to open it.

Lily stood there. 'Oh, thank goodness,' she said. 'You're all right.'

'Well, I am now,' I replied.

She glanced round fearfully. 'Can I come in?'

Grudgingly I opened the door wider and stood back. A conversation with Lily was the last thing I wanted right now.

Without waiting to be asked she sat down on the chair by the window, carefully removing my hastily discarded clothes and placing them in a neat pile on the floor.

She coughed and took a deep breath before saying, 'We are so sorry about what happened. So very sorry.'

I'd remained standing to make her aware I didn't expect this conversation to last long, but in my weakened state found I'd no alternative but to sit down on the bed. 'Yes, it was a bad experience, must have been the chicken. Did you hear if anyone else has been ill?'

She regarded me thoughtfully before saying in a voice so low I had to ask her to repeat herself. 'It wasn't the chicken, Alison. I'm afraid it was the Major who was meant to be ill.' She fiddled with the top button of her cardigan.

'What?' In spite of my debilitated state I sprang to my feet. 'What on earth do you mean?'

'He's such a nasty man, Iris and I thought we'd teach him a lesson, put him out of commission for a little while.' She shuddered. 'All those rude sayings, disturbing people.'

It was proving impossible to focus. 'But didn't the Major have the beef?' And how on earth would Iris have poisoned only my chicken? I'd fetched it from the Carvery myself.

'It wasn't the chicken, it was the fruit juice.' She sat up straight. 'We did try to warn you but you insisted on exchanging your orange juice for the Major's grapefruit.'

She looked fearful. 'You won't tell on us, will you? You're fine now, aren't you?'

This request left me astounded. Not tell? 'How much poison did you put in the drink?'

'Not much,' she replied hastily, 'only enough to make him ill. We were very careful this time.'

It was possibly a sign I wasn't back to normal, but I couldn't take in what she was saying and as though to persuade me, she said, 'He's a nasty, nasty man. People like him shouldn't be allowed.'

She looked so old, so vulnerable and she had come clean. With every passing minute I was feeling better, so I took the decision. 'I won't say anything, but you must never do anything like this again.' What good would it do? At their age being accused of a crime might prove fatal and I was now feeling fine.

'Oh, we won't,' she said eagerly. 'You can be sure of that.'

She rose shakily from the chair. 'Thank you for being so understanding. It was all my idea in the beginning and Iris took some persuading to go along with it. She's not in the best of health.'

With much twittering and expressions of thanks she eventually left and I sat back on the bed, exhausted by this revelation.

It was only later that I remembered exactly what she had said and had this most horrible sensation of dread. What did she mean by "we were very careful this time"?

49

In spite of my promise to Lily, the more I thought about it the more I realised it was impossible to let matters rest. It was my duty to let someone know and I phoned down to check if Clive was available.

Lily's words rang in my ears as I headed somewhat shakily to the Manager's office. Quite how, or what, or even how much I would tell him I'd no idea and it was likely he wouldn't believe me, would dismiss Lily as a crank, or one of those people who haunt police stations confessing to crimes they haven't committed. But the more I thought about it, the more it made sense.

Truth was, I couldn't pretend the visit to my room hadn't happened, not when she'd hinted there had been other episodes. Surely these sweet old ladies couldn't have been responsible for the deaths that had taken place? There was no motive I could come up with for killing Hamish or Effie. Hamish had certainly been annoying, but Effie?

There must be some other explanation.

As I approached the Reception desk I saw to my dismay that Iris and Lily were there, deep in conversation with Clive Timmons and Yvonne. Too late I tried to sidle off before I was spotted.

'Alison, good to see you're back on your feet. How are you feeling?' With what was evidently a sigh of relief Clive detached himself from the sisters and headed towards me. 'I believe you've some information for me? Something important about the recent deaths.'

I hadn't said any such thing and it was clearly a ploy to allow him to escape, but Lily didn't know that and a look of fear crossed her face as soon as she heard him.

She caught Iris by the elbow and without a word pulled her away. 'What's wrong, Lily, what's wrong?' said Iris, grabbing at her stick to steady herself.

Lily started muttering under her breath, all the while pushing and pulling her sister out of the front door, crashing it shut behind them.

I made to go after them. 'They shouldn't be out on a day like this without coats,' I said. 'There's something wrong.'

'Don't worry. I'll go and check on them as soon as I finish this invoice,' said Yvonne, heading round the desk to the computer. 'It won't take long.'

Clive shrugged. 'They'll come back in soon enough once they feel that chill wind off the bay. And,' rubbing his hands together, 'thanks for coming to the rescue. Dealing with guests like the Herringtons does get difficult at times.'

'I do have something to ask,' I said and followed him into the office, looking round to see if the sisters had returned, but there was no sign of them. Sighing, he waved his hand towards a chair.

Determined to make him aware of what the sisters might have been up to, I couldn't think where to begin. Eventually, after a little prompting, I told him of my suspicions and his face grew darker and darker with every word I spoke.

'But are you sure?' he kept saying after every question. 'There could have been any number of reasons for your sickness.'

'As sure as I can be,' I replied. I stood up. 'I really think someone should see where Lily and Iris are - if they've come back.'

Then something else came to mind and I swallowed hard. 'Do you remember the chef becoming agitated because some of the guests were in and out of the kitchen? He only mentioned Sylvia but I'm sure the Herringtons were the people he meant when he said "other elderly ladies".'

Clive groaned. A sheen of sweat glistened on his forehead and he wiped it away with the back of his hand. 'And I was blaming the chef for this. Good grief. What do we do now? We'll have to call the police again. I'd better...'

But he didn't have an opportunity to finish his sentence as Yvonne came rushing in, banging the door behind her. 'You have to come at once, Clive. There's been a terrible accident.'

50

'It all happened so quickly...I'd no time to help. I did try, I did try.'

Bertie stood at the side of the pond, gazing round the little group of horrified onlookers, seeking reassurance.

Clive came forward and patted him awkwardly on the shoulder. 'Of course you did, of course.'

The bodies of Lily and Iris lay stretched out on the damp grass in front of us, so still they might have been sleeping, pulled from the freezing water, but too late to save them.

'What happened? Was it an accident? What on earth were they doing wandering around the grounds in this weather?' said Bertie.

'I should have stopped them,' said Clive guiltily. 'I assumed once they'd realised how cold it was outside they'd come straight back in.'

Beside him Yvonne was weeping quietly, sniffling into a wad of tissues. 'And I should have gone out after them instead of finishing that wretched invoice.'

'So it wasn't an accident?' Bertie sounded mystified. 'I only saw what happened because I was up the ladder at the back of the building. I heard this great shout and turned to see Lily pushing her sister in before jumping in herself. Nearly fell off my ladder, I did.'

'Why didn't Iris struggle?'

'I suspect they were of a generation who didn't learn to swim,' said Clive gloomily.

As I was about to reply to Bertie, saying, 'No, I suspect Lily realised they'd been found out,' but something held me back. Any suspicions were for the police, not the general public.

As soon as the police arrived we were shepherded into the hotel where Sylvia was standing at Reception, clutching Jasper to her chest. It was the first time I'd seen him outside one of her many handbags and sadly he didn't improve on seeing his whole body.

'What is going on now?' she said. 'My poor Jasper is quite upset by all this commotion.'

'We've more to worry about than a dog,' replied Clive waspishly. 'The Herrington sisters have drowned in the pond over by the old greenhouses.'

Sylvia staggered back, almost dropping Jasper in the process. 'No, never,' she said. 'Why would they do that?'

'We think they were responsible for the deaths of Hamish and of Effie because...'

I kicked him hard on the shins to make him stop but it was too late.

Sylvia raised her eyebrows. 'It wouldn't surprise me in the least. They did take things to heart, were always talking about why so many wicked people should be left in the world when their beloved sisters had died.'

'That wouldn't make them killers, surely?' The words were out before I could stop myself.

Sylvia sniffed. 'Lily was very upset when she overheard Hamish calling them "silly old biddies" and he was a most annoying man.'

'But Effie?'

'That's easy. She made fun of poor Lily. She was very deaf, you know, but wouldn't admit it and it gave her the appearance of what we called in my day 'slow.' The thing about Effie was that she'd no patience with others, though she expected everyone to make allowances for her age.'

'But how would they get hold of poison?'

Sylvia made a face. 'Perhaps they used Iris's heart pills? My dear Tristan had a weak heart and was well warned of the consequences of accidentally taking an overdose. If Hamish and Effie unknowingly had problems then possibly…' She shrugged, letting us fill in the rest.

So Sylvia, always there, always in the background, was a lot more perceptive than any of us gave her credit for.

As we waited for the police to come in to question us, Kelly came running in. 'I heard the news,' she said. 'How awful.'

'Yes,' said Clive grimly. 'Thank goodness you've turned up. After this latest episode they're bound to want to turn the place over from top to bottom. It's going to be a terrible few days.'

Kelly turned pale. 'Why would they want to do that? There's nothing of interest in the hotel, surely.'

Clive shrugged, resigned to his fate. 'That's as may be, but this time they want to make sure they've missed nothing. Every last nook and cranny will be searched. They've demanded all master keys, so I'll have to ask you to hand yours over. I guess the place may have to close down. Just as well we're almost at the end of the *Turkey and Tinsel* weeks.' He looked gloomier than ever.

287

'There's something I have to do,' said Kelly, suddenly springing into action and almost running towards the stairs.

As she passed me I caught a whiff of her perfume, that same perfume I'd smelled in that room on the top floor. Wherever she was headed, whatever she was up to, I was determined to follow her.

51

I had to find out where Kelly was going, though I could make a good guess. Fortunately she opted for the stairs rather than the lift and I was able to creep up behind her. I doubt if she would have noticed me, so preoccupied did she seem.

We reached the top floor, me a little behind her, trying not to make a noise, not to reveal myself by the sound of my laboured breath.

My hunch was correct and she made straight for the room that had been the cause of all the problems, pulling a bunch of keys from her pocket as she went. She stopped at the door and fumbled for a few moments and I drew back into the shadows, willing her not to turn round. If she did she was sure to spot me and there was nowhere to hide.

The door opened with a soft click and she slipped inside. Now I was left with a dilemma: should I follow her in or wait here to see what she would do next.

As I was mulling this over, she suddenly re-appeared, clutching the music speaker and after locking the door, hurried off, but not in the direction I expected. She seemed to be making for the very last door in the corridor and I crept along behind her, ready to flee if I was spotted.

After several tries she opened this door with another of the keys and disappeared inside. I waited and waited, but there was no sign of her reappearing. What to do? And where had she gone?

I inched forward and pulled open the door, expecting to find her behind it, trying to come up with a reason for being there.

To my surprise what was behind the door wasn't a room, but another set of stairs. I stood and listened, but there was no sound from above and emboldened by this I began to climb the short flight of steps.

At the top I paused, unable to stand upright because the ceiling was so low. Then I realised from its conical shape that I was in one of the turrets of the old West wing. But where was Kelly?

'I'm right behind you, Alison,' a voice said and I whirled round to confront her.

'So, what are you doing here, spying on me?'

There was no need to be afraid of this slip of a girl so I said, 'I'm trying to find out the cause of that sobbing Anna and I heard coming from the room that had apparently disappeared.'

She laughed and pointed to the music speaker on the ledge over by the open window. 'There was nothing odd about it. It was very simple, but unfortunately it didn't work out as planned.'

'So what was it all about?'

Kelly sighed. 'It was my uncle's idea. The Coronet Hotel has suffered badly since the Hydro re-opened. My uncle invested every penny in that place, but the previous owner must have known what would happen. And if the plans for the Casino go ahead...' she shrugged.

'So what did that have to do with the sobbing?'

She took her mobile from her pocket and stabbed at it a couple of times. I jumped back as the sound of

290

sobbing issued from the music speaker. 'You mean this noise?'

'Exactly.'

She laughed. 'The idea was to scare the guests with stories of ghosts, of hauntings. We were relying on Sylvia and her belief in her powers of communicating with those who had 'passed over' but she refused to set foot in the West wing, never mind have a room there. We thought Anna would be the most susceptible of the guests and once the rumours spread among the others...'

I stood in silence, waiting for her to continue. 'Then instead of telling everyone about the noises, Anna tells Clive first and he threatens her not to mention it. That's why she enlisted you. She knew she could trust you. We thought we'd cracked it when you began asking about Gertrude. We'd no idea about that story, but it seemed as if it was all going to tie in nicely.'

'That was a long shot,' I said, trying to ignore the implication that I was so suggestible.

She laughed. 'Yes, my uncle had plenty of other ideas, like fusing the lights that night of your talk. I told him it was all a waste of time. If all these deaths didn't put people off, nothing would.'

'So what happens now?'

'Now I get rid of the evidence,' she grinned. 'Then it's business as usual, though I daresay I'll have to come up with some excuse to hand in my notice.'

I moved forward intending to seize the music speaker, but she was too quick for me and with a couple of deft movements she grabbed it, pushed the tiny window fully open and hurled it out.

I rushed over and stood on tiptoe, but all I could see was a series of shattered fragments scattered among the jumble of roof tiles. There was no way anyone would be able to retrieve what was left.

She gave a deep sigh. 'So that's it, Alison. All over. And I daresay the police will have other things to worry about rather something that can be passed off as a stupid prank.'

She pushed past me. 'Well, are you coming or not?'

With no desire to be left here alone, I meekly followed her back down the narrow twisting stairs.

If the Hydro was to close it would be nothing to do with Kelly. It was scarcely worthwhile mentioning what I'd found out, though I was reluctant to let her get away with it. In the end it would be my word against hers. And the story of Gertrude had had nothing to do with it in the end. There was no ghost.

EPILOGUE

The copy of *The Buteman* was lying on top of the pile of papers for recycling and I smiled as I glanced at the headlines again. Omens for the Hydro to gain a casino licence looked good and in the meantime it appeared to be going from strength to strength.

There was a picture of Clive on the front page, beaming from ear to ear, claiming the Hotel had secured a contract with one of the biggest Tour companies in Britain for all year round coach parties.

I heard no more of Kelly, but it was fair to guess all her efforts had been in vain. The Hydro's future was secure now. I wasn't as sure mine was.

It was strange wandering round the empty rooms of the house where we'd lived for so many years, knowing we were leaving, possibly for good. We'd decided to let rather than sell, mainly because I was so reluctant. 'What if this job doesn't work out?' I'd said to Simon and in response to his frown, 'And when you do eventually retire we may well decide to come back to Scotland.'

Clearly this wasn't in his plan, but rather than argue he gave in. I suppose he was grateful I hadn't made more fuss about returning to London, about leaving so much behind.

'It will be fine,' he kept reassuring me. 'Alastair isn't likely to return from Canada and surely it's a bonus that Maura and Alan and Connor are going back south after their time in Edinburgh.'

He didn't mention Deborah, but we had a feeling she'd soon be following us: she'd mentioned it often enough with increasing enthusiasm.

My footsteps echoed on the bare boards as I slowly moved from room to room, remembering so much about our lives here: the children growing up, the family Christmas parties, the summer evenings when it had been warm enough to risk inviting friends at short notice for a barbeque.

We'd been advised, 'Best to let a place this size unfurnished', so most of our belongings were in store, though we'd sold a few pieces of furniture to the incoming tenants, a young doctor, his wife and their two children.

I sat down on the window seat in the lounge and looked out over the garden. After a long winter signs of life were beginning to show: clusters of nodding snowdrops under the apple trees in the far corner sheltered from the wind, daffodils poking their heads through in the flower beds beside the kitchen steps, tiny buds of yellow on the forsythia bush over by the garden shed.

'Don't be silly, Alison,' I told myself sternly as I felt a lump rise in my throat. 'This is a family house and it will be good to have children living here again, playing on that swing at the bottom of the garden beside the old plum trees.'

But then another little voice said, 'Yes, but Connor could have been playing there. Not much chance of that in the flat in London you're renting meantime.'

Worst of all was leaving Motley our cat behind.

'He's getting on a bit,' said Simon firmly when I ventured to suggest he should come with us. 'And how would he adapt to living in a second floor flat?'

Ella, our next-door neighbour, who looked after him on the many occasions when we were away, professed herself delighted to take him on a permanent basis. 'He knows us well,' she said. 'And we'll be happy to have him.'

'We'll come back and visit: it's only London we're going to,' Simon said. 'There will be lots of opportunities to come north.'

I wasn't so sure. And what about Bute? Perhaps he was glad to have me living well away from a place where trouble appeared to follow me, but that wasn't how I felt about it.

I'd miss so much: the screeching of the seagulls swooping and diving for titbits, the long stretch of sand at Ettrick Bay, the arrival of the wild geese at St Ninian's Bay in the autumn, the cry of the oyster catchers, the activity of the town of Rothesay. We never did manage to walk the West Island Way.

It was too late now for regrets. We were going back to London, to where it all began, where Simon and I first met. Hopefully, after so many ups and downs, our relationship was strong enough now to survive whatever lay ahead.

'Ready, Alison? That's the last of the cases in the car.' Simon came bustling in, his voice loud with excitement.

He looked so happy, so pleased with the possibility of this new start, how could I do other than smile at him?

He squeezed my arm. 'Don't worry; everything will be fine, you'll see.'

As he turned away I stood up and followed him out to the car, gently closing the front door behind me.

I didn't look back.

Acknowledgements

Sincere thanks

To Joan Fleming and to Bill Daly for reading an early draft of the manuscript and making many helpful comments, to Judith Duffy and Joan Weeple for proof-reading and comments and to Peter Duffy for help with the idea and his continuing support.

Special thanks in matters geographical and historical

Brandanii Archaeology and Heritage
www.discoverbutearchaeology.co.uk

Lightning Source UK Ltd.
Milton Keynes UK
UKOW05f1220281114

242351UK00002B/10/P